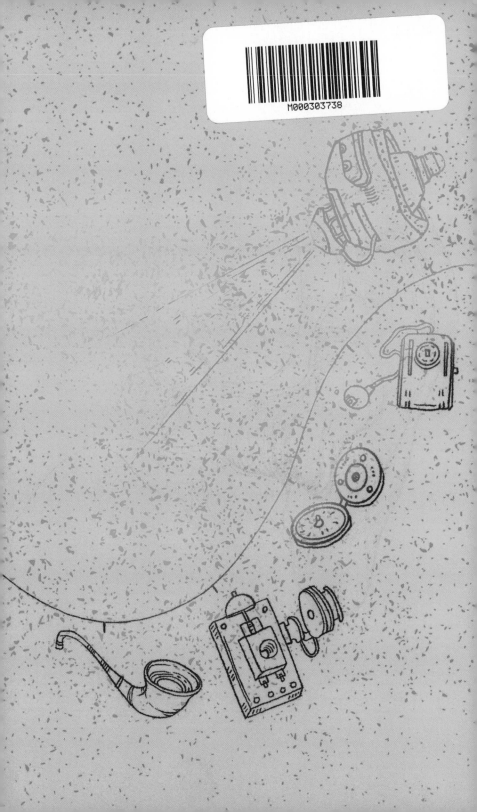

PRAISE FOR *THE SKINNY: A MEMOIR*

"One of the most vulnerable memoirs I've ever read, Jonathan Wells' *The Skinny* is the story of surviving the long, brutal gauntlet toward manhood that many boys who grew up in the 1970s and '80s endured. An important cautionary tale illuminating the devastating, lifelong harm caused by rigid gender rules and the parents who try to enforce them."

—BILL CLEGG, author of *Portrait of an Addict as a Young Man* and *The End of the Day*

"Layer by layer, Jonathan Wells unravels the father-son knot in ways both troubling and uplifting. I was gripped by *The Skinny*, a remarkable portrait of the most tangled of relationships, written with a poet's eye and grace."

—ROGER COHEN, author of *The Girl from Human Street: A Jewish Family Odyssey*

"This touching memoir of growing up in suburban New York in the '70s and '80s reads a bit like outtakes from *Mad Men*, if told from the perspective of a teenager with a more nuanced point of view on the overwhelming tropes of masculinity that dominated that era... This coming-of-age chronicle is lushly rendered and touchingly intimate, a critique that is loving and unsparing at the same time."

—CHLOE SCHAMA, *Vogue*, **Best Books of the Summer**

"A poetic remembrance of pain and forgiveness that rivals Tobias Wolff's *This Boy's Life* in its power to enthrall."

—*AIRMAIL WEEKLY*

THE STERNS ARE LISTENING

A NOVEL

JONATHAN WELLS

ZE BOOKS

Published by ZE Books of Houston, TX
in partnership with Unnamed Press of Los Angeles, CA

www.zebooks.com

Cover Design by With Projects, Inc.
Jacket Design and Typeset by Jaya Nicely

ISBN: 978-1-736309-37-7

Ebook ISBN: 978-1-736309-39-1

LCCN: 2023939772

Distributed by Publishers Group West

Credits:
Exploring the Fremont by Terry Tempest Williams
Shouting at the Sky by Gary Ferguson

Printed in North America by Sheridan

First Edition

2 4 6 8 9 7 5 3 1

"Listening is the most dangerous thing of all, listening means knowing, finding out about something and knowing what's going on, our ears don't have lids that can instinctively close against the words uttered, they can't hide from what they sense they're about to hear, it's always too late."

Javier Marías, *A Heart So White*

THE STERNS ARE LISTENING

PART ONE

1

I**T WAS A LATE AFTERNOON IN MANHATTAN NEAR THE END OF**
August when Benjamin's hope for relief from the heat, already
strained, neared its highest level. Hope seemed futile. Humidity
deepened the already heavy air, as though the weather was saving itself
for a final fury, a suffocation that would descend with exceptional weight
and an explosive yet lasting energy. People in the streets, those who
hadn't escaped the city, had pretended to ignore its force by invoking
the mantras of their childhood summers, sighing nostalgically, stoically,
about "the last warm days." But by the afternoon they slowed, moving
heavily along the schist-studded pavement, brushing the sides of buildings with their fingertips, clinging to the black spiked fence posts around
the struggling gingko trees for balance.

When the sun finally set it left an ochre residue on the brick facades
like a bruise. The light displayed a mottled palette with streams of green,
yellow, coral, and teal. Anything but golden. That was the shade of a
different era. Although most buildings were awash in it, the older facades
were more absorbent. Decades of wear gave them a fatigued look. Many
of the bricks had blackened, and the mortar had turned dry and crumbly.
Protruding air conditioners dripped on the sidewalks below while they
made their humming sounds, animating the ambient air like they belonged to a distinct species, an urban beast groaning or a reptile with a
churning heartbeat.

The building in which Benjamin and Dita Stern lived was not a notable one in spite of its age. There were no architectural flourishes to distinguish it from any of the other large apartment blocks that had been built before World War 2. Despite the building being boxy and brutal on the outside, its units had the classic, spacious proportions that certain New York apartment hunters craved. Aside from that, it was "worn out" in real estate agent parlance. The room in which Benjamin sat, a maid's room adjoining the kitchen, was the smallest in the threadbare apartment. White paint was thin on the moldings, and the dark framing underneath discolored them in places. Screwed into the ceiling was a smoked-glass fixture that hadn't been replaced since the fifties. The overhead light was sickly, and every time Dita turned it on, Benjamin turned it off as soon as she left the room. The sound of the air conditioner was intermittent. It cycled through shrill, whistling periods and then settled back into a deeper growl. Neither register was pitched loud enough to drown out the sound of the cable news show that played in the kitchen next door—the martial network music interrupted by attention-grabbing fanfares, the pious low notes of pundits dissecting the latest outrage with a distanced, steady poise, the cheerful commercials for new pharmaceuticals with names that seemed to come out of a random syllable generator.

Although Benjamin did his best to ignore it, the noise of the air conditioner still distracted him. He fidgeted in his armchair next to the window, glad to be indoors in spite of the interruptions as he gazed down at his fellow urban dwellers creeping along the streets. He switched on the table lamp and stood to take his tan linen jacket off. He ran his index finger inside his collar as though it was still too tight even though he had unbuttoned it. He had stopped wearing a tie years ago. Even the ventilation couldn't remove the close, uncomfortable feeling inside him. Only the prospect of his daughter Alessandra's visit for dinner that evening put a dent in his restlessness.

Alessandra was in her early twenties and still a college student. A big but pleasant-looking girl with hunched shoulders, an uneven complexion, a mass of tangled, black hair rising from the top of her head like a turban, and a scowl that was accidental, Alessandra strove to distinguish herself through her wardrobe, as if conceding that her looks weren't enough. Instead of wearing the standard neutral colors and plush fabrics favored by her classmates, she dressed almost exclusively in workout clothes of the 1970s that she'd bought at vintage thrift shops throughout the city: tracksuits in a range of colors from chartreuse to orange made only from synthetics, hoodies with forgotten sport logos heat-transferred onto their chests, and sneakers with rainbow designs on the side. Yellow was the color that Benjamin associated most with her. It announced her radiance, distinction and vivacious cheerfulness that was missing from his life. Her major, paleolinguistics, fascinated him. The last time she had come home for dinner she told him that she thought he was at least 3 percent Neanderthal, on the higher end of the Homo sapiens spectrum, and quickly added, "Sorry, Pop." Then she told him that it was something he should "carry with dignity." Neanderthals were far more developed than they had ever been given credit for in popular culture, she said, softening the blow. They even had toothpicks, Dad, she had added.

Troubled by the comment, Benjamin went into his tiny bathroom and studied himself in the mirror to hunt for signs of his primitive nature—the flattened, receding forehead, the extended upper lip, the curled-over lower one, and the protruding jaw. Because he was six feet tall he had to stoop to fit himself into the mirror's small frame. What caught his eye, in addition to the hair on his head that was still black and thick in patches, were the little stray ones that had sprouted from his nose and his ears. These were particularly worrisome. He wondered if these sprouts had become so thick that it had affected his hearing. A secret voice planted somewhere in his ear canal whispered that his body was a vacant lot and if he forgot to groom himself, it would be overgrown by Christmas. He opened the little cabinet door to find his pair of stainless steel German nail scissors and began pruning.

In the slanted mirror he could see Dita's profile. She still had beauty in her bones, he thought. Her planar face, which had once looked as if it had been chiseled from Carrara marble by simple tools, was a little puffy now, but it wasn't hard for him to see past that. Age was a sign of valor, he thought to himself. It was not the survival of the fittest but a stubbornness that didn't flag. She was loyal and hardheaded, and in spite of himself, he found that he loved her for it. And besides, he knew the fierceness of those qualities would never fade. He went back to his shearing, trying not to pierce the nostril lining with the scissors' pointy tips.

"Dita!" he shouted, hoping she'd hear him so he wouldn't have to come out of the bathroom. "Dita, I need help!"

Braced in front of the mirror, he could hear her shouting back at the television. She loved an argument with men who couldn't talk back almost as much as she loved arguing with those who could. The rare pauses that cable news commentary offered inspired her, and she flew into flights of Italian swear words. *"Stronzi! Cazzo!"* she repeated alternately. Her sense of her own dignity and righteousness swelled up with each curse, and that didn't account for the sheer pleasure the words gave inside the mouth, like baklava or sponge cake. The outrage was transporting if not completely orgasmic.

"I can't come this instant, *caro*. Let me just hear this," she shouted, but then he saw her lumbering toward him. She was beamy, he thought to himself, and wondered instantly if this observation was another sign of Neanderthalism. Did measuring her hips beneath the embroidered and sheer pale-green top define and condemn him as a man from the lower orders? He knew enough to know that that was a question he shouldn't ask his daughter if he was expecting a considered answer.

"Would you mind clipping my fingernails, dearest?" he asked her. He extended his right hand toward her. His left hand wasn't coordinated enough to do the job by itself. Being at Dita's mercy was not his favorite marital position. Sometimes she simply said do it yourself and turned back to the television. Other times she sat next to him on the two-seater and placed his right arm across her thighs, taking her time, smiling and repeating the day's stories. That was the tenderness he angled for. It didn't seem like much to ask, but sometimes it seemed to be.

"What are you making for Alessandra?" he asked.

"Pasta in brown butter and sage sauce," she answered. "You know that's the only reason she comes home, don't you? It's not to see us anymore."

"Not so true," he said as she finished clipping. "Aren't we part of the dish? We select and mince the leaves, crush the garlic clove, et cetera. We're all in the same family casserole, aren't we? And you combine and season and stir as if your mother had taught you in the old country."

There was nothing Italian about Dita except her name, which she mistook for an Italian diminutive but was really a Spanish abbreviation of Perdita, which translated to "lost woman." Her given name was Delores, which she abhorred, so she'd changed it as soon as she could. Dita was the only name Benjamin knew her by. She had grown up a single child in a small Tudor house in Larchmont, and every Sunday night she went with her mother and father to a Neapolitan restaurant on the banks of the Hudson River for cannelloni and spumoni. For her, Sunday didn't represent the end of the weekend as much as the freedom of the week ahead, and she couldn't think of a better way to celebrate than with a thick tomato sauce and frozen ice cream. In her teenage years she taught herself to make the dishes she loved. She added nuances of flavor and refined them, and by this time they had become an extension of her. She prepared them without thinking, combining the ingredients absentmindedly and intuitively as if she were a native.

Benjamin had grown up in the building where he and Dita lived. His developer grandfather had built it in the 1920s, and his cousin was the chintzy chairman of the board. It was the shabby, oversized New York version of a Parisian *maison particulière*. Its antiquated system of pipes forbade basic modern conveniences such as in-sink disposal units, forcing its tenants to squeeze their trash into narrow chutes that reeked of the Depression, when they had been invented, fabricated, and installed. Family members were sprinkled across its twelve floors, mixed with renters who had blundered into the building unaware that they were being admitted to a family colony as much as an apartment building. Benjamin could still remember trailing his grandfather's long outdoor coat down the speckled black linoleum tiles as he went from door to door collecting rent.

"Guess who called me today? Spence," he said without waiting for an answer. "It must be at least two years since I've heard from him. Asked me to come visit him in the office in the morning. Says he has a new project he wants me to work on. Some kind of device he said," Benjamin added before Dita got up to walk to the kitchen. "Headphones, I think. No, hearing aids. He said it might rescue us!"

"What would you do?" Dita asked skeptically.

"I'm not sure yet. I'll let you know tomorrow when we're done, but he said it was writing some kind of perspective paper and then maybe some other copy. He was vague. You know how vague he can be when he's trying to trap you," he said, following her to the kitchen.

"You don't know how to do that. You haven't written anything in twenty years, and I'm not sure your reference library will help you much. They're not exactly practical texts unless you think *The Ego and the Id* might explain Spence. Come to think of it, that might give you what you need to understand him. The ego part, not the id," she said, gesturing toward his shelves in the other room as if she were the hostess on a game show letting the contestants have a peek at the glamorous prizes behind her.

"Thanks, I'll keep that in mind," he said, and turned away from her. Standing in front of his bathroom mirror again he examined his torso and was surprised when he lifted his shirt by the slackness of the skin around his midsection, especially on the sides. It seemed to pucker and puddle in places that had never shown excess before, but a little pasta couldn't make matters any worse, he thought. Working for Spence, his pugnacious baby brother, flashed through his mind. The idea presented a multitude of problems.

Benjamin was older than Spence by five years. His brother was a profile of continuous prosperity and success. Benjamin had sat on the world's sidelines, collecting his meager share of the building's rental income, giving himself the alibi that fewer doers and more sifters were needed and he would never be one of the former. Spence had taken the path of direct action. Little by little he had accumulated a controlling stake in a retail franchise business selling hearing aids and related auditory gadgets. Benjamin didn't know exactly how he had accomplished this, but he feared the worst: intimidation and chicanery. He renamed the motley collection of stores and outlets Belphonics on Benjamin's recommendation. Spence had gone for the suggestion instinctively and impulsively, still believing somewhat reluctantly in his older brother's aptness and originality. The name combined the essential twin roots of *beauty* and *sound*. As the company grew, added franchisees, built a network across the country in the early aughts, payments rolled in and Spence became unaccountably rich. In thanks, he sent Benjamin a small check every month to supplement his share of the building income and to help maintain his brother's precarious financial position. His suggestion that Benjamin become more directly involved with him felt both tantalizing and menacing. It was unlike Spence to be involved with people or situations in which he didn't hold a dominant position. Spence's idea of control was at best whimsical and at worst despotic.

The sound of the front door creaking open disrupted Benjamin's thoughts. Before leaving his station in front of the mirror, he counseled himself to not think any more about the next day's meeting while Alessandra was there. If anxiety was a necessary component of his preparation for meeting with Spence, there would be plenty of time for that during the night. He buttoned his shirt and rinsed the tiny, dark clippings from the sink bowl. Alessandra presented herself in a burgundy-colored boiler suit in a shimmery, no doubt inflammable fabric, subdued for her, that showed off the new red tint in her hair. How exotic she was, he thought to himself as he went to embrace her.

In Alessandra's honor Dita turned off the television. She knew that Alessandra's patience for twenty-four hour news was limited and didn't wish to put up with her daughter's criticisms. How could Alessandra not understand that the day's news, no matter how recycled, was essential? Even Benjamin, who was a stoic about most things but especially his wife's peccadilloes, found Dita's obsession with nonstop cable irritating. She put the top on the large saucepan and carried it to the table. The giant blue dish on the silver accordion trivet was one of the few heirlooms to travel with her from the lower Westchester suburbs. The air was steamed with the humidity and aroma of its contents.

"Dad has some sort of news, darling," Dita announced. "Spence asked him to come to the office tomorrow to help him with a new project."

"Probably it doesn't mean anything. Not worth discussing," Benjamin said, bringing the conversation back to a less speculative reality.

"Are you still upset that I called you a Neanderthal?" Alessandra said, eager to take the sting out of her remark. "You shouldn't be. The Neanderthal brain was as big as ours, no, even bigger. That isn't what separated them from us. It was more their community and language. Their linguistic ability was far less developed than ours, but it wasn't nonexistent. Their social circles were small, and family groups were more isolated from other families. Apartment living wouldn't have been for them. They preferred living in small groups clustered around their hearths. They cooked together and migrated together on their massive legs. They covered distances we couldn't imagine doing today."

While Alessandra elaborated on her favorite topic between bites, Dita started fiddling with her phone. To expand her Italian vocabulary beyond curses, she had registered for an online language course that required her to repeat certain phrases into the phone's tiny speaker. A male voice pronounced, "Mi scusi, posso farle una domanda?" very slowly, and Dita imitated it as closely as she could. "Ti voglio bene," the voice said, and Dita repeated the statement. Then she uttered another phrase, a wish, a desire that wasn't part of the lesson, but no one paid attention as she pronounced it. "Voglio un uomo." She repeated it into the phone and then placed the phone facedown on the oak dining table. She sat solemn and still, as if she were squaring off with the question she had asked, one that had come to her out of nowhere. To whom had her request for "a man" been made? God? Heaven? What was she asking? It had popped into her mind so suddenly and unaccountably and vanished as quickly.

Benjamin and Alessandra paid no attention to her or her Italian. The inexpressive look on Dita's face hid the accretion of inner questions. Nor did she like their conversations about prehistory. The subject made her feel diminished and ignored. Sometimes, worse, it gave her a touch of vertigo. She preferred the immediacy of crushed garlic and wild country herbs to the abstraction of immeasurable time, remote strains of humanity living in caves and skinning the mammoths they had somehow caught and killed with sharpened cherts. She didn't want to have to imagine those lives, the damp discomforts, the danger and the wandering from place to place. She didn't want to see her life as the fulfillment of theirs. She liked this building and her apartment even if the bricks needed repointing, the hall tiles were scuffed, and some of the inner windows still had wire mesh running through them. If their building didn't equal better, fancier buildings, it was of little importance to her as long as she could travel to Italy as she and Benjamin planned to do in the spring. Her first visit.

"How did Neanderthals communicate?" Benjamin asked Alessandra. "Is there any way to know? Were their voices the same as ours? When I was a kid I used to practice saying words, and each time I'd pronounce one I'd lop off a syllable so that when I got to the end of the exercise there'd be this tiny vocal stub. Kind of like the particle of a groan. I thought it was my own special identifier, my sound print, the smallest noise I could make even if it had no meaning. Do you think that's how they talked? Just kind of grunting and pointing with their chins?"

"Not really. I don't know. Nobody knows. They have the same shape hyoid bones that we have, but their jaws and palates were shaped differently. I don't think we have any proof of how they talked or what they said. Some people think their voices were much higher pitched than ours, but who knows. Dad, I don't want to talk about this anymore. Mom's right. It makes you feel like a speck if you think about it too much, like you're not even a human, and I can say that without prejudice because I'm the one who decided to study them, but that doesn't mean they don't freak me out," Alessandra said.

Dita looked up from her phone and gazed over at her daughter. She has the same anxieties that I do, Dita thought with affection and solidarity. Her mother wondered if that was why primitive man fascinated her and why she dressed as she did. Dita considered this for long enough to think it might be too foolish a question to ask and dismissed it.

"Is that why you are always wearing Day-Glo?" Benjamin asked, introducing a topic that he and Dita had discussed between them. Maybe Day-Glo was the wrong word, he pondered. Personal questions of dress or behavior had on many previous occasions abruptly terminated their conversations as well as his daughter's visits.

"Yes, Pop. I imagine that a spaceship visiting from another galaxy will look down and if I am wearing bright-enough colors, they'll be able to see me. They will spot me from way up there, swoop down and rescue me. Whisk me away to their celestial Nirvana universe. Only me," she said with a faint smile.

Dita, fearing that the conversation might have reached an awkward point, stood up suddenly and started folding napkins. Benjamin carried the messy pan back to the tiny kitchen, emptied what was left of it into a plastic tub, and filled the dirty pot with warm water. When he squirted detergent into it he heard the sticky front door creak open. He recognized the sound of what he thought might be an escape. Had he driven Alessandra away again? He hadn't meant to. He was an ape. She was right. He cursed himself using the Italian words he'd heard Dita shout over and over. He had hounded her out when what he yearned for was the opposite. He wanted her to remain, to move back into her old room down the hall that still held her childhood drawings and photographs and little clothes and shoes and picture albums of long-ago summers when the heat was only intermittently unbearable.

He dropped the dish towel and rushed out to apologize for his rudeness and to beg her to come back and stay longer. The person he saw standing just inside the doorway took his breath away.

"Giorgio?"Benjamin shouted.

"Dad," he replied flatly.

Their son was back. Benjamin could feel the static in his ears break into a crescendo as he rushed toward him, straining to reach his arms around his wide shoulders. Giorgio had been absent for almost three years, since they had sent him away for his uncontrollable behavior, his rages and his angry hands, fierce when they jumped out of his pockets. He had been only fourteen years old, tall and spindly, when he left for the wilderness camp in the mountains of southern Utah. Benjamin and Dita had visited him there once, but that was over two years ago. They hadn't seen him since and had had almost no contact with him except for the occasional postcard or, even rarer, a phone call. The remedial school in Omaha he attended after the wilderness camp in Utah had also restricted their communication.

He was taller now, over six foot two. His body had broadened and strengthened. Even through his coat and shirt, Benjamin could see a thickness in his son's arms and shoulders. His lank black hair fell over his right eye, but that didn't hide the remnants of the cherubic roundness in his face that he'd had even as an infant. At seventeen he possessed authority and stature. He had left as a child and returned as a man.

Giorgio leaned forward slightly to hug his father.

"Are you all right?" Benjamin asked. "Why didn't you warn us?"

"I just need to sleep, Dad. I haven't been in a bed in days. I am so tired my bones feel like they are crumbling inside my skin."

"Oh, *Dio mio,* Giorgio!" Dita shouted when she saw him from the kitchen. She rushed to him, threw her arms around his neck, and pulled his head down to her. They both felt the dampness on her cheek. "You come out of the air, *carissimo,* a *miracolo*! We just finished dinner. Your favorite. Ravioli with sage. I'll get you some."

Giorgio lifted his duffel bag off his shoulder and set it down gently in the corner. He took off the long blue military-style coat he was wearing despite the heat and dropped it on top. He pulled out one of the dining room chairs, and it disappeared beneath him. With as much love as she had felt for him on the day that he was born, Dita brought out his plate and watched him put the first forkful into his mouth.

"Amore," she whispered in his ear. "Dove sei stato?" She asked him over and over again where he had been, as though no answer was satisfactory.

"Omaha," he answered. "Omaha. But I left. I told them I was leaving."

Hearing the commotion, Alessandra approached slowly from the other end of the hall. At first, like her mother, she thought he wasn't real—an apparition. But then she noticed the spotty stubble and whiskers on Giorgio's cheeks and throat and the familiar tilt of his head. They had corresponded and even spoken a few times while he was away, but it had never crossed her mind that she would actually be seeing him anytime soon. His physical presence overwhelmed her.

"When did you get back? Where have you been? Have you been in the city all this time hiding from us?" Alessandra asked him urgently. He didn't answer but looked up from his plate.

The scene was a tableau of surprise. His mother and father were huddled together again like survivors of a shipwreck, as they had been the night of his arranged abduction. His sister, who stood next to him, was leaning toward him, her coiled hair dangling. She had been at school and was told the next day that he had been sent away to a place where he could learn to live better with other human beings. She had been furious at her parents for not preparing her or consulting her.

"Too many questions. I'm too tired for that. I got a bus back from Omaha a few days ago. It was time for me to leave. I was ready to come home. New York City feels like Mars. The hostel in Omaha was so full, I had to sleep under this bridge in a park called the Heartland of America Park right next to the Missouri River. Dabbers' Bridge it's called because that's where they all live. They all hassled me. Smoke this. Try that. Dab this. You know. I don't get on with those people. Don't want to be around them." Giorgio stabbed at the food in front of him but it didn't appear to energize him. He was pale and strangely composed.

Except for the sound of Giorgio chewing and swallowing, the room was quiet. His large, unexpected body filled the small space, pushing his family back against the plain white walls and wainscoting as though they were experiencing blast waves from a massive explosion. Their former selves, the old issues between them, were broken into little pieces and were swept out into the hall to be crammed into the chute like other garbage. The enormity of his return made him larger than he had ever been.

2

FIRST OF ALL, MY NAME ISN'T FUCKING GIORGIO. WHEN I WAS born, Mark was the name I was given and that is my true, original name before my mother changed it four years ago. I know lots of kids are given nicknames, especially girls, but I had a perfectly good name and it is the one I wish everyone would use. When I was "transferred" to Camp Fremont the guides greeted me by calling me Giorgio. Even my goons called me Giorgio. My name is Mark, I am not Italian, I said, trying not to shout at them.

So I'm retracing my steps little by little. Be patient with me. This isn't easy. It forces me to review some of the terrible things I have done. I tell myself sometimes that I wasn't the one who did them. I was provoked, and the provoking was responsible for my actions. If the Program did one thing, it was to make it perfectly clear that it was really me who did the things I was ashamed of. I did have the power to act in other ways even if I didn't understand that while it was happening. But you spend a freezing night shivering under a tarp at eight thousand feet, solitary frigid fucking confinement, pissing into a plastic bottle so you don't have to get up and out of your sleeping bag and freeze your dick off, and it gets harder and harder week after week to convince yourself that you aren't responsible for something.

At first I hated the noise of the bristlecone and piñon pine trees creaking in the wind. It sounded to me like they were groaning, aching and bending in ways that were painful to their old, gnarled bodies. I thought they were trying to tell me how much it hurt, and I couldn't stand the thought of their pain. But the longer I spent out there alone, the more they became my chorus when I had no other company. They talked to me and consoled me. I started to think of them as this kind of heavenly forest choir and their straining in the wind was their daily warming-up exercise. We all have our music, I guess. When there was no breeze and they were hushed, I hoped the wind would rev up and their singing would start again.

During the first week or two, it was hard to get the city out of me. The hoodoos spooked me. They rose like stand-alone desert skyscrapers out of nowhere. During the day they were peculiar, kind of lopsided. At night they were terrifying and their tilting made zombie shadows fall across the dirt. The desert varnish, a topcoat of paint on the cliffs, our leader told us, gave the sandstone spooky human faces. But the worst was the stars banging away at me, competing for my attention when I was scrunched up in my sleeping bag and trying to duck their glare. It took days for me to get used to lights that bright that I couldn't switch off. And the fresh air choked me. There was so much of it, I almost couldn't breathe. I had to practice sleeping with my mouth closed so it wouldn't fill up with wind.

Although it feels like a long time ago now, it also feels like it happened yesterday. From my sleeping bag, I could see how my behavior turned from bad to worse. The first thing I did wrong was to smash Walt's head into the aquarium. Walt was my friend, my only friend in eighth grade. He was a pale, skinny kid who was shorter than the rest of us. His dad was sick, very sick. Cancer of the... I can't remember. He followed me around everywhere. I couldn't get rid of him, but I kind of liked him. He'd come over to my apartment after school, and we'd listen to records all afternoon. The same ones day after day. For my thirteenth birthday my dad had given me a turntable and a few vinyl records that he had saved from the olden times: from Cat Stevens to the Talking Heads. We'd play some of them so many times, my mom would come into my room and say, "Basta!" It's weird for your own mother to turn Italian and your dad to do nothing to save her. It's like living with an international transplant or spy. We listened to *Tea for the Tillerman* so often that we knew all the lyrics by heart. We could even hum the opening bars before Cat started shouting that there was "a lot of bad everywhere." I guess Walt and I bonded over that. I wonder what he's doing now. Poor kid. I learned that his father died in a letter Mom wrote me. I should have written to tell him that I felt sorry for him, but I didn't. Not writing was just another sin. I know that's bad, but it's not as bad as what I did to him on that late-fall day.

I was in the boys' bathroom at my school. I'd closed the stall door and sat down on the toilet seat. I heard noises outside, and I could tell that there was some kind of ruckus going on, pushing and shoving. I recognized each one of the voices. The next thing I knew, Walt burst through the stall door that hadn't closed securely and four other boys from my grade were staring at my naked parts because I reflexively stood up to slam the door as fast as I could. Walt stammered, "Sorry, sorry, sorry." The other boys started laughing and pointing at me, saying "Giorgio, Giorgio," over and over. Joining them, Walt laughed a little too although I now think he did it just to fit in with the others. They knew I hated that name, and so they taunted me with it. I pushed Walt out and banged the door closed.

When I sat down to try and recover from the invasion and humiliation, I could feel my head start to swell like that time my thumb got slammed in the taxi door. It turned a sour numb purple even though Alessandra, formerly Claire, said she was sorry and it was just an accident. She hadn't seen that I wasn't completely out of the cab and my hand was left behind. That's how sore my head felt now. Somewhere inside my brain there was a fuse like the ones on cherry bombs. It was lit. I could hear it crackling and feel the prickly heat and picture the sparks it threw off in my head. They were flying all through me from the back of my neck to the top of my forehead. I knew I had to snuff them out, but I didn't know how. My brain had never hurt so badly before.

I flushed the toilet, stuck my hands under the cold water tap, and slapped water on my cheeks and eyelids to try to cool off. I wanted to stick my whole face under there, but it wouldn't fit. I ran back to the classroom, and by that point my head was on fire. I could feel the burning on my skin and smell it sizzling. Our homeroom teacher, Ms. Leesar, was standing at the blackboard, her hand raised above a column of numbers that she was asking the class to solve, and she was saying something about ratios. I was unable to listen, wasn't interested in the ratio of anything to anyone. I wanted to punish Walt for what he had done to me. The shame and embarrassment he'd caused me. Exposing my nakedness to others. He was sitting at his desk all twisted up, arms and legs crossed, limbs too long and thin. I grabbed him by the throat of his shirt and lifted him up out of his chair. He felt so light and life-less, like a puppet, and I had a superhuman strength in my arms like the mother I'd read about in *Life* magazine who had lifted a car off her son's body saving his life, even if it was only a Volkswagen Beetle. Walt felt weightless. It was only a split second before I saw the aquarium on the low shelf in the classroom and I knew that I wanted to put him in there with the fish that he fed every day and loved. I didn't really want to hurt him. I wanted to stun him, to astonish him, to do to him what he had done to me minus the embarrassment.

As soon as I heard the crack his head made when it collided with the glass wall of the aquarium, I knew that I was in trouble. Not only dis-ciplinary trouble with the school but trouble with my soul. Mortal trouble. The glass on the long side of the tank cracked and burst like a dam unleashing water from a reservoir. It gushed onto the floor and the fish tried to swim in the bubbly streams of it without getting stuck dry on the linoleum. Goldfish, Siamese fighting fish, guppies, tetras, and zebra fish flailed and flapped across the tiles under the desks and chairs. Kids lifted their feet to let them pass. Panic broke out. Ms. Leesar shouted, "Scoop them up, scoop them up!" and threw little Dixie cups around the classroom in a cyclone of Styrofoam. Walt lay half-soaked in a ball on the floor. There wasn't any blood on his face or shirt, but I saw that a shiny, pinkish bump had swelled up on his forehead.

Ignored in the mayhem, I sat rigidly in my seat. I felt creepy calm while the teacher and other students shot around the room in a frenzy rescuing the fish, shouting directions at each other, and giving stray advice. I loved those fish, especially the blue betta that Ms. Leesar had let me name. I had called him Barry, for our president. I knew Walt would be all right without being sure how I knew it. I just did. Walt would recover. The nurse would hold a bag of ice on his lump and send him home. He'd get all his parents' sympathy and attention. I bowed my head in my hands and kept muttering, "Barry, Barry, Barry," and tried not to sob for my pathetic self.

As soon as the fish had been rescued and most of the water mopped up, Ms. Leesar called Dr. Feigel and my parents from the wall phone in the corner. She marched me down to his office without saying a word. Although Feigel was director of the upper school, he wasn't known for his guidance as much as his pettiness. In fact, everybody hated him, even the teachers. Once, after he complained that we hadn't hung up our coats after he had repeatedly asked us to, he gathered them up and threw them on the outdoor terrace and locked the door. He was the only one who had the key. We couldn't retrieve them until we had sat through his interminable lecture. Accidentally, he had swept up several teachers' coats in the same bundle. We overheard their seething whispers in the common room.

The only image that consoled me as I was being walked to Feigel's office was imagining Barry swimming in a tight circle in his little cup.

The beautiful, smooth waving of his tiny fluttering fins, the radiance of his cobalt blueness, and the little nibbling lunges he made with his mouth, like kisses, when food was dropped near him moved me. His littleness and his elegance brought me to the verge of internal tears.

Feigel's fat pink face stuck on top of his thick body leaned toward me across his desk. He didn't say anything. He just stared at me as if he couldn't believe that I was human.

"Before your parents arrive," he said, "would you like to explain to me what made you act in such an irrational and violent way? Or was there no provocation? Were you just in the mood to hurt someone and so, naturally, you picked on your best friend?" Feigel didn't know anything about me or Walt, so Leesar must have signaled to him that Walt and I were friends. I wasn't going to answer him or look him in the eye, so I watched him tug at the collar that cinched against his swollen neck. That made the fat stack up in wrinkles. Dad had taught me how powerful silence could be.

"If you don't say something, I can give you more than a warning," he said, trying to scare me. "The school can ground you. No time in the common room. No outdoor sports, but you don't like sports anyway, do you?" Because I was tall, he had tried to get me to try out for the loser basketball team he coached. All of his pet students were tall. I didn't have any interest in him or his team of suck-ups. Luckily, my parents arrived so I didn't have to give the obvious answer to his question.

As soon as they walked into the room, I felt they had my back. My father was wearing a tie, which he used to do when I was little even though now he rarely left the house, and my mother wore a brown tunic top with sequins on it, and her long blond hair looked as if she had just taken the curlers out. It fell midway down her back and bounced when she walked. She gave me a big hug and pressed my cheek against the hard sparkling discs. Dr. Feigel stood up and extended his hand to my father, shaking his without looking up.

"We at Blethen School as you know think of ourselves as a learning community more than a disciplinary institution. Giorgio is a valued member of our community, as is Walt. So how are we to interpret what happened this morning? Giorgio, can you shed some light on the situation for us? Was there something that made you do what you did?'"

I squirmed in my chair. Maybe I'd tell my parents what happened, but I would never reveal a word of it to Feigel. Too humiliating. Too wild. Too risky. In my now calmer brain, I was trying to break down the events into smaller, digestible pieces. I had been minding my own business. I was intruded upon. I was gawked at and exposed, and even though I made an unsuccessful effort to control myself, it felt as if a monster had been uncaged inside my body and turned it into a lunatic's rag doll.

"Say something, darling," my mother urged, and smiled in Feigel's direction.

"I can't find any words, Mom. I'm sorry. Is Walt all right?" I said.

"Obviously, Giorgio, we believe that infractions have consequences. Your parents will take you home. Think about what happened and why. If you think it'll help, write down some of your thoughts and come see me tomorrow morning when you get in. How's ten minutes before class. Let's say eight o'clock?" Feigel said. I nodded.

I grabbed my backpack from my locker, and we walked out to the avenue. As soon as we left the building, my mother snarled at me to put my coat on. I still felt too hot and didn't want anything to suffocate my skin. When we were jammed into the back of the taxi, my mother reached around behind my father's neck and slapped me on the back of my head. It didn't hurt, but it stung.

"How could you be such a fucking idiot? What did I do wrong with you, Giorgio? I would do anything for you. Defend you to anyone, but tell me what I didn't teach you? Did I teach you to torture your friends? Is that how your father and I live? Is that what you see?" Then she slapped me again. This time it stung more.

"Dita, don't hit him. That doesn't help anyone," my father said.

"It helps me!" she said with a vengeance. "It is proof that I care about him."

"Walt walked in on me when I was on the toilet and laughed at me. They all laughed at me," I said.

"That could make anyone angry, Giorgio," my father said, squeezing my arm. "But you can't behave that way toward people, especially your friends. The next time you feel like that, you have to hold yourself in check. It takes practice, but I think you can do that. Do you think you can?"

"I don't know, Dad. Maybe. I can try," I said without a trace of confidence or energy.

"Why are you coddling him, Benjamin? There are no excuses in a crisis like this. It doesn't matter what made him do it. He's never going to behave like this again. And you're calling Walt this afternoon or you're going to reform school tomorrow. Do you hear me, Giorgio?" she asked, her voice strained by rage.

When we got home I shoved my things into my cubby as I always did after school as if nothing different had happened that day. I went into the kitchen and got a glass of cold water. I looked at my fingerprints in the mist on the side of the glass. Those were my swirls and curlicues, my traces. But at that moment I thought to myself that if I wasn't more careful, they might end up in a police file someday.

3

BENJAMIN HADN'T VISITED SPENCE AT THE BELPHONICS office in many years. It wasn't only that there had been no invitation, there'd also been no desire on either one of their parts. He regarded Spence as he regarded any volatile substance, something to handle with extreme caution and as rarely as possible. Wear protective gear.

The office was in a prestigious Midtown building near Grand Central but the place itself was shabby. Inside the front door, a receptionist sat propped on a purple swivel chair with stray threads sticking out behind the padded shoulders of her black jacket. Where the front door opened, the lime-green carpet was worn down to its tan fibers. The logo Benjamin remembered from long ago was still on the wall behind her. It was an ear trumpet made of handworked metal.

As he was shown the hall to Spence's office, he noticed a new series of hearing devices through the ages displayed in immaculately clear plexiglass boxes on the wall. A small curatorial note hung beside each device giving its name, material, date, and origins. On the other wall were reproductions of famous ear paintings from Hieronymus Bosch to Salvador Dalí. The final one showed Vincent van Gogh with a soiled bandage around his head covering the bloody spot where he had lopped off his ear. The displays must have been chosen and designed by Anna, Spence's pixieish ex-wife, who Benjamin hadn't seen in almost a decade. They displayed her sly sense of humor. With the hope that omission would erase her from history, Spence never mentioned her name.

When his brother entered, Spence stood up. While Benjamin was on the lanky side, Spence had the body of a middleweight. He was five feet six inches tall with a beaming smile, unnaturally white teeth, jags of brown gelled hair shaped into a surfer's curl circa 1965 that dangled over his forehead, and the heedless movement of a mechanized vehicle. He plowed forward no matter whom he was walking toward or in what direction he was headed. He threw his short, thick arms around his brother's chest and nuzzled his shirt with his cheek.

"God, it's good to see you, Benjy!" Spence exclaimed. "I have really missed you. How long has it been since you came to the office? How many years? The number doesn't matter. You're here in the nick of time. How is everyone, by the way?"

"All fine. Giorgio came home last night. We were all in shock. He's taller than I am," Benjamin said.

"How long has he been gone? I can't remember."

"Close to three years."

"Three years. Wow! That is a long time to spend in the desert. I don't think I'd last a night out there. I still can't understand why you sent him away. Just makes no sense to me. How could he have been that bad? He was such an angel. I'm no father. Obviously. How long has it been since you saw him?"

"Almost two years."

"How could you stand that?"

"We couldn't. But they convinced us that minimal communication was best so kids can figure out how they went wrong away from home."

"Didn't you want to visit him and talk to him and hug him?"

"I visited him every single night at four in the morning. I obsessed over the decision we made, but he was just too much for us. I don't know what else we could have done. The Omaha school called this morning to say that he had been discharged. Can you believe that? No warning. Nothing."

"So, I had an idea that needs you. Do you want to hear it?"

"Of course I want to hear it. I wouldn't have come here otherwise."

"Okay, so how old are you now? Fifty-five or something, right? Maybe a little closer to sixty?" Benjamin nodded. "How's your hearing? Have you ever had it checked?"

"No. My hearing's fine, Spence."

"I'm not so sure, but we will get it tested by a professional. It's part of the job I have in mind for you. I made an appointment for you at ten with Dr. H. She's the best. She does a lot of our technical work. I hope you don't mind and don't have anything else scheduled for later?" He smiled, suspecting that Benjamin had nothing to do all day. Spence failed to understand his brother's philosophy of life, seeing it only as a blank diary that was waiting to be filled.

Spence swiveled his high-backed black leather chair to a small glass-fronted medical cabinet that rested on a table behind his broad desk. He extracted an otoscope with a gold handle from a gleaming leather holster. Of course, Benjamin thought, stainless steel would be too common for Spence. No doubt he had had it custom made. Spence changed the plastic protector covering the tip and came toward him holding the scope as though it was a tomahawk.

"Do you mind if I have a look? Don't worry. I have a lot of experience doing this. And since we are brothers, I trust we haven't kept too many secrets from each other," Spence said with a grin.

"If you have to," Benjamin answered, repeating a phrase that he suddenly remembered uttering many times during their earlier lives. Spence would describe one imaginary, reckless adventure or another and repeat it until, to Benjamin's ears, it had lost all its meaning or, worse, sounded normal. Fatigued, Benjamin would say, "If you have to," and Spence would do whatever he'd been insisting on—jumping off the top bunk, tossing pennies or Idaho baking potatoes off the tenth-floor balcony of the family apartment. Spence had always possessed a quality that Benjamin defined as harmful carelessness, but he wasn't without charm.

Spence yanked the top of Benjamin's earlobe up, inserted the scope into his right ear, and flicked on the light button on the scope. He hummed slightly as he maneuvered it inside his brother's inner ear. Benjamin stared at the wall and prayed for the examination to be over.

"You have to take better care of your ears, Ben. It's a swamp in there. Ever heard of a Q-tip? But still the mechanism is so beautiful, so perfect. The tympanum is like a shimmering cymbal. The cochlea is curled around itself, and those little hairs that trap the sound waves and dispatch signals to the brain are still in perfect condition. Dr. H can give you the whole rundown, but I don't see anything wrong." Spence said in a tone of momentary rapture, withdrawing the otoscope. Benjamin felt defenseless against his brother's diagnosis. Spence returned the otoscope to the medical cabinet and signaled that his brother should follow him to his office seating area—a couch, two chairs, and a glass-topped coffee table.

"So let me tell you what I have in mind. Ideas are dangerous, I know that, but listen to the whole thing before you tear it apart. First, how many times did you go to CBGB's?" he asked, staring straight into his brother's eyes. Benjamin hadn't thought of the dingy, raucous club on the Lower East Side that reeked of beer and vomit in decades.

"A few times," he answered, struggling to remember the details of a place he hadn't been to in over thirty years. The excitement of the cab rides downtown to the Bowery, the exhaustion of the return home came back immediately as did erratic moments of rapture. "Maybe more."

"Not true, Benjy. You went at least fifty times and I went even more, since we didn't always go together. Remember the bands we saw there for the first time? Talking Heads. Television. The Ramones. Voidoids. Suicide. Remember those amazing nights? We memorized every word they sang. Knew every riff. We wanted to be them. How they danced, how they flopped on the stage. How they didn't care what anybody thought of them. We were so young but nobody ever carded me. We were high. We drank beer and puked in the toilets. Remember the graffiti on the walls? If those weren't the greatest nights of our lives, what were?" Spence spoke with a phlegmy, contagious rapture that made Benjamin feel as if they had been temporarily rejoined as brothers and adventurers.

"There were some great moments. I agree. That was over thirty years ago. What has it got to do with us now?" Benjamin asked, growing impatient.

"So I don't know about you, but my hearing isn't that great. My theory is that it must have been those nights at CBGBs that caused the damage. Tom Verlaine's guitar. And Richard Lloyd's too. God, they sang and played together like angels, didn't they? Anyway, it can't just be me. There must be hundreds or thousands, maybe millions of us who lost some or all of our hearing at CBGB's or other clubs or stadiums around the world, right?"

"Maybe, or maybe they just got older like we did and the hearing decline was organic. And you're right, Spence. Ideas are dangerous. So what is it?"

"When CBGB's went out of business in 2006, it started licensing its name. They even have a gift shop at Newark Airport. So my idea is this. What if we acquired the rights to the CBGB name to create a line of hearing aids for all of us who were wounded by rock and roll? One of the most difficult obstacles in the hearing aid business is that people don't want to admit that they're aging and need them. They resist, yet almost eighty percent of people who might benefit won't use them. It's the same as walking with a cane or having a patch over your eye. It proclaims that you are old. It also says that you're checked out, no longer a player in the external world. You're adrift on your inner sound waves, since you can't exactly hear the ones outside you. That's why they make them smaller and smaller so no one will be able to see them. But what if we designed a hearing aid that stood out, that was a badge of honor? One that proclaimed that you were proud of your impairment, not embarrassed by it. What if by wearing them you showed the world that you had lost your hearing for something you loved and that you knew that it had been a worthy sacrifice. A sacrifice for rock and roll? What better reason could there be than that? The theme of our lives. The heart of our youth still beating, still alive. Wouldn't that be glorious? Wouldn't that transform us from being hobbling, aging men into esteemed veterans, into actors in a great drama? It would be a vindication of the life we lived. It would affirm our devotion to what we loved, what we followed and believed in. Wouldn't that make us greater and more beloved?" Spence paused to give his brother a moment to digest what he thought of as his most original idea. Spence's fervor reminded Benjamin of the early days of Belphonics when he had been the first sounding board for Spence's ideas.

"How many people went to CBGB's?" Benjamin asked.

"Enough. But you're missing the point of the tie-in. Far more people have heard of it than ever went there. Remember what they used to say about the first Velvet Underground album?" Spence asked.

"No," he answered. "What?"

"They say only ten thousand people bought it, but they were the ten thousand most important people in the world. And all of them started a band!" Spence declared, pounding the heel of his fist on the glass table, which reverberated from the impact.

"It wasn't mainstream, and not everybody liked the punks who went there, including us. They were drunk and they stank. We didn't even like all the bands," Benjamin said.

"Hey, it was far bigger than you think. It may have started off as only a punk club, but they took over the radio. Talking Heads and Patti Smith and Blondie. They became world-famous. And I still listen to their records, don't you?" Spence asked.

"No, never. So what do you want me to do?" Benjamin asked, skeptical.

"This is all just a hunch so far. I need someone I can trust to keep it quiet to tease it out, turn it into something solid and dress it up. Do some research, pull the numbers together and write them up so I can convince the Board to let me do what I want. I'm a much bigger company now than I used to be. I'm not a one-man band. I have to sell it and you have to give me the ammo. I think you can do this, Benjy, don't you?"

"So this is just a research project. Nothing else. Do I work here or from home? Who do I deliver my report to?"

"So many questions, Benjy? You're already exhausting me! I haven't thought about any of that yet. I thought I'd just kick it around with you first, and I knew I could trust you. We have to keep this project totally secret. I don't want any of my competitors to get a whiff of it. What do you think? Do you like the sound of it?"

"I need a little time to reflect on it. Can I have a day or two?"

"Of course, take all the time you need, but I'd love it if you could get started right away. Maybe tomorrow. Talk to Dita. Talk to your kids. Or Alessandra or whatever her name is now. But remember, it's only a little, short-term project, not a lifetime appointment. Almost time for you to go. The girl outside will tell you where. Come back and see me for a minute afterward. Have fun. I love Dr. H!"

Benjamin walked back down the hall lined with primitive instruments and images. The receptionist handed him an appointment card with a name and an address printed on it. He examined the card as the elevator plummeted down the fifteen flights, depositing him in the cool lobby. He clutched his umbrella and prepared himself for the layers of flannel heat that awaited him outside the front doors. During the time he had been in Spence's office, the fine sweat that had coated him as he walked in had congealed on his skin. The other pedestrians looked wilted and pale, the opposite of Spence with his splotchy, red face and bluster. They slouched along the pavements as if they were in a trance of humidity, barely lifting their feet or swinging their arms.

Although he stuck to the shady side of the street and Dr. H's office was only a few blocks from Spence's, Benjamin was dripping again by the time he opened the door to the refrigerated lobby. His white shirt stuck to his chest, and his sweat formed a ragged bull's-eye in the middle of his back. Even the inside of his wrists felt sticky. As though the heat was a different kind of smothering blanket, the city seemed as quiet to him as it did during the freak snowstorms that struck in March. Traffic in the heat was reduced by more than half, and the taxis brave enough to keep driving on the buckling asphalt crept along, not even beeping their horns. A muffled, woolen silence accompanied the atmospheric conditions. Had his hearing been eroded by time, or, as Spence insinuated, was it the effect of those raging bands that cranked the amps to their maximum volume?

Sandwiched between the Swiss American Amity Society and the headquarters of The Astronaut Food Digest, Dr. H's office was inauspicious. A simple brass plate with a finely profiled ear in black below it was followed by a short parade of letters listing her qualifications. Entering, Benjamin was struck by how small she was. Almost as if she were trying to compensate for her size Dr. H had an exaggerated cascade of dyed auburn curls that were too large to be natural. There were so many of them that he wondered how long it took a curling iron to get the job done. Hung on the wall above a rickety electric organ were Fender guitars signed on the fretboard by unknown lead guitarists.

Even with the advantage of patterned and multicolored stilettos that seemed to be her trademark, Dr. H was barely taller than five foot two. On the wall behind her left shoulder was a calendar where the weeks were marked off by assorted pairs of equally garish footwear. For Rosh Hashanah it featured a clunky wedge covered in aquamarine sequins. For Yom Kippur, a six-inch-high silver heel that was a triumph of structural engineering.

"Such an honor to meet you, Benjamin. Spence has told me nothing about you. Of course. I didn't even know he had a brother until yesterday. And an older, taller, handsome one, too. Are you here because you want to be, or did Spence force you to come?" she asked in a tiny, nasal voice.

"He didn't force me, but he urged me. Let's leave it at that."

"Yes, that's fair. He urges me to do all sorts of things I wouldn't think to do. Not all of them are terrible," she said. A smile flickered across her face. She gazed out the window as though she needed depth of field to reflect on her spontaneous statement. Benjamin, a poor judge of cosmetic surgery, noticed her chiseled features and wondered how many of them were naturally hers.

"So, let's get started," she said, and led him to the soundproof booth. She gave him a set of instructions. She mimed blocking one ear and then the other while she played a series of squiggly noises that were not even notes through the earphones. At first he watched her reaction through the dusty horizontal window to see if he had given the correct answer, but when she saw him watching her she covered her mouth with a sheet of paper. He closed his eyes; the ventilation slowed. He pictured the little sounds in his ears like flashes of fireworks that appeared and vanished over a ridge on a dark horizon. They flared and fizzled out in an instant before dissolving. No residual light was left behind, and the sky in his mind went black again until the next small efflorescence. He stopped worrying about what he answered correctly and sank into the panorama of sound in front of him. He didn't notice that the sequence had ended until the door clicked open and he felt Dr. H behind him. She put her tiny left hand on the right shoulder of his damp shirt and left it there long enough to let him know it wasn't a mistake.

"You have such beautiful hair, Benjamin," she said, tousling the top of his head, then running her fingers toward his neck. The compliment hung between them in the tight booth like a mummy that might burst into song. He didn't know what to say. Was she flattering him for a reason or because he was Spence's brother? Was she trying to tell him that she wanted something from him in a language that he didn't speak? In a hidden frenzy he searched for a reply. Should he compliment her back? Her hair, perhaps, or her high heels? Or how clearly she pronounced the random words he heard through the headphones she had placed over his ears? He wasn't sure, so he said nothing.

After another test, she asked him to sit next to her desk where he had sat before. He saw that she wore a locket around her neck that had a speckled stiletto composed of pavé diamonds on its little front latch.

"You have a shoe obsession, I guess," Benjamin muttered.

"Yes, I have a closet full of them," she said, and extended her leg toward him.

"A closet of obsessions?" Benjamin asked with a stony face. Dr. H's dark eyes ignored his intrusion.

Once her foot swung closer to him, he could tell that her shoes were covered in overlapping sequins that hypnotized him. The iridescent colors pooled together so he wasn't able to distinguish them. At first he thought they were golden, but then they turned silver and then a slate blue before changing back to their original color. He could feel himself being pulled in by her and didn't notice at first that she had lost interest in flattering him. She had become professional again, turning her attention to plotting the results of his hearing test on graph paper. Her pencil made solid black marks that formed a sloping curve. Each ear had its own scale of decline.

"Have a look at this, but remember that it's not definitive. The final results will be emailed to you tomorrow. These are preliminary, but they give us an idea of what you can and can't hear," she said, tracing her index finger along the curve.

"So on the left is the low range, and that covers low frequency. Certain letters like *f* and *b* even *j* and *r* are well within your hearing range. But as the decibel level increases and crosses over into the high range, your hearing loss is significant. Those letters are represented by the sibilants *s* and *z* This also means that it's hard for you to hear specific higher pitches like birds chirping or a kettle whistling. On the other hand, some sounds, like blenders and vacuum cleaners, are very loud for you and drive you crazy because your hearing distorts the sound and is amplified," she said in an analytical monotone.

Benjamin listened, and every word she spoke was at the perfect pitch. Was she making an extra effort to articulate for him? he wondered. He remembered that he hadn't responded to her compliment and thought about what he might say instead of listening to the details of his condition. As she leaned over the sheet and pointed to the lines and dots on the pages, he noticed that buried inside her tresses was a porcelain sulpha blue butterfly hairpin that shone like one landing in a field of wildflowers.

"I.....I.. like your little blue butterfly," he stammered, and didn't know what else to add.

"Thank you, Benjamin," she said. "So I will need you to come back next week for a follow-up appointment."

"Do I need hearing aids?" he asked nervously.

"Do you want them?"

Benjamin had never contemplated the idea before his meeting with Spence. Occasionally, when Dita muttered to herself or spoke to him from another room, which she did frequently or while the tap was running, he was unable to guess what she was saying, but it hadn't occurred to him that that was hearing loss as much as it was knowing so little Italian. Or maybe he had become indifferent to what Dita said. Often she spoke aloud not to communicate with him but to hear how her thoughts sounded. No confirmation was required, and none was offered.

"I need to think about that," he said.

"Take your time. Say hello to Spence for me. He said you were going back to his office after our appointment," she said.

"I will," he answered, and remembered, in spite of the numerous distractions, to retrieve his umbrella from the closet.

Back on the street, ambient sounds seemed brighter. Sonic details were sharper. The garbage trucks rumbled thunderously like boulders avalanching down a hillside. The horns of vans and taxis wailed; the brakes squeaked and pierced his aural defenses. Each minute sound took on its own life as if by hearing everything he was refuting Dr. H's initial conclusions about his condition. This was proof that her numbers and charts were exaggerated, if not wrong.

He went directly back to Spence's office and pushed open the door without knocking. Spence was talking on the phone with his feet propped on his desk, his tie loosened. He covered the mouthpiece and looked at his brother as if to say, "So?" Benjamin tossed the sheet of paper that Dr. H had handed him across the desk. Spence glanced at it, one ear glued to the receiver, and set it back down.

"So you know what this means, don't you?" Spence said in his heavy, raspy whisper, keeping his palm over the phone.

"No, I don't really understand it at all yet. What does it mean?" Benjamin asked as Spence examined the sheet of paper.

"It means you don't hear high frequencies too well, and you know what the significance of that is, don't you? It means that you don't hear women's voices as well as you hear men's. Maybe you don't hear them at all. That's what the little bird icon there stands for. Obviously due to social sensitivities, they couldn't put a woman's face on the chart, but that's the gist of it." He started cackling, his teeth glimmering as he traced the line Dr. H had drawn. It seemed to fall off a cliff into the depths that were labeled "severe" when it reached the higher registers.

Benjamin waved as he left his brother's office without saying another word and trundled down the hall. He couldn't wait to leave Spence's strange realm and see if Giorgio had woken up yet. But as eager as he was for his conversation with Giorgio, his brother's joke about women's voices preoccupied him. Spence and Dita had disliked each other from the instant they met. Her loyal, protective instincts for her husband had been jolted awake. She could sense the grip that Spence had on his older brother's mind, and she vowed to keep Spence as far from Benjamin and herself as she could. In Spence, she recognized the grabber, the taker, the possessor, and she determined that if anyone had to possess Benjamin, it would be her.

4

THE MORNING AFTER THE WALT AQUARIUM DISASTER I woke up early. It was still dark, but I could see that little clusters of crystals had formed in the corners of the window panes next to my bed. I can still feel some of the outdoor chill slithering through the cracks in the old wooden frames, although it was a long time ago. I turned away, but the cold air that snuck in rushed down my spine and made me curl into a ball.

Whether it would do any good or not, I couldn't help looking back at what had happened the day before. In slow motion I could see Walt burst through the door to the toilet, his pale face with its sick grin and the other boys crowding next to him to gawk at me and point at my naked midsection. The echoes of their laughter as they walked down the hall to our classroom made me hot with rage. I could feel the heat start to prick the backs of my eyeballs and press against the pulp inside my temples. My forehead throbbed and then froze like an ice cream brain freeze. I couldn't make it go away by breathing slowly or imagining a bright-green canary in its cage, as Mom had advised me to do once before when she saw that I was getting unstable. A mood adjuster, she had called the image. She could be full of helpful little tricks like that, although they didn't always work. Was that how being crazy felt? I wondered, and a panic streaked through me like I had gone swimming naked and a prankster had stolen all of my clothes.

To restore myself, I opened the drawer of my child-sized desk and groped through the odds and ends that had accumulated over the years until I found the bag of Skittles I'd stashed there. I poured out a bunch onto the blanket, and even in the near dark I could recognize their bright colors and taste their bright flavors. Friends of mine said they only liked certain ones and would throw the rest away, but I loved the whole Skittles rainbow mashed together in my mouth. A banquet of fake fruit. Before that incident I had never been one of those wild kids. At least not that I remember. I didn't talk much. Mostly, I was easygoing. Kind of happy even. I didn't have tantrums or bang my head against the radiator until somebody dragged me away. I'd heard about boys like that. We all had. They stood out like blinking red caution lights that flashed the word DANGER. Having your mother change your name was not the coolest thing that ever happened, either. It was disorienting, like being awakened in the middle of the night, kidnapped, and then being told by someone you vaguely recognized that you were another person. Names were meant to be unchangeable, timeless things, I thought, not something that could be switched on a whim by someone else. I tried to accept my new self, but I never could. And there was no reason for it, either. It's not as if our family was on the verge of moving to Italy or Alessandra and I were about to be transferred to La Scuola d'Italia Guglielmo Marconi on Ninety-Sixth Street, although Mom did mention that possibility from time to time as the straightest path to fluency. Everything else stayed the same: my room, our apartment, and my big sister, formerly Claire.

Mom had also said becoming Italian wasn't a big deal. I trusted her. Maybe she was right. Maybe it wasn't. So she changed my name, told the school and made only Italian food and spoke Italian phrases at dinner into her phone that I couldn't understand. Dad had tried to talk her out of it or at least blunt the impact, but I noticed after a while that he started to call me Giorgio too. Think of it as a nickname, he recommended, as if he knew that he didn't have a chance against the onslaught of her will and making it seem casual and natural was the best way to get used to the damage. When I tried to protest that it wasn't right, she scowled at me as if I had wounded her. I never wanted to hurt her even if she made me feel like an alien.

Claire, at least, had the fierceness to fight back, which was more than my father and I could manage. She said it was like switching our souls and souls couldn't be switched. And no one should even try it. I thought she had a strong argument, but it got her nowhere. Finally, she relented too. "Let Mom have her fun," she said, counseling me in a tone that I thought was a little dismissive.

Dita never wavered in her positions no matter how whimsical or wrong they were. I wondered if this was another aspect of her Italian conversion, as though she had come to possess some bit of ancient Sicilian wisdom, like the Mafia's idea of *omerta*. I'd heard Dad use that word once, and when I asked him what it meant, he made the zipper gesture across his lips and gave me an evil look. Then he explained that it meant that you never have to explain your actions. You just do them and never show a second's doubt.

That morning I realized that I had been hijacked, too. As Mom had been stolen by Italian food and the Italian language, a belligerent, out-of-control psychotic beast had decided to build its nest inside my body. I didn't recognize the "me" who had grabbed his best friend and smashed his head into a fish tank. Some alien had wormed its way inside me and was snacking its way through me. Although I couldn't tell who or what it was, I could sense a mobile, dark, pea-shaped object floating around inside my brain when I closed my eyes. Was that another sign of the alien inside me? It never stayed in one place, and I couldn't say for sure when or where it slept, if it ever did. At the same time, I could feel a warm, shadowy presence brushing softly against my back and shoulders. That came and left too. When I turned around to see who was behind me, whose body and skin it was, it was gone. But when it was quiet or I'd stopped worrying about it, it would sneak up on me again like the fuzzy ghost of a dead family dog rubbing against my leg, except we had never had a dog.

I walked to school along the same route as I always did once I was old enough to go on my own. The familiar corners, streets, and shops gave me comfort. I pictured Feigel's fat face blasting at me across his desk as he leaned forward. Perhaps he would have special words of advice to give me, although I had my doubts about that. My parents didn't have any particular wisdom for me either, or rather I hadn't given them the opening before it was time to go. I left before eight without saying good-bye. I didn't want my father's stock encouragement or my mother's stern advice rattling in my head. Instead, I focused on the image of that canary's chartreuse feathers that Mom had planted in my brain and the tranquil little trill that played in its small body. That was all the guidance I could handle.

The school halls were half-bright, half-shadow as I walked in. It was an earlier arrival for me than usual. Men in maintenance uniforms moved briskly along the hallways pushing giant brooms as if they were performing for the closed-circuit cameras. Teachers appeared around corners and slipped through doorways and up staircases that we kids weren't allowed to use. I thought I saw Ms. Leesar hurrying toward her classroom.

"So you've had some time to think about your actions, Giorgio. Any conclusions?" Feigel asked as soon as I sat down in his office without saying hello.

"Yes, I thought about it a little. I don't understand it, so how can I explain it to you? I don't even know you! He embarrassed me and then something got into my brain and that thing made me want to hurt him. That's it. Is he all right?" I couldn't say his name.

"All right, I guess. Walt will be back at school anyway. So we have a few options. Obviously, staying in detention for a couple of weeks could give you some time to figure it out. You could get your homework done, too. But I had another thought. Why don't you assist with the basketball team? You don't have to practice or play or do drills or anything like that, but maybe that's a way to get you involved without it being too official. What do you think?"

"What would I have to do?"

"You know, minor stuff. Carry the equipment, towels, and basketballs to our games. Mop up the court after practice. Small things like that. Nothing too time-consuming. That way I could keep an eye on you and you'd be part of something, not on your own all the time. And by the way, you have to talk to Walt, but I'm sure you were going to do that anyway, weren't you?"

"Yes, but I don't know what to say."

"Tell him what you told me, and maybe, since he was there, he'll be more understanding than I can be. Aside from being 'embarrassed,' you haven't told me what happened. What made you angry enough to do something like that? Most kids, even you, don't suddenly act like that out of the blue. There's more to it than that, whether you want to say exactly what it was or not. And I guess I don't need to tell you that it can't happen again. I have to protect the other students. Part of the job. So, what's it going to be?"

"I don't see myself with a mop," I said, annoyed. In my head, I repeated my vow to never tell Feigel what Walt and his friends had done that made me so upset. As I did, I remembered the word *omerta*. My stubbornness made me think that Mom and I had a lot more in common than I wanted to admit.

"No, are you sure? It's not that bad compared with suspension This is your first disciplinary warning. Let's not make a habit of it, okay? I don't want to see you in that chair again." Feigel smiled in an institutional way that had nothing to do with me. He probably used it in all kinds of situations.

"I'll try."

"Remember, my door is always open when you want to talk about it some more," he added. We both knew that I would never go back unless I had to.

When I got up from Feigel's desk, I could feel the hovering again over my head that I'd felt earlier that morning. Nothing was touching me or leaning over me, but I could sense a ghost behind me. I turned around to see if anyone was there, but there were only Feigel's bulletin boards jammed with odd-sized pieces of paper piled together with thumbtacks: daily school announcements and schedules with red felt pen underlinings and multicolored stars to denote some peculiar schedule of information. I jammed my hands into my pockets and made a fist to keep them quiet.

As I was leaving, I couldn't help glancing back at Feigel's desk . I saw a pathetic snapshot of him with his wife and kid kneeling on the grass in front of a suburban ranch house with a phony black lantern at the top of a few stairs, and they disgusted me as much as I felt sorry for them. Having Feigel for a father was going to suck for that kid, if it didn't already. It was only a matter of time. But what fourteen-year-old boy doesn't think his parents are weird? My parents, by contrast, felt steadier and larger despite their idiosyncrasies.

It was halfway up the student staircase that I saw Walt and he saw me. Instantly, I felt shame. The lump over his left eye stood out like a beesting. It bulged and shone under the fluorescent lights hanging above the stairwell. It stared at me like it was a third eye. I could feel its heat. The high windows above us caught it too and made it seem brighter, bigger, and rounder. I knew what I was supposed to say. I could picture my body walking toward him and my remorse and apologies spilling out of my mouth even if I could only stare at the tops of my sneakers. The high sunlight flicked from him to me as I got closer, and I felt sweaty inside my undershirt. My throat turned dry and catchy. My eyes were splashed with so many sun discs and sequins that I could barely see him next to me. Thoughts that didn't feel like my own circulated around my brain. Maybe I wasn't the one who needed to apologize. Maybe he should apologize to me first. He was the one who had burst in on me and brought the other idiots with him. He was the one who had exposed, humiliated, and jeered at me. I had only reacted the way any kid would have in that situation. Only a chicken would have done less than I had.

As I walked up to Walt, I could feel my righteousness surge. It had a warm and fuzzy feeling that convinced me that I was sticking up for myself. With a burst of energy, it carried me up toward him and lifted me past him without my uttering a word. No doubt that would seem wrong to him and Feigel and my mother, but at that moment I didn't care. It felt like a way of protecting myself, putting my clothes and armor back on, which I had been stopped from doing the day before. Saying I was sorry would only make me feel naked all over again, and I refused to do that, to feel that. When I was a few steps above him it was as if we had never been friends and I barely knew him. He was just another kid in the stairwell.

This doesn't mean that I had forgiven myself. I hadn't. It burned inside me. It was more than that. In that single moment, I didn't want to make my responsibility for my actions public. I wanted to keep all of the guilt and shame inside me, get to know its full size, its weight and shape, for myself before dismissing it by apologizing too quickly because Feigel or someone else forced me. I wasn't ready for that. I wasn't prepared to be ready. Yet.

5

B Y THE TIME BENJAMIN REACHED THE FRONT DOOR OF his building, he was dry-mouthed and perspiring again. The standard summer sweat patches across his chest had spread to cover the lower front panels of his thin cotton shirt. He nodded to the doorman as he rushed past so he could duck into the elevator in the shortest possible amount of time. Although Rick was one of his favorites and had worked in the building since Benjamin was a young boy, he didn't wish to be seen drenched like that in public. He raced into the elevator and jabbed the button.

As soon as the elevator doors opened on his floor and he headed down the erratically painted hallway, he knew that Spence had been wrong about his hearing diagnosis. He heard Dita's voice even before he opened the front door. It was operatic. Only the stone deaf and the brickwork would have been able to ignore the threats and curses bursting from the kitchen. When she was being furtive, she spoke in whispers and inaudible asides, but that wasn't her usual volume. More often her voice soared, exhorted, and performed in both of her languages. Sometimes in her rants in front of the television, confronted with political facts and positions that were abhorrent to her, she stood up to her full height and unleashed a torrent of righteousness. Leaning her torso forward, she flicked her long, blond curls over her shoulders and, without meaning to, howled as if she were a wounded hyena. That timbre made him want to run to her as much as it made him want to flee.

"Can you believe how they defend themselves now? How is it possible?" she asked in a voice of outrage. "And why isn't Giorgio up yet? He can't sleep all day. He's exhausted, I know, I know, but I need to hug him. What mother wouldn't want to do that when her son comes home after three years away. Three years! What did we do, Benjamin? He needs me now, and I want him awake!" she exclaimed and lamented in one long exhalation.

Benjamin walked behind her and placed his hands flat on her shoulders. He wanted to share his steadiness with her, his focus, his patience. After a minute her arms went slack and her shoulders drooped. He knew how to slow her down even if he didn't know how he knew. An intimate intuition, he named it in his head. A few seconds later, feeling that she had become calmer, he wanted to leave to change his foul shirt but his hands remained fixed on her shoulders.

"Thank you. You're sweating. Go take a shower and then come back and talk to me," she said. Benjamin let his hands drop and headed away from her.

As he stood in the shower, he felt like the hot water had finally given him permission to release the burden of the day's heat and the fallout from Giorgio's return. Now that his son was safely back, Benjamin could review the agony of his departure with less self-blame and less remorse. The ache of guilt that he and Dita felt remained within them. Opening the front door, handing him over to the agents of a program that they had researched and probed but didn't fully grasp still felt alien. As much as Benjamin had researched it, he could barely make his way through the verbiage of its claims. So many abstractions: calm, healing, balance, wellness, embodiment. The information read like an invitation to a destination spa rather than a wilderness rehabilitation center for adolescents. They also charged so much that he'd had to borrow most of the money from Spence, putting him in an unenviable, indebted position. Dita wasn't more hopeful than he had been. Giorgio had forced them to realize that they didn't have the equanimity to handle him. His issues had escalated at a pace they couldn't match. They were at the end of their joint tethers. The school was too strict for him or too lax. Home was volatile. His studies were hopeless, his friendships shattered. It was the best they could do for him, maybe the only thing. Let him be on his own. Establish himself in a different setting in the hope that he could transpose what he learned there back to his regular life. The limited contact that they would have with him seemed drastic, but they had no choice but to accept it. The idea of him being torn from them was excruciating, but if it saved their son, it would save the family.

Benjamin emerged from the shower refreshed if not relieved. It was too soon to tell how Giorgio had changed, and he promised himself that he wouldn't jump to premature conclusions. He wouldn't pry. He'd attempt to sever the past from the present, act as if it had no bearing on the boy who had returned. He dried himself, put on fresh clothes, and went back to Dita's station in the corner of the kitchen.

"Can we turn it off for a minute, or at least turn the volume down?" Benjamin asked. A glance at the screen showed the usual panel of cable news experts nodding to one another and then shaking their heads in practiced disbelief, droning on about this new government transgression or a previous one that had resurfaced in a new guise. Dita nodded and pointed to the remote.

"I've been thinking I can get him a job working for Cherise," Dita said, referring to one of her closest friends. "That way at least he could learn some basic skills. The world will always need film editors, won't it, even in digital? Film, television, advertising. I don't understand how this new technology works. We are so useless, the two of us. And then we can see about getting him back in school. No, we can worry about school later. I just don't think it's a good idea for him to be home the whole time. I'm afraid of what might happen. I'm not sure I can trust him right away. Do you remember what it was like just before he left?"

"I don't want to think about it."

"It was *un matricidio*!" she shouted as she exhaled, slipping into the past.

"No. It wasn't. And why do you say it in Italian? It's the same word."

"It feels better in my mouth," she said.

"You are exaggerating. You slapped him. He slapped you back. If you cuff someone enough times, that might be their reaction. It's not at all far-fetched, is it? It's a normal response for a stable adult, and he wasn't close to that," Benjamin said. The air and energy went out of his body as they rehashed the old conflicts. He barely had the strength to lift his head to look at her.

"I'm his mother. A boy doesn't slap his mother no matter what she has done. A mother always deserves to be protected. That is a law of nature. It's in the Bible. It's in every book of wisdom, every book of human knowledge that has been written. Every book of history. And you didn't back me up, did you?" Dita shook her head.

"I wasn't here when it happened. I came home later, remember? He had locked the door and you were howling. I burst in and you and he were on the floor. I couldn't even tell if you were breathing. I thought you were unconscious."

"Let's change the subject. Talking about it more doesn't help what happened. It's over. How was your *pazzo* brother?" Dita asked.

"He has a wild idea about hearing aids and rock and roll. Imagine, he says to me while we're sitting on his office couch, creating a product for the unfortunates who lost all or some of their hearing standing too close to the speakers. That's his idea. By the way, this was after he pulls out his scope, looks inside my ears, and tells me how murky it looks in there. Can you believe that?"

"Ma che sei pazzo?" she answered.

"Translation, please."

"He's out of his fucking mind? Who the hell would buy them? That's my translation."

"He said it would be like a rock-and-roll badge of honor. People would be proud, not ashamed, to wear hearing aids if they could buy ones that made them seem heroic, not frail. It would mean that their bodies weren't really failing. They were celebrating. Or something like that. Anyway, that's what he's thinking. He wants me to write a report full of numbers and persuasive prose. How many and how much. He'll pay me, he says."

"Caro," she said, coaxing him in her most sympathetic if condescending voice. "*Cretino!* Do you really still trust him even a little? How could you? He'll pay you and then what? What will he ask you to do for him, or what has he already done to you in advance that we don't know about? I wouldn't trust him to park our car."

"We don't have a car, Dita."

She shrugged. "You know my meaning."

"I know, I know, but he always helped us when we asked him. And he sent me to get my ears tested. A nice lady, although I'm not sure whether their relationship is strictly professional. Knowing him – "

"Of course, he's involved with her in some way. He doesn't have relationships that aren't tangled. He's not capable of it, and if you were as chaotic as he is, you couldn't either. That's why I chose a simple man like you, not a firecracker. So what was her assessment? Knowing Spence, he probably sent her the results he wanted before she examined you!"

"I hadn't thought of that. It's not very serious. I can't hear high pitches. Birds tweeting. That kind of thing. And my ears distort certain sounds. The blender and the vacuum are the worst, she said. And barking dogs. I think Spence sent me so that I could start to think about hearing and hearing loss and what it means. Maybe he thought that would help with the assignment."

"Maybe, but I am *dubbiosa*. At best," Dita said in her most skeptical voice.

Between pieces of their conversation, Benjamin reviewed his session with Dr. H. Was her caressing his neck and roughing his hair merely courteous or a prearranged seduction? Dita, had she known, would have surely assumed the latter, but she was so innately, profoundly suspicious that to her even the most innocent gesture represented a terminal threat.

Benjamin preferred not to see people in a doubting way. He liked to negotiate the world in a state of openness that allowed him to picture himself as free and unprejudiced. That attitude made him expansive rather than enclosed, and when he was wrong, as he had often been about Spence and others, he promised himself that he would be more careful in the future, even though caution wasn't part of his nature. If vulnerability led to betrayal, that was the price he was willing to pay for living without paranoia. Dita believed he was either naïve or ridiculous. Perhaps both. Her philosophy was that the world and its people were a brutish, sharp-elbowed bunch and any person who insisted on being as naïve as her husband must be a masochist.

"I'm not just *dubbiosa*. I'm certain your brother is setting some kind of a trap," she said, rising on the balls of her feet to her greatest height. Dita was never more stunning than when she resembled a wild animal. Her pride, her loyalty to her family, her fierceness, the fierceness of her distrust made her strong and flexed. Her golden mane lifted from her forehead and cascaded down her back. Her strong face jutted forward, her torso lengthened, and her shoulders rounded and rose up. She was the queen of her kingdom, and even if it was only a cramped three-bedroom New York City apartment that housed them, this was her realm and she ruled over it.

"I'm supposed to go back to see her next week for a follow-up visit. She said she needs to give me another test to find out more about my hearing loss in the higher register," Benjamin said, and felt stripped before his wife's scrutiny. He fiddled with his hands, then realized that he was acting as if he had already done something wrong and hid them in his pockets.

"It can't hurt, I suppose," she said. "Are you going to write the report for Spence?"

"I haven't thought about that yet. Should I?"

"I don't know, *caro*. That's for you to decide. I support what you decide."

When she looked up from the floor, Giorgio was standing in the kitchen doorway. The top of his head grazed the doorframe, and some of his staticky hair stuck to its top. He was wearing boxer shorts and a light-gray sweatshirt that had POMONA spelled on it in white block letters. His arms curled around his sides as if he had caught a chill and was hugging himself for warmth.

"What time is it?" he asked groggily. "I think I need to go back to sleep."

"Won't you sit down for a minute?" Benjamin asked. Giorgio didn't move.

"Why did you leave? Your mother spoke to the school. They know you're here. You have been discharged."

"I'm not ready for this talk yet, Dad. You have to give me a little more time. I just got back. I'm exhausted. I didn't eat or sleep much getting here, so can you give me a break before we discuss it?" Giorgio asked. He stared blankly at the wall behind his parents' heads.

"Of course, darling," Dita said in her most reasonable voice. "Of course. Don't push him, Benjamin. You tell us when you're ready, darling." Giorgio nodded before he turned around and walked back down the hall to his bedroom. The living room was silent. Benjamin could almost see the conditioned air wafting across the room. The cooling machine downshifted as if it were chugging up a steep invisible hill.

Dita stood up and appeared to follow Giorgio to his room, and Benjamin was on the verge of rising to stop her when she turned around to grab her dark blue purse from the kitchen counter. She slipped out the door without looking back at him. In the void of their sudden absence,

Benjamin was unsure how to occupy himself. Maybe he should do some preliminary research on Spence's report. Dig into statistics, familiarize himself with the rock-and-roll casualty hearing aid market, he thought, and smiled to himself.

Benjamin had no idea where his research should begin. He opened the door to the closet in his study hoping that the vinyl albums he had saved from his ancient collection were still there. He hadn't thought of them since he had given some to Giorgio years before. The closet that shrank in size as it receded was black inside and had a damp smell. Yanking on the pull string hanging from the bare bulb at the front only cast light on the clothes hanging right before him. He groped his way past winter jackets and wooly, matted scarves and snow boots, wishing that it was cold enough to wear them. Wooden tennis rackets in presses blocked his way along the floor, as did lamps with broken necks and bent prongs. His fingers could find the shelves along the low rear wall, but his old stuff was packed in so densely that it made it hard to reach farther back. Pushing his hand into a small alcove on the side close to the floor, he thought he could feel what were the thin spines of album jackets. He lunged for a wedge of them and snagged a few, nearly falling face forward in the process. He crawled in reverse back into his room to see what he had discovered. The first one was *Marquee Moon* by Television. The faces that peered out from the cover photograph were hollow-cheeked and spectral, staring at him from a distant era. He slid the record out of its jacket, held it up to the light, and wondered if it would still play, since it had assumed the shape of a parabola.

Benjamin switched on the boxy portable record player that he had given Giorgio but reclaimed after his departure and set it on the credenza in the living room. He turned the power on and flicked his index finger across the stylus. The small but functional built-in speakers emitted the familiar scratching noise of anticipation. He scanned the titles of the songs on the back of the album cover. Some sounded familiar. The only track that he was certain he knew was "Venus," so that was where he lowered the needle. The tinny, descending chord sequence came back to him immediately, as if he'd heard it in a dream a few days before. Tom Verlaine's strangulated, splintering voice cracked between the notes and gathered at the chorus. Benjamin found himself moving to the music and mouthing the lyrics as if he had never forgotten them, as if it were his story and he was the one who had fallen into the arms of Venus de Milo and wasn't sure whether that made him feel well loved or unloved. The lyrics were full of resolutions and questions. Did he feel low? Was he happy in the arms of Venus de Milo, or should he flee? Should the lover abandon the beloved in a lunge for freedom once the initial infatuation was over? Benjamin thought that the song was as mysterious and captivating as it had been when he first heard it, as sublime and mercurial as its subject. Maybe even more so to the complacent man he had become. He picked the arm up and set it back to the beginning. He didn't just want to hear it again, he wanted to live through it and in it, to find there the fearlessness that he had felt when the music had been alive, before he had become measured and afraid.

Maybe Spence was right this time, he thought. Music might have damaged them, but it had enheartened and healed them, too. It had spoken to them in a fluent, incantatory language. It had been their shibboleth of pride and devotion. That was the moment that he decided he must participate in Spence's project in spite of all the risks of working with his brother. The music that had inspired them and brought them to this brink would make working on the project a privilege, not just the "the badge of honor"nonsense copy that Spence had cynically used to describe it.

When the needle skittered across the rest of the side, Benjamin went over to lift it and set it back in its cradle. Even misshapen the record was vital, and he placed it carefully in its sleeve. He turned and saw Giorgio staring at him.

"How long have you been watching me?" Benjamin asked him with an edgy tone to his voice.

"Probably a few minutes. It looked like you were kind of in a trance. What were you listening to? I never heard it before. Play it again," Giorgio said.

Benjamin put the record back on and closed his eyes. He felt himself pulled by the same power that he had felt a minute before, but this time he was standing next to his son, who, he could tell as soon as he had reappeared at their apartment door, had his own power to impart. Although he felt self-conscious that Giorgio had seen him in his mystical state, he realized that the music might have the same effect on Giorgio that it had on him. The intro began, the strained voice lurched, but when Benjamin opened his eyes, Giorgio was gone and he was alone. He sat down on the blue loveseat. His hands had a slight tremor that he couldn't make stop by spreading his fingers on his kneecaps. He leapt up and replaced the record in the stack of albums at the back of the closet before closing the door firmly, as if it were the door to a vault that protected something essential and rare.

6

WHEN I GOT HOME FROM SCHOOL THE NEXT AFTERNOON, Mom was sitting at the kitchen table. Her hands were folded resting on the wood surface, and she looked superficially calm, as though she wanted me to believe that she often sat there idly waiting for me to return. It wasn't like her to be motionless. Her eyes avoided mine. I knew this was a performance to conceal what I was sure was her rage. I felt like a defendant at a trial in which the guilty verdict was known to all even though witnesses hadn't been called yet. From fourteen years of experience, I knew it could only take a split second for her to be turned into a banshee.

Even if I could explain how Walt and the other boys had humiliated me and laughed at the body that I was trying so hard to believe was strong and brave, I didn't think she would be able to hear me at that particular moment. Maybe it was difficult for mothers to understand how a boy could feel weak and exposed and, when he did feel like that, all his muscles and reflexes could seize up and snap and, once he was uncoiled like that and spinning, he could turn into a cyclone. And when the cyclone occurred he would be as powerless and as incapable as any other natural disaster to say what happened and why. Or to stop it.

"Sit down, Giorgio," she said.

As soon as I was seated, she raised her hand, and almost before I could see it, it was already huge, three inches from my face and a blur of motion.

I didn't have time to flinch or dodge it. It landed on my cheekbone. It was the blunt heel of her hand, not a fist, but I toppled off my chair from the force and crashed to the floor.

"How many times did I tell you not to tilt back in your chair? Get up," she said. "Get up!" she shouted at me. Her face was transfigured into a mask of hatred, not merely a look of strict, maternal discipline. Like she didn't just want to give me a lesson. She wanted to punish me in a way that I would never forget. The hurt on my skin would fade, but the judgment would last forever.

I picked myself up, brushed the dirt from the floor off my shirt and pants, and righted the chair. It felt weightless to me, or maybe adrenaline made me feel like Superman. I sat back down as she glared at me.

"You're a disgrace. A disgrace to me. A disgrace to our family. Your sister is ashamed of you, although she wouldn't tell you that, but she told me so herself. Your father is ashamed of you. You let him down again and again. But I am the most ashamed," she said, establishing the supremacy of her injury. "You can't stay here for two weeks of suspension. We're going to have to send you somewhere. Where? To whom?" I had heard of the fight-or-flight impulse, but I'd never heard of the freeze one. I was unable to move or speak. My jaw locked. My eyelids were stuck open. My fingers were stiff and ached in my lap.

"I'm sorry," I mumbled.

"Feigel called and told me that you saw Walt and didn't say anything. Nothing! No apology! No hello! And the suspension. I taught you to think of the calm little bird in its cage, didn't I, and keep your hands in your pockets, *not* use them to shove your best friend's head into a fish tank!" She screamed the last part, as if I might not be able to hear her. As if I were in another room. "What did I leave out, Giorgio?"

"I'm sorry," I said again.

"Why did you do that, *carissimo*?" she asked. A second's sympathy washed over her face. Her features softened. For an instant, I thought she might smile. She took my hand. I wasn't sure whether she meant it or it was a trick.

"I was embarrassed. A little." I managed to say, but I didn't want to go any further.

"Why?" she asked.

"I'd rather not say. I'm sorry."

"What did you say?" she asked.

"I said I was sorry. That I don't want to tell you any more."

Suddenly her face was six inches from mine. I could feel the heat of her cheeks on mine, the humid clouds of her breath. "How dare you!" she shouted, and pushed me backwards with furious, unknowing strength. I could feel myself toppling. For a second, teetering in the air, I thought I might be able to lean forward and grab onto the table so I wouldn't plunge. I lunged for its long side but only grazed the edge with my fingertips before collapsing sideways on the floor. But this time when I fell, my head slapped on the wood and bounced and dropped back down again. The chair twisted and landed on top of my sprawled legs. I looked up at the candelabra. It had crystals dangling from the metal arms that held tapered bulbs. They made a tinkling noise. The room felt like winter, snowflakes and Christmas. I wanted to smile in an interior way that she couldn't see, and then I reached for the back of my head. It was seething. I moved my hand to rub it and sensed that there was a little blood on my fingers. They smelled like some of the minerals in the science lab.

Inside my head at that moment, I remembered how I felt before I attacked Walt, the shadowy ghost, like some foreign presence pressing against my shoulders and a pod or an amoeba-shaped seed swimming inside me, moving randomly from spot to spot. The goblin or whatever it was brushed against my neck. A blur of orange, red, and navy fabric burst in front of my eyes and faded like fireworks, and I felt the crazy tension that I had felt with Walt.

I was wobbly, but I was able to get my feet beneath me and lift the chair off me. She was still staring at me when I was on my knees, and all I could think of was her solid, animal body darkening mine, blocking the light, and how her eyes were fixed on me without seeing me. There was no feeling in me, either, neither warmth nor contrition. Not restraint or remorse.

I stood up slowly, like I was stumbling out of the grave. My shirt collar was damp with sweat, and I could taste blood on the inside of my lip. Once I was on my feet again, I felt a surge of power shoot through my limbs. I lost control over my arms and legs. My hands flew out of my pockets. I had been straining every muscle to hold them there. They flailed when I approached her. She stepped back until her hands groped the bare wall behind her. My eyes couldn't focus. Her blond hair was a tangled mess that hid most of her face. I windmilled my arms at her, and I could tell that my hands had struck some part of her upper body. I wasn't sure where exactly. She stepped to the side, hugging the wall and holding her hands out for balance, and I was moving with her. Suddenly, I could feel my fists ball up, and using all my strength I yanked them back and shoved them into my pockets. We caught each other's eyes for a split second. She lifted her hands out toward me as if she were begging me to stop, and I collapsed on the floor. I felt as if I had been shot or someone had pulled the plug and all the air whooshed out of my plastic body. I could hear her wailing, her rushing, snorting breath. I could sense her loathing and her fear. I could feel her fending me off, staggering away from me, disowning the heap on the floor at her feet that was her son.

I'm not sure when Dad came in. I heard the balanced tone of his voice that had always steadied me. Even the disastrous scene before him didn't disrupt his equanimity. I heard him gently asking her questions, but I couldn't hear her answers or didn't want to. He crouched down beside me and put his hand on my shoulder and let it hang there. I could vaguely hear him say, "Giorgio, Giorgio," in a tender way, but that was when I realized that I never wanted to be called by that name again. I wanted my original name back, the one I had been given and lived with for fourteen years. Even in my freezing brain, that vow felt like one I could keep. She had chosen the name Mark for me too. That had been her original choice, and she had told me the story of how she had arrived at it, which I couldn't remember in that confused minute, but I did remember how I had liked the shortness and sharpness of the single syllable that ended in a hard consonant, and I liked that it stood for a specific place whether it was in time or space and that place could be mine and mine only. I didn't like that she had stolen my "mark" from me. She had left me unmarked, displaced, anonymous.

"What have you done?" my father asked suddenly and desperately, but I wasn't sure if he was asking me or her. Neither of us was able to answer. I don't think it was meant for either one of us. It was a question for the universe, but the universe answered in a way that I grew more accustomed to the longer I spent under my tarp at night in the wilderness. A gust of wind blew through the room and the curtains moved and the lights flickered and from the floor I could hear the windows rattle loosely on their runners and feel the chill as we headed deeper and deeper into winter.

That was how Alessandra found us when she walked in. Mom and I were stretched out on the floor. My father was kneeling next to me, his hand still on my shoulder. It was as if she had stumbled on a battle scene seconds after the firing had stopped. She paused and surveyed the room. It was unlike her to say nothing at all, but probably the whole thing was so confusing that she didn't know what to say or think. She walked over to where Mom was sitting, her hands clasped between her knees. Alessandra sat next to her and started fussing with her hair, putting every strand back in place, recomposing her.

Dad put his arms under my shoulders and lifted my limp body to my feet. We walked down the hallway to my room like injured soldiers bumping our elbows against the walls. He was kind but not too kind. I could tell he wasn't sure how kind to be considering what I had just done. He sat me on my bed and turned on the lamp.

"Why don't you read a book," he said, and closed the door behind him.

Reading was the last thing I wanted to do. I wanted to smash something. No, I wanted to smash everything. I jumped off the bed and thought I'd start with the prizes I'd won at school. Not just the cheap tin ones, the ones they give kids just for having a pulse and showing up. I wanted to smash the main one, which Feigel had given me for long distance running. He had patted me on the back and said I was the best runner my age in the middle school. I picked it up and lifted it over my head like it was an axe. It barely weighed anything. I held it up there for a second trying to think what I would smash it on—the desk, the bedpost, the windowsill. I was stuck in the simple, frozen moment that comes before destruction.

I felt someone lift it from my outstretched hands, set it down on the shelf, and guide me back to the bed. It was Alessandra. In spite of her chaos and bright colors and cavemen, she was the only one who knew how to make me calm.

"I know how it feels," she said. That was all. We sat next to each other not speaking. It was probably only twenty or thirty minutes. Every so often I thought she was going to say something or I thought I might, but all that came from either of us was the thinnest breath of air from our throats. It made me think of Dad telling us about how when he was a kid he would try to make the smallest human sound. Not even a syllable. A nub. And that made me think that even the tiniest human noise, the littlest note, could have meaning.

7

DR. H LEFT THE DOOR OPEN TO HER OFFICE, AND BENJAMIN could hear her speaking to one of her patients in that hushed, clear tone she had. He could tell that it was a grave conversation, not an initial diagnosis as Benjamin's had been. The patient's hearing aids had stopped working, and it wasn't an electrical short circuit, he heard her say. A more muted dialogue followed the diagnosis. Pauses were interrupted by remarks that Benjamin couldn't make out no matter how much he leaned in their direction.

When he was called in, Dr. H was all business. She instructed him to sit down in the chair next to her desk. The calendar of shoes had shifted to September and contained the familiar array of wedges, platforms, and beaded, sequined sandals with four-inch heels. She fiddled with the mouse attached to her desktop computer searching for an icon on her screen that he wasn't quick enough to see. All of the coyness and flattery of his last visit had vanished.

"I'm going to read a passage to you and then ask you a question or two about it. It's not long or difficult, but you have to pay attention. Oh, and there's going to be music playing at the same time. Ready?"

Benjamin nodded. A Fleetwood Mac song from the Stevie Nicks era cranked up from the desktop speakers as she read from a manual, covering her lips with a blank sheet of paper so that he couldn't cheat.

"Every year the farmer's son _____ his father that he needed a _____ tractor. The _____ were starting to wear thin and one _____ he might have an accident. The farmer_____ a crop when he_____. He could hear the ambulance_____ but didn't think it was for him although he was lying at the bottom of a _____." In the gaps where the words had been omitted, Stevie Nicks pushed her reedy voice through the lyric that proclaimed, "She was just a wish," or maybe, Benjamin thought, she was saying, "just a witch."

"Why did the farmer need a new tractor?" Dr. H asked as she switched off the music and shook out her voluptuous curls. "Was it because he felt like it, A, or because his son was pushing him, B, or had the brakes started to wear thin, C?"

"C. What a terrible song!" he said.

"How could you say that?" she asked, instantly indignant. "It is so beautiful and yearning and dreamy, and Stevie's voice harmonizes so perfectly with the instrumentation and the rhythm. Can't you picture the girl in the song? She's lying on the rug on her bedroom floor playing with her girlish things, right? She's imagining herself twirling in a gypsy skirt, and then she confesses everything by saying that it was all up to him. How could you not be moved by that?" Dr. H asked, as if his lack of appreciation was a more profound failure than hearing loss. She dangled her left red stiletto in front of him in a way that was impossible to ignore.

Benjamin didn't have any idea what she was asking of him. His mind had wandered to the metal soundproof booth that occupied at least half of the space in her office. He pictured himself squeezed inside it again, sitting uncomfortably in the tiny metal chair, wedged against the sound-board as if he were inside a space capsule. Dr. H was tugging gently but firmly on the top of his earlobe, stretching it so that she could insert the earbud. It felt like an affectionate gesture, even a loving one, in addition to its diagnostic purpose. The cavity was filled perfectly. Inside the close space, he imagined that she pressed herself against him as she tried to squeeze through the doorway to get to the control panel on the other side of the picture window. As she maneuvered past him, her breasts pushed against his shoulder and flattened. He could smell the fresh natural flavors of her soap or her lotions. He imagined that she didn't look back at him as she brusquely closed the steel door behind her, shutting out all of the ambient noise of the street and the sky.

"Hello?" she asked, annoyed by his inattention or wounded by his lack of appreciation for her beloved song. "Did you hear me? Or are you pretending not to hear?"

"I heard you, but I don't know what to say. I was trying to come up with an explanation, but I'm at a loss," he said, dissembling.

"That's because you were never a teenage girl. Obviously. Don't you get that all of those things in the song are jumbled together? She's young, she's innocent. She's trusting and hopeful, putting all of her trust in you, in him. Isn't that what is going on?"

Benjamin paused. He couldn't stand the wavering, febrile voice that he was supposed to feel compassion for or the throatiness that was meant to be a sign of its urgent authenticity. It brought back to him all of the unanswerable questions he'd been asked by girls when he was a teenager and had not just not answered but had not even begun to comprehend. They made him feel stunted and inhuman, a Neanderthal, a lesser form of human life, as Alessandra had suggested. He was unable to imagine how Dr. H felt about the song. He was perplexed by the moaning, baffled by its insistence, mystified by how the singer saw herself—a fantasy, a wish, a wandering figure, artfully dressed, receding into the background.

"Let's continue. We don't have to argue about the song," she said after an uncomfortable silence. "I had another look at the chart. You have some hearing loss, Benjamin. How shall we proceed from here? I can do some more tests that would tell me a little more about it and suggest possible treatments. But let me ask you this. When you are out to dinner with your wife, I assume you have one, and the waiters are moving around the room, clinking plates and glasses, and other diners are tinkling their silverware and talking and pushing past each other and laughing, are you still able to hear the conversation you're having with her? Does your comprehension come and go? Do you watch her lips when she's speaking to confirm what you think you're hearing? Do you find yourself nodding along because you've had a lot of practice reading lips? And that seems safer to you than admitting that you haven't heard what she said because you have already asked her to repeat herself too many times? Does that sound like a familiar scenario to you?"

"It may have happened a few times," he said, surprised by his own reluctance to admit how frequent it was.

"In that case, hearing aids might enhance your life, married or otherwise. But think about it and then come back for another appointment. Is there anything else I can help you with today?" she asked.

Benjamin wasn't ready to leave, although he didn't know how he could prolong the appointment. He wanted to remain in the chair next to her for a while, even listen to the song again if he had to. The idea of returning to Spence's office was forbidding, more forbidding than staying near her. He racked his brain for an excuse.

"There is something else I wanted to mention. I wake up early in our apartment. My wife is still asleep. The bedroom is quiet, and there isn't much traffic noise on the streets before dawn. It's mostly dark. I lie in bed and listen, and when I do the silence whooshes louder and louder. It's a fuzzy, staticky noise, as if my ears are being filled with cotton and then drained. What is that?"

"Probably tinnitus. I need to do more tests to be sure, but it isn't a difficult diagnosis. Millions of people have it. There's no real cure, but if you take care of your sinuses, steam twice a day and take turmeric and some other herbs, it may reduce. Before your next appointment, follow the instructions on the sheet." She looked at her sparkling watch and turned to him. "It's time for you to go. Spence is waiting for you."

When Benjamin arrived at his brother's office, Spence was standing behind his baroque desk. The big grin on his face matched the splashy colors of his bow tie: burgundy, royal blue, and forest green, with a seam of ivory in between. It flopped artily below the spread collar of his shirt as it had loosened. Except for its vivid preppie colors, the casualness of it reminded Benjamin of the type of bow tie a plantation owner might have worn in a daguerreotype of the pre– Civil War period.

"How are you getting on with Dr. H?" he asked. "I thought she might be your type."

"My type?" Benjamin asked. "My type of what? Audiologist?"

"Yes, Benjy. Of course. Your type of audiologist. What else would I mean?"

"I'm not sure. I've never been to an audiologist before."

"Tell me about Giorgio. Is that what we still call him, or did he change his name back to Mark? Would you mind if his uncle invited him out to lunch one day, or a concert? The Stones are supposed to be here soon. It's their Fifty and Counting tour, believe it or not. He might like that. I haven't seen him in such a long time. He must have grown up. He must be almost an adult by now. How tall is he?"

"I guess there couldn't be too much harm in that, but let's give him a little more time to stabilize. He's not used to being back in the city yet. Anyway, I started to think about your project, and I want to participate. I put *Marquee Moon* on the turntable the other day, and I couldn't believe how good it was. When is the last time you listened to it? I forgot how much I loved those songs. How good they were. It has to be over thirty years!" Both brothers paused to consider how big the passage of time had been.

"It was very long ago. Maybe this means something, Benjy. Maybe it means that what we used to love is as good now as it was then, as it always was. It wasn't just some nostalgia piece of junk or novelty. It was profoundly good in the seventies or eighties, and it's just as good today. It has a kind of power that doesn't go away, a complexity that lasts." Benjamin turned to Spence, surprised by how philosophical he had become. "Now back to business," Spence said. "How long do you think it's going to take you to dig up the data on people like us and write a persuasive report to help me sell it to the Board? And how much do you want me to pay you for it?"

Spence sat back down at his big desk and opened the top center drawer. He leaned over it and started rummaging around inside with his stubby fingers, as if he had dropped a pencil in a heap of autumn leaves. Benjamin couldn't tell exactly what he was doing until Spence placed three checks on the leather surface of his desk.

"What are all those?" Benjamin asked.

"Payments," Spence answered.

"I can see that. Payments from whom? For what?"

"Franchisees. Now, I picked three out. Here's one for five grand," he said, pushing it toward Benjamin. It was made out to Belphonics. "Here's one for ten. And here's one for twenty. What do you think your work is worth? Or maybe we should just pay down some of the money you owe me."

"How much is it down to now?" Benjamin asked. Spence picked up the phone and shouted "Stephanie" into the receiver. A minute later a disheveled woman wearing large pink framed glasses and a pale pink blouse opened the door and poked her head in.

"Stephanie, how much does Benjamin still owe me? Go check and come straight back."

They waited in fidgety silence for her report. Spence sifted through more of the checks in his drawer, picking one up and flipping it over to examine the endorsement line before replacing it in the pile. Benjamin squirmed in his chair. In his head he tried to calculate the size of his debt.

He'd borrowed sixty thousand dollars to pay for Giorgio's program and the school afterward, he thought, or was that just the first part or just the second part or both parts together? Whether it was in bits or pieces or all at once, he couldn't remember. Money had been the least important concern at that dire moment compared with the chaos and despair he and Dita had sunk into. He recalled the depression he'd felt. Its dimensionless darkness mixed with the frenzy of guessing what his son needed from him and whether he could supply it. Stephanie's return interrupted Benjamin's rumination.

"He owes you forty-five thousand, Spence. He hasn't paid us anything in the last year," she said, and slipped away again.

"Well, it's not worth that much to me no matter how good a job you do," Spence said. He opened his drawer and sifted through more checks. From the other side, Benjamin could smell the aroma of the airless drawer's wood lamination mixed with paper and glue.

"Here's one for twenty-five thousand. Take this and we can worry about the rest of the debt later. That's a lot more than the work is worth. I could get some business school student to do it for less than half that, let alone a professional consultant, but I'd like you to work with me. That would make me happy. Shared experiences and all that shit," Spence said, and showed his toothiest grin.

"And if the venture goes well and you stay interested, I'll think about canceling some or all of the remaining debt. After all, you went to those clubs too. You were the first one to take me there. You know what it was like back then. This isn't just some exercise for you, either, is it?"

"What's the deadline? Yes, I liked hearing the songs again. They made me want to do this not you. I already told you what I think."

"Tomorrow?" Spence said, with a devilish child's glee.

"And how am I supposed to deposit this check? It's not even made out to me!"

"Banks don't give a shit, Benjy. It's just money to them. They don't care anymore whose money it is or where it came from. The days of verifying signatures and those little rules are gone. But in case you have a problem, just tell them that you're me. They know who I am."

"If they know who you are, then they'll know I'm not you."

"You were always too smart for your own good, Benjy. Deposit it and don't worry about it. If there's a problem, then call me or tell them to call me and I'll sort it out for you, okay?"

Benjamin nodded and began to walk out of his brother's office. Before sticking Spence's check into his pocket, he glanced at it. It was made out to Belphonics, Inc. It was from somewhere in Pennsylvania, a town he'd never heard of. Sugar Creek. Where the hell was that? he wondered. How could a town he'd never heard of need twenty-five thousand dollars' worth of hearing aids?

The humidity had dissipated enough so Benjamin could walk the forty blocks home at a faster than deep summer pace without fear of heatstroke or red splotches on his skin. He patted the check in his pocket, and it made him feel purposeful and manly. It was more than he'd earned in years, and that alone was enough to propel him through the uncrowded late-summer streets.

As he walked up Third Avenue, he noticed a buzzing in his ears that intensified as traffic thinned out above Fifty-Ninth Street. He heard the usual bus and horn noises, but they were buffered by a layer of sound that he could only describe to himself as an enveloping field of baffles. It wasn't aggressive or torturous, but it still invaded him and didn't retreat. On one block, he thought it had vanished, and on the next one the volume returned. He tried to think of it as a form of swaddling, as being wrapped in a mohair blanket of sound. That made it cocoonish and cozy, so he continued and marveled at the splendors of the day to distract himself: the sunlight, unoccupied tables and chairs on the avenue cafés, and the legions of dogs being walked by their owners, barking, straining sideways on their leashes to lean toward other dogs, momentarily roused from their corner dog beds or couches in all the apartments and in all the buildings that rose around him.

Benjamin wondered if hearing aids might dissolve that vague, erratic noise. If they made other noises sharper and more distinct, wouldn't the ringing fade into the background? As an experiment, he focused on a piercing sound and tried to notice the subtler effects. A van blowing its horn sliced through the aural fog, but it didn't last long enough to dispel it. He tried to imagine brightly colored plastic molded to his ear and lodged inside it. Even the thought of being overwhelmed by sonic information seemed to him like listening to Dita launch her chain of invectives at the television without pausing to take a breath. That did not increase his desire for sonic clarity.

Benjamin was barely sweating when he opened his front door. The television was silent, but he could hear chopping sounds coming from the kitchen. He saw Giorgio standing next to his mother at the sink. He wielded the knife as she handed him the vegetables to slice. There was an agile, easy fluidity in their movements, as if this was a routine that they had been practicing for years. Since they didn't hear him, he turned away and sat down for a minute at the dining room table. He took Spence's check from his pocket and looked at it again, as though he suspected that there was something phony about it, if he could only figure out what. The amount was accurate, and the names on it were correctly spelled, as far as he could tell. He turned it over and saw that "Spencer Stern" was signed on the endorsement line. Maybe it was real, he thought, but it was hard to be sure in a situation where his brother was involved.

"Did Spence give you that?" he heard Dita ask through the ringing in his ears.

"Yes. It's an advance payment."

"How much?"

"Twenty-five thousand dollars," he said, and tried to conceal his excitement.

"*Tesoro*, that's not an advance. That's a bribe. What is he bribing you for?"

"It's a big project, and he wants me to be part of it. Do you want me to give it back?"

Benjamin knew that no matter how much Dita objected to Spence, how deep her suspicions of him ran, that she would not push him that far. They both knew that they needed the money, and not many moral qualms would prevent either of them from depositing it. He showed her the check proudly, as if he had earned it and expected recognition for that.

Giorgio appeared in the doorway and walked slowly into the room. "What's that?" he asked.

"Spence gave your father a check for doing nothing as far as I can tell. At least nothing yet. It's supposed to be a big project. Big men, big plans, but it sounds like caca to me."

Giorgio took the check out of his father's hands and scrutinized it. "Shouldn't it be made out to you if the money's going to you and you're going to be his partner?"

"I'm not his partner in this. But maybe I will be. He asked after you, Giorgio."

"He did? Why?"

"Because he hasn't seen you in almost three years. He asked me if I'd pass along a lunch invitation to you. Or a concert. The Stones he said are passing through, and he thought you might like to go."

"I'm not ready to see other people yet, Dad. Even family. Especially him. My Fremont counselor had said to me a long time ago that in aftercare you have to take it slowly. I never forgot that. They say coming home is like going for a swim in an alpine lake. You can't just leap in no matter how refreshing and inviting the water looks. It's too cold and might be a bad shock to your system. Even a kid could have a heart attack. You have to take it one joint at a time. Don't go up to your knees until your feet get used to it, et cetera."

"Well, put it in the back of your mind and let me know when you're ready," Benjamin said.

"It's going to take me a while, Dad. Maybe even a long while," Giorgio said.

8

FOR THE NEXT FEW DAYS AFTER THE CONFRONTATION WITH my mother, I barely spoke. I wandered through my daily routine like I was sleepwalking and none of it was real. I could remember my father helping me down the hall and sitting with me on my bed and my sister taking the statue out of my hands. I could remember wanting a red Skittle so badly that I could almost taste the sharp flavor on my tongue. But I couldn't recall many details of the incident itself. I knew enough to know that there was nothing good about them. Silence and sticking to myself were as close as I could get to a dressing for my wounds.

On the nights that followed, I sat at my desk and tried to focus on the textbooks my mother propped in front of me so I could keep up with my classes during the suspension. Every hour or two she would pop in with a fresh glass of cold water. She set it down and cupped the back of my head in her palm for a second, as if her touch could soothe the pain she'd caused there. What had happened between us was too big for words, so she brought me cups of calming tea, offerings of truce, and I drank them. Spoken apologies were not part of our family vocabulary.

The water glass was the only contact between us. At the dinner table while I was staring at my food she studied me as if trying to fathom how a mild, mostly smiling boy had become nasty. I studied her, too, thinking that if I looked hard enough, I could find the place where her anger toward my recent behavior lived. I thought that if I could locate it, I could hunt it down, snuff it out, and be safe. But I couldn't see any trace of it, so I thought it must be somewhere very deep inside her, a buried, covered-up spot of shame. That left me on the friendly surface of her face, on the flickering smile that made wrinkles at the corners of her eyes and her pale, non-Italian skin.

My father was unlike himself in the days that followed. He acted twitchy, and I could sense a jumpiness in his voice and his body. Patience had always been his trademark, but it had been replaced by strange traces of panic. From my bedroom, I could hear him pleading with her and her asking questions that he didn't have the answer for. He was begging for something. What was it? Tolerance? Empathy? For me, or someone else?

I imagined that he was admonishing her for what she had done to me. He was taking my side in the story and standing up to her. He was saying that I was just a kid who had reacted terribly in a bad situation and her actions had been too intense. I fantasized that the more he spoke, the more carefully she listened, and finally she heard and then understood how she had been at fault, too. But when I listened more closely, those were not the words I heard her say. I heard "safety," "safe," and "you must." "You must." I heard him say "program" and "Spence." But when I tried to put those words together into a complete sentence, I came up empty-handed.

Alessandra didn't reappear after she had soothed me. She didn't have to. I could feel her in my room. She was always reasoning with me about something. It's hard to be a mother, she said. She's like that with me, too. But maybe not so brutal because I'm a girl. You'll be all right, she kept repeating. Whatever they have in mind for you, you'll be all right.

After dinner, before I went to my room for more studying or, more likely, staring at the page because I couldn't take any of the material in, I saw my parents huddled in front of the desktop, turning to each other, their faces aglow and a little spooky, asking each other simple questions. "Not see him? I couldn't stand that," I heard her say. Dad nodded. I knew it must be serious because there was no lightheartedness between them—no Italian, no teasing, no dicing or cooking.

It was on the third or fourth evening of this uncomfortable routine that everything changed. I had said good night to them after Chinese takeout and given them each a weak hug before I shuffled down the hall to my bedroom. I sat down at my desk, turned on my little lamp, and opened my math book. Within minutes, I felt sleepy. The formulas blurred into a black jumble of numbers and letters, and the geometric shapes slid off the page. It was hopeless. I was too sleepy, and closed the book. I put on my pajamas and lined up my Skittles on the edges of the bedside table as I usually did before going to sleep, and turned out the light.

I had a sweaty dream that I was on a trip to a place I'd never been before. It was a glacial landscape with high green hills strewn with large rocks. I felt healthy and energetic, but I knew that the real test of my stamina lay ahead of me. Then I heard a kind of rumbling thunder, as if there were a rockslide in heaven, yet it was happening very close to me, maybe in my own room. I looked around quickly, trying to assess how to protect myself from being crushed. I saw a huge boulder in the open field no more than thirty feet away and started running toward it, thinking that I could shelter myself behind it, before I was pulverized by a tsunami of stones.

In the dream, as I was running toward the safety of the boulder, two men I didn't recognize came toward me. For a second I thought I was still asleep and they had come to rescue me from the rockslide, but when they were closer I knew that they were too big to be part of any dream. I bolted upright in my bed.

"You don't need to take anything with you, Giorgio. Just put on the clothes you were wearing last night. We've got the rest."

"Who the hell are you? What are you doing in my room?" They moved closer, and I could feel their enormous bodies towering over me.

"Your parents asked us to come, Giorgio. We're here to help you."

"Dad!" I yelled. "Mom!" But there was no reply. It was as if my room had been walled off from the rest of our apartment and it was now floating somewhere in space on its own weird, solo orbit.

"Your parents said you needed help, and we're here to help you on your way," one of them said. He was a giant man, the size of a fullback. His head was shaved to stubble, and he had chains around his neck and tattoos on the insides of his arms. He reminded me of the nightclub bouncers you see in the movies. "Now, get dressed," he said, with some urgency this time. When they scanned the room, they didn't see me sweep the Skittles off my bedside table and stick them in my pocket.

"My parents sent you?" I asked, disoriented and incredulous.

"Of course. We wouldn't be here otherwise. They hired us to look after you," one of them said, repeating what he had already told me.

"Can I talk to them before I go?"

The question hung unanswered in the gloom. I put my feet in my shoes and tied the laces in a double bow while they hovered over me. I stole as much time as I could to pan across my room. Unlike the night before, now my awards and citations took on an importance that I tried to fix in my memory so I could bring them with me wherever I was going, a touchstone. The few coins in my pocket, the small bills in my wallet, and the handful of Skittles wouldn't be enough for that.

"How long will I be gone for?" I asked them.

"That's up to you."

"Time to go," the smaller one said. "We'll get your coat on the way out."

As I left my room, they followed closely behind me. I could feel the overhang of their massive shoulders and heads like a heavy coat on my back. The chains around their enormous necks made little tinkling noises. I had walked up and down this hallway thousands of times without thinking about it, but this time, followed by two giants, it took on unforgettable hospital features. The light was flat and sad. There were no shadows. It was a tunnel that led to a river that separated one part of my life from the other, and I had to get across it somehow. One of the goons opened the closet and grabbed my winter jacket.

"Where is my phone? Can I call my sister to say good-bye?" I asked.

"No, sorry. You have to leave it here. We don't have time for any calls right now. The plane is at seven."

"What plane? Where is it going?"

"We'll tell you at the airport."

"Which airport are we going to?"

"We'll tell you in the car."

The plane, the airport—what the fuck was going on? I asked myself in a screaming inner voice. Then I saw my parents in their pathetic robes, hugging themselves, sliding their slippers back and forth on the wooden floorboards. They watched my every move as if they might never see me again. I wanted to ask them all my questions. I opened my mouth to scream "Why?" but no words came out. Their plan, whatever it was, was too far along to reconsider.

"We love you, Giorgio! We forgive you," my mother said, weeping. "Don't be angry at us. We're doing this for you, not for ourselves." I didn't know what she meant. "For our family. We will be visiting you soon."

"Forgive us, Giorgio" I heard my father mutter in a meek, whispery voice as I was ushered out the door. "Forgive us," he repeated, but he couldn't even raise his head to look at me.

The goons took me downstairs and lifted me into a black Suburban. It was still dark outside, and cold. The city was asleep. The car glided through the mostly empty, mostly quiet streets. We were alone. No, I was alone. As alone as I had ever been, with no idea where I was going or to whom. Wherever it was, I had a feeling it would be like a foreign country where I didn't speak the language or like the food.

9

THE BELPHONICS CONFERENCE ROOM LOOKED AS STRANGE as it always had. It was an oddly shaped space, a trapezoid, he thought, stuck between two hallways. On the walls were an assortment of silver and gold shellacked records and their jackets in plexiglass boxes. The citation on the bottom read, "Presented to Spencer Stern and Belphonics for their service to hearing and music." Benjamin suspected that Spence himself had bought these gilded records in one of the shlock shops on Broadway and had the plaques engraved himself. The albums ranged widely in genre from Big Joe Turner to Richard Hell and the Voidoids to Twisted Sister, but most of all, Benjamin thought, Spence wanted them to signify that he was an esteemed figure in the field of music, worthy of respect and recognition, even if it was self-appointed.

Inside the conference room, Spence, Benjamin, Dr. H, and Dutch, a Belphonics sound engineer and marketing expert, flanked a table made of plywood boards glued together and littered with paper clips, a squawk box, pads of paper, and pencils. Spence smiled beatifically and kicked his feet up onto the table. From the carpet next to him, he grabbed a bottle of Grey Goose vodka by its long neck and lifted it to his lips. He took a deep swallow, and the assembled team watched the clear, almost frozen liquid flow slowly through the smoked glass. He let out a heavy sigh to make sure that his employees knew how much he had been refreshed by his slug. A slash of light from the high hallway windows slanted across the table.

"This is officially the first meeting of our new product team. I declare it open. Let's dazzle," Spence said with a flourish and banged his fist on the trembly table. "Shall we start with the obvious. What is the name of this incredible new product?"

The question was met with silence. Without turning their heads, the three participants stared slyly at one another out of the sides of their eyes. No one wanted to speak first and risk Spence's retribution. Benjamin, who had no broader ambition than being a researcher, stared at his shoes. Dr. H, their audiologist consultant, flexed her lips and shook her head to loosen the curls that had gotten stuck inside her collar. Dutch, a man of all trades in his late forties with a crew cut and a military bearing who had worked for Spence for almost a decade, was the least self-conscious, but he had survived at the company for that length of time because of his instinctive sense of caution. He was used to letting Spence go first and waiting to express his feelings in a reduced form later.

"I want them big and bright colored. I want them to glow in the dark like lighters. And flash and send Morse code. We're not going to hide anything. We're proud of who and what we are. We're going to proclaim and shout. Questions?" Spence said, balancing as he lounged further back in his chair. "Is this topic of no interest to you, Doctor?"

"Women may want something a little more discreet, Spence. Or sleek. I'm not sure they'd go for a colorful clump of plastic with lightning bolts on the side emitting random signals. Most of the ladies I know never liked those metal bands anyway. Yes, they went to the concerts to humor their boyfriends, but that's not the same as liking the music for itself. As for the technology, that's a different story."

"Thank you for giving us the female perspective, and please tell us what story that is?"

"As a professional audiologist I can't make people buy hearing aids just because they make a statement or look different. The technology has to reinforce the style, and it must be new, too."

"What do you think, Dutch? What's new for us to add on?" Spence asked, not too interested in the answer. The mechanics of wave patterns and sound technology were not among his areas of interest. He was more of a proselytizer, a salesman directing other salesmen.

"We can go analog and digital with this," Dutch suggested, stating the two obvious solutions. He spoke with a nasal Brooklyn accent that had become more and more rare. Dutch was a withered veteran not only of Belphonics, an admittedly warlike environment, but also of rock and roll, which he knew was its own gauntlet of small skirmishes. When Spence met him, he had been a roadie for a punk revival band that was so faithful to its act that it required a man of Dutch's military background to drag the members out of bed in the morning or, more frequently, the afternoon. Usually, he had to resort to the drill-sergeant whistle that he had saved when he retired from the marines. Nothing gave him more pleasure in life than busting into a hotel room at noon and blowing it. His cheeks ballooned to their maximum muscular size, and that only deepened the pleasure of watching the musicians' drooling mouths struggle for animation. Stupefied, hung over, dazed by the random drug assortment they'd ingested the night before, they barely stirred, but their catatonic state only gave him another opportunity to blow the whistle and to pierce their sticky, opiated slumber.

"What do we call it is the first question. Any ideas?" Spence asked.

"What about the Listener," Benjamin said, before he'd even had time to reflect on the words that came out of his mouth.

"Terrible name. Pervy too. Suggests eavesdropping to me, or wire-tapping. Nice try, Benjy," Spence said, without a look in his brother's direction or a trace of feeling.

"Anybody else?" Spence asked.

"1975," Dutch said.

"1975 what?" Spence asked.

"You know, Spence. That was the year, wasn't it?" Dutch answered.

"Too long ago. Ancient," Spence said. "Benjy wants to listen. Dutch says what was that? I want it to rock, so why don't we call it the Rocker, and it comes in scarlet, forest green, and other colors. We can put little lightning bolts on the side or lilies for ladies. I'm not sure about the decoration, but I know we want something grabbing, something vibrant and loud. This is not the moment for subtlety and nuance, is it? We're proud, remember? Can we get it for Christmas? I'm imagining a launch party at CBGB's late November."

"Christmas?" Dutch exclaimed. "Impossible. We'll be lucky if we can make them by National Vinyl Record Day next August!"

"So, Christmas it is!" Spence declared.

The team shook its collective head and the meeting ground to a halt as they contemplated the rushed timeline and Spence's suggestion for the name. Instead of a lone silhouetted figure arching backwards, his gelled, spiky hair standing straight up as if he'd stuck his toe in a live socket, throttling a Fender guitar in the spotlight, Benjamin imagined a rocking chair on the porch of a nursing home, a quiet place to read the classics.

"We can't call it that, Spence. People might misinterpret. The name has too many connotations that are the opposite of what we intend. Like the cradle that rocks. I don't think that's the image you want, is it?" Benjamin asked.

Instantly, Spence's mood and complexion changed. The fervor went out of his eyes and was replaced by a perplexed darkness that Benjamin hadn't seen on his brother's face since they had been boys and Benjamin refused to jump off the top bunk.

"Why not just call it the Punk," Benjamin added to make sure he wasn't just being contrary. "That says authentic, new, real, doesn't it? What that music meant versus the bloated, rich arena rock tours of the era."

"Another terrible idea, Benjy. You should know better than that. What codger wants to think of himself that way now? Scruffy. Penniless. Methadone. Homeless. Back then punk was new, elite but edgy, a small club of insiders, but now it's historical. And worse."

"Isn't that who's going to buy this? Aren't we all codgers now?"

"Speak for yourself. Any other ideas, folks? Forgive my brother. He doesn't get out in the world very much. He's a recluse. The universe is shouting at you to wake up, Benjy. Clean the wax out of your fucking ears!" Spence bellowed in a rising voice that bounced off the walls and the clerestory. He pounded his fist on the table again, and the pencils jumped in their holder. The team's other members stared at Spence, but there was no emotion, no sign of surprise or purpose on their faces. Or on Spence's. They were unfazed by their boss's attack, as if they had witnessed such outbursts so many times before that they were inured. Benjamin, on the other hand, felt as if he was bleeding from an internal wound. Shock waves rippled through his gallbladder and spilled into his large intestine. His extremities felt tingly, his brain went fuzzy and dull, and he wanted to ball up like a caterpillar that had been poked by a child. Why had he made himself vulnerable again? Spence smiled and seemed pleased with his dissection.

"Okay, let's get back on track," Spence said. "Punk is a terrible name for a hearing aid product. A punk steals your car! Rocker may not be perfect, but it conveys what is most important about this launch. It is brash but dignified. It admits to no weakness or failure. It is how we picture ourselves in our best moments." The rest of the team nodded. Dutch nudged Benjamin's leg with his foot under the table and gave him a warning look that meant "You better agree too this time, mate," but Benjamin felt too morose to respond to the cue. "Benjy," Spence added, "don't worry about it. I believe in the free give-and-take of ideas. This is a forum. You can say what you like. Make any suggestion you like. I just happened not to like yours, okay?"

"Okay," Benjamin mumbled. How had he blundered back into his brother's distortion field after so many years of independence? Separating himself from his role as big brother hadn't come easily or naturally to him. He had disciplined himself to stay away, and Dita had reinforced his instincts even if she did it in a heavy-handed way. That respite now felt like a decade-long reprieve although he had missed his brother's antics from time to time.

"All right," Spence said. "We need to mull this over without losing sight of the calendar. But let me leave you with this. In spite of Benjy's word games and pseudo distinctions that nobody will care about but him, what expresses our concept better than the Rocker? Next time we meet I want to hear all your ideas no matter how rough or stupid they are."

Benjamin knew that the only answer that mattered to Spence was his own. The rest was gibberish. Other suggestions and ideas interfered with Spence's clarity and certainty. Benjamin saw that Spence thought no one could plumb a concept, any concept, as quickly and as concisely as he could. Even he, Benjamin, his older brother, was sluggish and dull, although Spence seemed to have a statutory respect for him in other areas. When Benjamin came up with the company name, Spence had consoled himself with the notion that it was only beginner's luck.

The signal to them that the meeting was over and they were no longer needed was that Spence pulled out his phone and started speaking as if the team was no longer present. They shuffled out of the room and headed down the hall to the front door.

"Too early for a drink?" Dutch asked no one in particular. "If he had one, why can't we?"

Silently, they traipsed to the elevator and rode it down to the lobby. By habit or instinct, Dutch led them to the pub next door. Even though it was cooler in mid-September, the air-conditioning purred in the background just below the hum of the televisions that were tuned to different sports channels. Assorted teams in vibrantly colored uniforms chased balls of different sizes and shapes and ran drills across dazzling green fields. The pitch of ringing and static in Benjamin's ears had risen by at least one level.

"Not too bad," Dutch said when they were seated. "Not too bad for him, I mean." Drinks arrived without an order having been placed. Stillwater's, as the sign announced in Gaelic script entwined with clover leaves on the dark wood siding above the bar, was the beneficiary of Spence's temperament. There was a smell of pure anesthetic alcohol in the air. Judging by the number of tables that were filled at three thirty in the afternoon, that odor described a broad prescription. Men and a sprinkling of women hoisted their beer glasses in the air as if their arms were attached directly to the taps.

"That was awful," Dr. H said. "He is an awful man. Sorry he's your brother, Benjamin. Excuse me." She stood up, smoothed her skirt, and disappeared from the table.

"Benjy. May I call you Benjy too?" Dutch asked. He passed his hand over the black-and-gray stubble on his scalp and cocked his head. His glasses, which Benjamin hadn't noticed before, had an odd yellowish tint to the lenses. Considering the touring life he had maintained for over a decade, he didn't look half bad. His eyes, though, had a stupefied sadness to them that was impenetrable and unwavering. The small-time rock-and-roll life had given him glimpses of horror.

"I prefer Benjamin. My brother is the exception. He couldn't care less what my name is, but I like the whole thing if you don't mind."

"All right then. Benjamin, has your brother always been such a jerk? Hold on. Before she gets back I have to warn you to be careful what you say in front of her. She is lethal. She may seem all friendly and a team player to you as if we were all in the same cesspool slash lifeboat, which we are, and she may be sweet toward you since he picked on you today, but she will repeat every word you say to Spence, especially the negative ones, so think about that before you open your mouth. Belphonics isn't for sissies."

"Oh," was all Benjamin could muster, more in agreement than surprise. Had he thought of it beforehand, the need for caution wouldn't have surprised him. But his eagerness to participate in the new venture and the time and distance he had put between himself and Spence had damped his instincts and paranoia. When he remembered Dr. H's flattery and her playfulness with him, it crossed his mind that she might be part of Spence's plan to lure him back into the Belphonics fold that he had left soon after Spence started the company. He had insisted that Benjamin go see her and made sure he returned to her for further consultations. Benjamin's head snapped up as he watched her returning from the ladies' room.

"So, what are we going to tell him? We have to come up with something different. Rocker is boring and obvious," Dr. H said, looking refreshed.

"What's the point?" Dutch asked. "Unless we can think of a much better name and convince him that he thought of it first, Rocker is what it'll be."

"But does it matter?" Benjamin asked. "Do people think of hearing aids as having a brand name? Isn't the technology the biggest selling point? Do they need a specific profile?"

"Yes, they do, for marketing purposes. You have to be able to call them something. Throw in a graphic. Maybe a testimonial or two."

"Testimonial?"

"Well, think about it a minute. Dream big. If Mick Jagger or Eric Clapton endorsed them, they would sell themselves. We could spend the rest of our lives at a matinee. We wouldn't have to lift a finger. And maybe never see Spence again," Dutch added as an afterthought.

"I thought we were licensing from CBGB's," Benjamin said.

"Whether we do or don't, it doesn't matter. If a rock superstar, not some punk has-been, endorsed them, your brother would make a gazillion dollars. That would validate the whole "concept." Dutch used his hands to add the quotation marks. "Didn't Mick Jagger say that he'd lost a lot of his hearing on his left side because that's where Keith stood when they were onstage? Isn't that the perfect symbol for us? Mick's hearing loss makes him noble and vulnerable at the same time. He wasn't ashamed of it. He was proud. He was admitting to his fans that it had been an honor to stand next to Keith for fifty years in spite of the damage."

Benjamin was seized by Dutch's vision. Dr. H, by contrast, was disinterested. They fell silent at the prospect of what an endorsement of that magnitude might mean and how unlikely it was, as if even imagining it made it ridiculous. Everything would be tainted by the attempt to achieve it, they knew collectively, especially as the most likely outcome of such an effort would be failure, a failure for which they would be blamed.

"Whatever you do, Benjamin, don't repeat the Jagger quote to Spence," Dutch said. "That's all we need. He'll torture us to find a way to get to Jagger and talk him into it. We'll be better off if we stick to the original plan. CBGB's is manageable. There's a guy we can call. A licensing agent. They'll be hungry to make a deal. The odds of Spence getting Jagger or one of the Stones interested are ridiculously low. Infinitesimal. So let's just not bring it up."

"Why did you even have to go there, Dutch?" Dr. H asked, not expecting a reply, her voice disdainful and low.

They finished their beers and got up to leave the bar. When they reached the sidewalk, Dutch waved and peeled off toward the subway. Dr. H and Benjamin looked at each other as if they weren't sure what they should do next. Benjamin began to walk to the corner, and Dr. H turned with him. The sun was at their backs, insistent but not stifling.

"Are you in a rush?" she asked, and smiled, her lips stuck together.

"Sort of, but not really. I'm trying to digest what happened today, so I'm going to walk uptown slowly. You?"

"I have no appointments and don't want to go back to the office. Can I keep you company for a few blocks?"

They walked slowly. The rush-hour crowds swirled around them. Everyone was in a hurry but them. They became slow-moving obstacles on the pavement that the other pedestrians were forced to circum-navigate.

"Calling it the Punk wasn't such a bad idea, Benjamin," she said. "He just gets worked up over nothing. To him everyone is an adversary. Even his brother. It's kind of sad, isn't it? He can't trust anyone. How did he get that way?"

"I have no idea. I don't know how dangerous he really is, but he could always be scary. Impulsive. He'd get an idea in his head, like throwing grapes at pedestrians from our window. "We'll never get caught," he'd say. "I could never predict what he'd do next or how he'd react or what he'd say. And I learned that anything could happen at any moment."

Because of Dutch's warning about Dr. H, Benjamin wanted to edit his comments, but he couldn't help himself from confiding in her. He needed to confess his anxiety and frustration about his brother to some-one who knew Spence and who wasn't completely biased against him. Dita's distrust was too deep and entrenched to be helpful. She hated him unconditionally. At the same time, he refused to believe that Dr. H was as treacherous as Dutch made her out to be. He wanted her to be the ally that he could confide in. Furthermore, he thought she might have sympathetic feelings for Spence, and he knew what a minefield that could be. It made him protective of her and sorry for her at the same time.

The sun hid behind the phalanx of buildings as they walked up-town. It was Rosh Hashanah, he remembered. That was why so many people were in a hurry to get home before the sun set. He and Dita did nothing to celebrate the holiday beyond marking it on the calendar. He stared at the pavement as they walked and then realized that Dr. H was wearing the red stilettos that matched the occasion on her shoe calendar. It hadn't occurred to him that it was prescriptive. Without thinking, he slowed his pace as he noticed that her heels had to be at least five inches high.

PART TWO

10

THE ENGINES ROARED, THE PLANE LIFTED, AND THE SKYLINE shrank. What I could see past the bulge of my seatmate were fields of lights: streetlights, house lights, and headlights. When I glanced again a few minutes later, they had thinned out and there was only white. Maybe clouds, maybe snow, I couldn't tell, and not knowing what was up or down made me dizzy.

I fell asleep, and when I woke up my head was resting on the massive shoulder of my kidnapper. He was asleep too, and his snoring sounded like a steel cable grinding on a rusty wheel. The guy on my other side was awake, but barely. He opened his eyes and caught me staring.

"My name's Frank, by the way, and that's Sal you were sleeping on. You've been very cooperative. We really appreciate that. You wouldn't believe some of these kids," he said, and shook his head. "Maniacs!" he exclaimed.

"Where are you taking me?"

"Salt Lake we hand you over, but we gotta change planes in Denver," Frank said.

Sal woke up as the plane landed, and my bodyguards escorted me silently through the Denver airport. People stared at me like I might be famous or a killer or both. They led me to a small corridor down an escalator at the back of the main runway. The next flight was already boarding. The people in line didn't look like people I had ever met before or even seen except on television. They were wearing jangly cowboy boots and cowboy hats. They must have thought that there were steers loose in terminal C. I popped a red Skittle into my mouth, and it relaxed me instantly, as if it were a tranquilizer.

The next plane was a much smaller one. Frank let me sit next to the window so I could stare out. We flew over the mountains that rose up out of the plains like caped monsters. Geologic Draculas. Snow was already socked into the highest chutes between the slate-gray peaks. When the plane cruised over the valleys, I thought I could see trails cut into the snow fields and a tiny wooden hut standing by itself that reminded me of a photograph in my American history textbook of a lone miner wedged in the doorway of a crooked cabin that has been almost swallowed by snowdrifts. The memory of school kept the question of how far I was going and for how long in the front of my brain. Again, I saw my parents staring at me as I left and felt a sharp pain inside my chest.

The plane descended over a lake as big as an ocean. Mile after mile of unrippled water stretched out like a mirror, making the cloudless sky even broader. As we approached, I could see the wide sandbars and rings of lake debris crusted with salt. The plane's reflection skimmed the surface before we landed.

Sal and Frank grabbed my coat as we pushed to leave the plane. They flanked me again down the corridor past the other gates and led me to a tall, unshaven, grinning man who was wearing chewed-up sandals and rugged outdoor clothes that looked a little slept-in. There was a lady next to him in a forest-green fleece with thinning blond hair. She had tiny city shoes on her little feet, with black, velvet bows on the toes. They both had a raw, burnt look to them, as if they had been left in the sun too long.

"Welcome to Utah, Giorgio," the happy man said. "I'm Hal, and this is Susan. Let's get out of here before the traffic gets up." Susan, who had a professional air about her, nodded in agreement. Hal clapped Frank and Sal on the back, and they nodded to me before walking away, their package delivered.

I followed my new abductors to a big Suburban in the parking lot and climbed into the backseat. The interior was totally torn apart. The leather covering the dashboard was ripped open, and the fabric on the roof was tattered and hanging down in strips like flypaper, as if there had been a block party in there the night before. The seat backs were scratched and ripped too, allowing the yellow padding to sprout through them.

"What happened?" I asked, unable to contain my curiosity.

"Dave left the door unlocked last night, and a bear followed his snout and then couldn't find food in here, he got ticked off, but he didn't really mean any harm. If you were a bear and starving, I promise you you'd have done the same thing. Speaking of food, let's stop at Carl's Jr. before we get off the highway. We always get the new kids a Thickburger and some of those natural-cut fries before the slow part of the drive. This is the last meal you won't be cooking for a while," Hal explained in a rote voice despite the bemused look on his face that didn't read as the slightest bit sadistic.

I pressed my forehead against the cool glass of the window. The sun was low but still intense on the other side of the car. The towns south of Salt Lake were just rows of small houses curving over hillsides that looked exactly alike. They were spaced farther and farther apart the longer we were in the car. Soon the towns became smaller and had strange names that sounded as if they had been stolen from the Bible. There were still groves of trees on either side of the highway, low foothills that rose in the distance tracked by telephone towers, but between them the earth was red. Dust swirled when the wind stirred up and blew across the road. A fine reddish film stuck to the window.

"Is this your first time in the West, Giorgio?" Susan asked, bringing me back from the alien surroundings.

"Yes," I answered. My hunch was that Susan was the psychologist. From the one I had met once at home, I knew they had that knack for starting conversations out innocently before leading you to where they really wanted to go. I was trying to process where I was and how I got there, so I couldn't expand on my answer. Obviously, my parents thought that a change of scenery might help me be more stable. Did they realize that they were sending me to a place where the bears were so hungry that they would eat the inside of a truck? Did they remember that I was only fourteen?

Hal exited suddenly and pulled into the Carl's Jr. parking lot. He and Susan flanked me as we entered, as if I were a suspect in a crime who might try to escape at any moment. They asked if I wanted to use the restroom. When I was done, they were both standing propped against the wall outside waiting for me. They seemed as afraid to leave me alone as Frank and Sal were. I was one precious package, I thought to myself, and grinned internally. It was the first time I didn't feel depressed or confused all day.

"You may not eat all of it, but we're going to get you the biggest burger meal they've got," Hal said.

"That's what we always do, by the way. It'll give you something to boast about when we get to camp," Susan added.

We sat at one of the fixed tables, and I didn't have any trouble eating. After a steady diet of Italian recipes, American fast food was a treat for me, especially under the circumstances. We ate silently. The door admitted a blast of wind when it was opened, and the repetition of orders through the microphone to the line chefs were the only sounds besides our chewing.

"Do you know why you're here with us, Giorgio?" Hal asked in a gentle way that made me wonder if he was a psychologist too.

"Most kids don't, by the way," Susan said, her tone supportive. "A few of them know that they're unhappy. Do you feel unhappy?" She had an empathetic, almost maternal quarter tilt to her head. It felt to me that no answer I could give, no matter how obnoxious or outrageous, would upset her. It was all usable material. I stalled and took a sip of the Pepsi that tasted watered-down. Her question made me squirm. I had a flashback to the lump on Walt's forehead. And Mom and me in a heap on the floor. Of all the things in my life, I was unhappy that I had done that to my friend and my mother, but I covered over the feeling as quickly as possible with justifications for my reactions. Those felt thinner and more flimsy as the days went by.

"What did they tell you?" I asked back.

"Anger. Reactive anger mixed with violence and aggression. Does that sound about right? I don't want to put words in your mouth, Giorgio. How does it feel to you?" Susan asked, using the therapeutic tone of infinite patience that always sounded a little fake. She had an earnest look in her eyes, as if she truly believed that I was capable of giving her a deeper answer and if I didn't, she might be profoundly disappointed in me.

"It feels like you're trying to get me to say something I might regret later. I can't. I don't want to say anything about it," I said to her. My tone was fiercer than I felt.

"That's not our practice. We don't use what you tell us against you. We're just trying to get to know more about you. That's our job," Susan said, and fiddled with the sunglasses that were holding back her frizzy blond hair.

"So what's my job?" I asked. "To make yours easy?" The question felt stupidly belligerent. Hearing it echo in my brain, I instantly regretted it. They stood up at the same time, as though they had heard the same alarm bell.

"We're here to help you, Giorgio," Hal said. "Not punish you. You don't have a job. All you have to do is adjust to this new place. That isn't easy. You'll see if there's anything here that changes your mind. We want to help you do that if we can."

"Hal's right. How can we help you, Giorgio? You probably don't have a clue about that yet, but when you do, will you tell us?" Susan asked. I nodded reflexively. My resistance dropped a notch.

"You done?" Hal, now a little more somber, asked. "If we leave now, we'll get there before dark. It's better that way. Nobody stays awake too much past sunset."

We drove the rest of the way with a country radio station coming and going. The music sounded like one long complaint. An hour or so later we turned off the highway onto a two-lane road and started to climb into the hills. The red earth that had been mostly concealed by the trees two hours before was now bare and even redder. There was scrub and the occasional pine or cottonwood, but mostly it was barren and bleak. Clearly, they had chosen to situate their camp where there was nowhere to hide. I could see a few lights in the distance, but I felt like I was on the other side of the planet from where I'd started the morning, a side that was empty of people, houses, streets, and cars. It reminded me of pictures of the moon. I realized at that moment that I would do anything to be home, even if I had to play on Feigel's fucking basketball team.

Twenty minutes later, Hal pulled the car into what I guess you could call a parking lot because there was one other vehicle in front of a large rock. I followed Hal and Susan on a path, and for some reason I was worrying about the red dust staining her tan patent leather shoes. When we came around the last bend, I saw a shed and tents and campfires in the distance. The temperature was dropping quickly with the sun, and I was getting cold. I was hoping that they had some warmer clothes for me. It wasn't as if I had had time to pack.

First, they led me to the shack that looked like an outfitters' store. Gear of every kind was hanging from the walls and from a pole that ran the length of the ceiling: tarps, tents, ropes, carabiners. A big man came toward me holding out his puffy hand.

"I'm Dave," he said. "Maybe they told you about me. I'm the idiot who left the truck doors unlocked. I guess you saw what the bear did. I should know by now that they can open car doors. I've been here long enough. Are you a large, or too skinny for that?"

"How's medium long?"

"Nope. Put these on, and I need everything out of your pockets and your belt and your shoelaces."

"My laces?"

"Yes, nobody gets to keep those. You'll get everything back when we know we can trust you not to do something extra stupid," he said, and handed me a stack of clothes. In the makeshift changing room I wolfed down the rest of my Skittles, suspecting that they would be confiscated too. When I emerged in my new clothes, Dave introduced me to Ron, the director of the camp. Ron was a small, intense-looking, ruddy-faced man with a bristly mustache and eyebrows. His shoulder and arm muscles strained against the fabric of his neat short-sleeve outdoor shirt. He didn't seem to possess the smallest trace of humor. He neither smiled nor looked at me. He sat me down on a wooden bench outside the shed. In the smoky distance I saw shapes of what I assumed were other kids moving around, building and poking fires, placing small pots in the coals.

"So here we are, Giorgio." His voice had an uninflected, inhuman rhythm to it. I guess his mother had never taught him intonation like mine had. Its high pitch surprised me, too. "We're going to get to know each other well, real well." That sounded threatening. "That's your group," he said, pointing to a spot in the distance where the wood smoke smudged up. A small but indistinct shape leaned over a campfire. "There are eleven kids here, including you. Six girls, five boys. We have some basic rules. We need to know where you are at all times. If you have to wake up to pee, even in the middle of the night, you have to count off out loud so we know how far you've gone. You have to stay with your partner.

Leave the girls alone. If you steal stuff, you're going to be spending a lot of time by yourself. If you try to run away, good luck. There's nowhere to go. Bicknell is over five miles from here. There are washes all around this place that you can't see in the dark. And there are animals out there, too. Are you following me, Giorgio?"

"What kind of animals?" I asked.

"Mountain lion, bobcat, coyote, rattlesnake. They won't attack you unless you bump into one of them. That happens a lot easier at night. So, what are we doing here, Giorgio? Do you have any idea?" Ron asked. He didn't wait for an answer. "You probably haven't had much time to think about that, so let me put it as simply as I can. We want to build your confidence. We want you to start to see yourself as the capable, intelligent young man you probably are in spite of the stupid shit you did that got you sent here. Being separated from your family and your friends is a punishment, but you have to try and see it as the best kind. It doesn't hurt, it builds something new. It teaches you when you don't think you're learning. We want to believe in you, but you have to give us a reason to do that. You have to earn our trust." He stared at me in a way that made me want to hide. He seemed more like a football coach than a guidance counselor. Did he want me to call him sir?

"Any questions? Are you hearing me?"

"No and yes," I answered.

"I'm not interested in no, Giorgio. Only yes. You got that?

"Yes, sir," I said a little too sharply, and it was all I could do not to give him a mock salute.

"Kenny is going to be your partner," Ron continued, ignoring the sarcasm in my voice. "Bring your sleeping bag and stuff. Kenny's not a bad kid at heart. He's a city boy like you. Chicago."

"Why is he here?" I asked.

"We can't discuss that with you. If he wants to tell you, that's up to him. He's been here a few weeks already, so he's got some miles on his boots. Watch your stuff. I tell that to all the newbies in case you're wondering. Kenny isn't any different. They're all thieves."

I reviewed what I had: absolutely nothing. What Kenny might steal was beyond the power of my imagination. Didn't we all have the same stuff? I'd even exchanged my underwear for thermals, handed over my wallet and my belt and shoes, even the undershirt I had slept in the night before. Kenny could take what he wanted. I was wearing their uniform; hiking pants with eight pockets, shirts that "breathed," Dave said, whatever that meant, and hiking boots. All of it was the same boring color. Like sand or like sand that was stained a shade darker with piss. I carried the lumpy sleeping bag in the backpack they'd given me. I could already feel fine grains of red dust on my skin.

As I followed Ron, we passed a campfire with two girls hovering over it. I was pretty sure they were girls because they had long hair, but when I glanced at them, there wasn't much feminine about them. Their cheeks were streaked with charcoal and dirt. Their fingers were mostly black. Their clothes were covered with marks, as if they had just been in a food fight. They shrank back as I walked by, as though they were a little self-conscious about how filthy they were. I wished I could ask Alessandra if this was how Neanderthal girls used to look in the old days.

Kenny was about five inches shorter than me, with dark curly hair that hung over his forehead and bounced up and down. He had hollow, grimy cheeks and a wisp of a beard, or maybe it was just dirt. He was dressed in the same nondescript clothes that I had just put on. He stuck a stick into the coals he was tending, and sparks swirled up into the twilight sky. As my eyes followed them, it occurred to me that there was something wrong with the stars, as if they had exploded into millions of pieces and those were spread everywhere, not just wedged between apartment buildings and rooftops. And the stars were bunched in clusters. After Ron presented me to him, Kenny poked the fire again, and the orange glow of the coals wheezed out a blue-orange flame that fluttered and lifted to the horizon that had its own embers.

"Sit down," he said, and pointed to where I should put my stuff. "Did you bring any real food?"

"No, they didn't let me. I thought there'd be food when I got here." I sat down on a rock not too close to him.

"There is food but not the real kind," he said. He turned and squinted at me, and his whole face crinkled.

"They said you've been here a few weeks."

"Five, maybe six. I've lost track," he said.

We stared silently into the same fire for a while. I felt around behind me for a stick so I could poke the coals the way Kenny did. I followed the sparks up into the bluish sky and watched them spin. In that moment of beauty I lost track of my anger at my parents for sending me away. It felt like a relief not to face the rest of the term at Blethen with Feigel breathing down my neck and my mother waiting to catch me doing something else wrong.

"So why are you here?" I finally asked Kenny.

"You know Keats?" Kenny asked back.

"I haven't met anybody yet."

Kenny shook his head in pity at my ignorance: "No, he's not here. He's not one of us. He died two hundred years ago. He was English. One of the most famous poets who ever lived. He got tuberculosis and died when he was twenty-five. I got obsessed with him. I guess it's hereditary," he said as he stuck a pot directly in the coals. "My father is a fucking English teacher!"

"What's in there?" I asked.

"Different kinds of beans. If you don't soak them right, they give you cramps, but that's about the worst they can do and they're pretty filling. Long hike tomorrow. It's a practice run for the lake trail. It's over five miles. They say we can do it, but I don't think some of the girls are up to it." Kenny paused for a minute and looked west, where there was still a rim of yellow orange light along the mountain ridges. Cicadas chirped from time to time. "Keats wrote, 'Heard melodies are sweet but those unheard are sweeter,'" Kenny continued. "My dad has a Keats quote for almost every occasion, so I apologize in advance, but I've got so many of them crowded in my head and I can't get rid of them. Like that one. If you start to listen out here, there's a lot to hear when you don't think there's any sound at all. So what did you do?"

"I don't want to talk about it," I said.

"No worries, Giorgio," he said, pronouncing it like Georgey. "You've got a lot of time to stew over that. Nobody is going to make you talk or do anything else. Even the shrinks. Ron is an asshole, in case you couldn't tell. I was a drinker and a glue head. And a thief. I was so proud of how invisible and quick I was until I got caught. Then they were all over me. The day I got here it was hailing golf balls. I couldn't dodge them, and they hurt like hell. What was I supposed to steal here? Nobody has anything worth taking. I was so pissed at my parents. I was pissed at the hail like it was the hail's fault that I was here," he said.

"So you were a klepto?" I asked. I knew kids like that at Blethen. Sooner or later they all got caught. But as far as I know the only kid who ever got sent to Utah was me.

He took off the red cowboy bandana he wore around his neck and waved it in my face. "Smell that," he said. "Stinks, right?"

I nodded. It reeked— as if he had sweated through it every day for the whole time he had been there and hadn't washed it. "How can you sweat so much when it's freezing?" I asked.

"Tonight it's freezing, but when you're hiking up a mountain at this altitude and carrying a heavy pack, it's a lot hotter. Believe me."

"Then why don't you wash it?"

"You may not have noticed yet, but there isn't a lot of water around here. Besides, I'm used to the smell, and now it reminds me of stuff. Like the fact that I'm alive enough out here to produce that smell. My sweat is proof I'm not dead. I'm not in juvie. When I got here, I thought there was no way that I'd survive. No car, no booze, no glue, no grass. How could I get through it? The first night, I refused to sleep under the tarp like Hal told me. I didn't care if I was cold and wet. I didn't believe anything they told me. Then I started to think, who am I going to get angry at? The rain, the desert, these old trees? They don't give a fuck and aren't listening, so what's the point of shouting at them? That's why I put on that dumbass bandana every morning, and the more it stinks, the more it reminds me that I survived another night. And that's when I started to hear all the sounds that I couldn't hear until then, and they just get better and better."

Kenny talked without stopping, and it crossed my mind that maybe he hadn't talked to anybody in days or he thought I'd have to listen since I was new. Or he had no friends. I liked what he said, but most of all, I liked watching his face and how it turned from being twitchy and crumpled one minute to being relaxed the next. It just flowed back and forth, and it was impossible to catch what made it switch directions. He didn't look at me while he was talking. He stared into the fire as if that was where all the truth was stored.

The day that had started before dawn in New York City and transferred me through two cities, two time zones and many pairs of hands had worn me down. I couldn't keep my eyes open. When I pictured my parents standing at the door as Frank and Sal took me away, I jerked awake. I unrolled the sleeping bag under the tarp next to the fire and inched closer to it. I wanted its little tongues of heat to lick me so that I'd fall asleep and the next day would arrive as fresh as a clean sheet.

The next thing I knew the sun was a taxi yellow and somebody was watching me. She was perched on a rock maybe five feet away and two or three feet above me looking as comfortable as if she had been settled there for hours. But it couldn't have been light for very long. She wore her own uniform: fingerless purple gloves and layers of shirts and sweaters over a long, pleated skirt above dusty black hiking pants. On top of those bulky layers was a sweatshirt that had POMONA written on it in block letters. She sketched in a large pad. The pencil moved with slow, hard strokes. She looked up and saw that I was awake and watching her.

"What the hell are you doing?" I asked her, embarrassed that she had caught me in my sleeping bag. "How long have you been staring at me?"

"Shh. Don't wake Kenny up. He's such a grump. I draw all the new kids when they arrive at camp."

"Does Ron make you do that?"

"Nobody makes me do anything I don't want to do. Ever. My name's Lainey," she said, and made a pointless attempt to stretch her hand out to me. Her long, dark, frizzy hair fell forward as she leaned toward me, almost covering her narrow face. Her nose was so thin I didn't know how she could breathe through it.

"Did you go there?" I asked her, motioning at her sweatshirt and wondering how she got to wear her own clothes.

"No, it was my brother's. I stole it. What's your name?" Lainey asked.

"Giorgio," I said.

"Giorgio," she repeated. "Giorgio, are you Italian?"

"No, my mother changed my name. It used to be Mark."

"I like Giorgio better. It's so chewy. What are you doing here, Giorgio?" Lainey asked, lengthening the syllables. That seemed to be the standard opener at Camp Fremont, the first thing that everyone wanted to know, like the "What are you in for" question in the prison movies Claire and I loved watching.

"I was a danger," I said, and my chin sank to my chest.

"To yourself?" she asked, not looking up from her pad. I decided not to answer her. "To yourself," she repeated, like it was no longer a question. "I was a danger to myself," she said, nodding gently, and pushed up the sleeves of her shirts. She stuck her wrist toward me, and I could see the many stripe marks and the pale, milky scars that had almost grown over them. "That was a while ago," she added. It took me a minute to realize that those scars were where her skin had grown back after she had cut herself. Maybe I was a danger to myself, but not like she was. She was in a different league.

"You know there's something strange about your eyes and your eyebrows, right? Did anybody ever tell you that?" She spoke in a casual way, as if we were discussing our homework.

"No, what's wrong with them?"

"Well, you're going to have to find that out. I'm not a very good drawer," she said, "but I'm a good seer, and I see that there is something dark between your eyes. I can feel it. Not inside them. Your eyes look normal. It's more like there's a darkish knot between your eyebrows. I can't tell exactly what it is. Maybe it's a secret you're keeping to yourself that you want to show or a secret you buried there that you don't remember and now it's pushing through your skin. You aren't sick, are you?"

"Not as far as I know, but my head has been feeling funny lately. Like there's a worm in it."

"Never mind. I'm probably just imagining things," she said.

The sun's rays flashed around her body as though she was their source. Behind her, giant cliffs with red and white bands of sandstone went as far as the eye could see. A broad valley spread out beneath us. Where am I? I asked myself. All of it seemed so strange. Then I smelled something familiar. Almost immediately I knew it was sage, and it became more and more distinct. It was my mother's favorite herb. Salvia, she called it. She used it on everything. It perfumed our apartment.

A bell rang and I could see Hal walking toward us. "Time to pack up, you two. Since you're new, Giorgio, check your shoes before you put them on. You don't want to wake up a scorpion. They love warm shoes and don't like surprises. Fill your water bottle from the blue container over there," he said, pointing at a water container a hundred feet away beyond the lumps of other kids stirring in their sleeping bags.

Lainey slid down off her perch and pulled the cleaner part of her skirt around to the front. She made half a smile at me. "Can I see your drawing?" I asked.

"Later, if we survive the hike," she said, and walked over to the group that had begun assembling around the water jug.

When I got there, Ron looked freshly showered and was dressed in neat, pressed clothes. "Listen up," he said in his public voice. "Remember to fill your water bottles to the top. And drink the water. You *have* to drink the water. We're at eight thousand feet. For the new kid that means that there is one third less oxygen. Your brains need as much help as they can get in normal situations, which these aren't, so don't deprive them. This is the *only* water you're going to get all day. Let's go."

"Now you know why his nickname is 'How's your water, Ron,'" Lainey whispered from behind me.

We headed to a trail near the campsite, and even though it was mostly flat, Lainey was breathing hard. I could hear her sucking air deep into her chest and her long and loud exhales. After a few cycles of that, she would stop and gaze back to where we had come from, hands on her hips, elbows jutted out, bottom leg braced against the slope of the hill. She'd lean her head over to suck in more oxygen and then pretend she was studying something by the side of the trail, like a withered flower or a lizard that was glued to a rock. She'd take another swig of water and then look at me to give me a sign that she could continue.

We walked for another twenty minutes, and then her breathing became heavy and deep again, so we stopped. It wasn't even ten o'clock and my bandana was already damp. I was glad Kenny thought the smell of sweat was reassuring, but I didn't like the idea of it drying on my skin. I wanted to scrape it off me. Lainey was bent over by the side of the trail, and I could see little tremors running down her back. I wanted to put my hand on her sweatshirt to reassure her, but I didn't know her well enough for that. I didn't know her at all.

After we started walking a little more, we reached a boardwalk where the rest of the group was already gathered. A wooden sign announced that we had reached the Fremont petroglyphs. I moved next to her against the railing and helped her take her backpack off and set it on the ground. When our eyes met, I could see that not only was she exhausted but there were tears streaming down her white cheeks. Her eyes were watery. I wanted to comfort her but I didn't know how.

With his back to the cliffs, Hal was grinning and waiting patiently for us to pay attention. Kenny was wringing out and refolding his bandana. The other kids were sipping water and sweating. I rubbed my sleeve across my forehead to soak up as much perspiration as I could.

"The Fremont River was full of fish back then," Hal began. He pointed to an empty riverbed in the distance. The vanished water left behind murky red and sandy white paths of junk that showed where it had last flowed bouncing from bank to bank. "The Hopi people knew how to make baskets that held water, and the children's job was to carry them full up the steep slopes to the mesas. I want to leave you with something to think about. A lady named Terry Tempest Williams said, 'Of what value are the objects of past people if we don't allow ourselves to be touched by them. They are alive. They have a voice. They remind us what it means to be human; that it is our nature to survive, to be re-sourceful, to be attentive to the world we live in.' That's part of what you guys are doing here. That's part of your job. You are being reminded of what it means to be human."

Instantly, I thought of what I had done to Walt and how I had launched myself at my mother. Had I forgotten that they were human, or had they forgotten that I was, or, in the moment, had all of us forgotten everything? I looked at Hal standing there. He pulled at his boots, slapped some of the red dust off his pant legs, and scanned the landscape as if he could read what was written there. The intensity of his attention told me that he knew and understood the secrets of this land. Translating the signs and clues and warnings was effortless for him. The panorama was neither passive nor inscrutable. It was alive and filled with legends, myths, stories, and messages, and they were written in a language he was fluent in.

Lainey had listened to Hal's talk bent over at the waist. An oval sweat stain showed through the back of her gray top. Kenny stood on the other side of her and kept rolling his eyes at me, as if to say, "This guy really believes this shit." Then he winked at me, nudging his chin at Lainey like we were conspiring against her. But I liked her already, the way you like someone who spots something in you that you couldn't see for yourself and she wasn't going to beat you up with it.

Hal waved to us to follow him to the trail. I was in a daze. The next thing I knew we were a third of the way up a long incline and Hal was running past us as fast as he could. His face had a grim, strained look on it. All of us turned around to see what the emergency was. Maybe fifty yards away from us we could see a figure sprawled in the dirt that I knew had to be Lainey. She was the only one missing. Kenny and I sat down and watched Hal bending over her, offering her water from his Nalgene bottle, talking to her and holding her arm. Her face was a few inches off the ground and her body was buckling in waves. Her back was arched and her neck was bent. She pushed herself up on her hands and vomited into the dust. Hal kept holding on to her.

"Is this normal for her?" I asked Kenny.

"Happens many times a day. Ron is so sick of her. Hal must be a saint."

"Maybe he's in love with her?" I asked out of nowhere. Kenny didn't answer.

"She's a cutter, you know. Did she show you?" Kenny asked me. I nodded. "Yeah," he continued. "She shows everybody the first day."

I wanted to ask Lainey a million questions. They shouted out in my head. Some were about her, and some were about what else she had seen in me. When the rest of the group stood up and resumed hiking, I hung back. Hal ran past me to the front of the line, and soon Lainey reached me. She was sunny and smiling, as if nothing had happened.

"Are you all right?" I asked.

"Are you waiting for poor, pathetic me?" she asked me. "You're a sweet boy, but you don't have to stop. This is as fast as I go. I prefer going slow. The conversation is better at the back of the line."

I wasn't sure what conversation she meant, one within herself or one with me, so I kept quiet for a bit and tried to walk as slowly as she did. That took way more effort than I thought. My legs wanted to rush forward, but I forced them to take shorter steps, go at minimum speed. That discipline made them ache more than the climb did. Whoever said going slow was easy never tried it.

"Thanks for waiting," she said between her held and rushed breaths. "I don't feel like being alone here. The desert is a scary place even if you don't see anything dangerous. You know they're watching you."

"Who is? Mountain lions? Snakes?" I asked.

"All of them, but please don't say the word *snakes*. Tell me your name again?"

"Giorgio."

"What a beautiful name. Giorgio. Let's not talk about venomous animals, Giorgio. It's hard enough for me to get through the night," Lainey said.

"Why do you draw the new people?"

"Because I like to watch them change. Take your friend Kenny," she said. "He's completely different. If you think he's tense now, you should have seen him on his first day. It was like he was being chased by mobsters. He was breathless and his eyes were haywire. I want to see how you change, too. Maybe that weird bump will turn out to be nothing. Or maybe it's everything."

"What?"

"Maybe it's a secret buried so deep that you don't have any idea what it is. What is it, Giorgio? What's in that little lump?"

"There's no lump there. You're imagining things."

"I have a lot of problems, but delusions aren't one of them. Let's not worry about it now. Stay with me."

I could tell how difficult hiking was for her, but it didn't seem to get in the way of her talking. Until I met Lainey, I didn't know that talking was another form of breathing. Or it was for her. And as she spoke, it seemed to me that she was able to breathe better.

"Okay, so tell me again," I said.

"Only because you're being so nice to me," Lainey said. "So I think there is something hiding in you and whatever it is has consequences, consequences that you don't understand yet. It isn't fixed or solid. It's floating, and that's why you can't see it."

I could tell that she was being sincere. She wasn't like a shrink trying to trick me into revealing something by accident. She didn't seem like someone who would do that. She was too nice to be making stuff up just to mess with me. Her intuition felt truer than anything I had heard before, as if she could tell that there was trouble inside me even if she didn't know what kind it was. She was trying to alert me.

"How old are you?" I asked her.

"Seventeen," she said. "How old are you?"

"Fourteen. Where are you from?"

"California. Have you ever been there?"

"My parents took me when I was a kid, but I don't remember it. Can I ask you something?"

"Yes, Giorgio. Ask."

"Why did you hurt yourself?"

"Sure," she said, and paused. "I was numb after my brother died. I loved him so much, and I looked up to him so much. He always knew what I was thinking when I couldn't figure it out. I couldn't get over the

fact that he would do that to himself without warning me. I still can't."
Her face, turned away from the sun, was darker now, with a somberness
that was deeper than the smudges of dirt on her cheeks.

"How did he do it?" I asked timidly, ashamed by my curiosity.

"He hung himself in his dorm room."

"Sorry," I muttered, but I felt speechless. That was the saddest thing
I'd ever heard.

"No, it's good to talk about. It really is. I was so shocked, I couldn't
feel anything. I couldn't cry. My parents thought I didn't care because I
had no tears. That's when I started doing it, and then I couldn't stop."

"Did it hurt?" I asked her.

"Of course it hurt. That was the whole point. So tell me, my dear
Giorgio, how are we going to get through the day?"

"It's my first one, so I don't know," I said.

"Well, I do. We're going to dream together about something delicious. Describe to me the last thing you ate before you got here. Don't
leave anything out just because you think it's not important," she commanded.

We kept trudging, lost in the features of my meal at Carl's Jr., its color
and flavor and texture and temperature. We discussed it for so long that
I barely noticed that Hal was standing next to us.

"Can the two of you make it to the plateau?" he asked, pointing to a
bench in the land a few hundred yards above us. "The rest of the group
is already there, and Ron is pissed off."

"Ron is always pissed off," Lainey said matter-of-factly. "You know
that, Hal. We don't do it on purpose, Giorgio, although it's kind of fun
to watch him turn red. Do we?"

"I'm glad you think it's amusing, Lainey," Hal said. "I wish I could."
I didn't say a word.

When we reached the flats, I could hear a gurgle of water in the
background near the ruddy cliffs. The other kids were gathered in small

groups sprawled on the ground. Kenny was sitting with some of the boys I hadn't met yet. They seemed surprised to see me, or surprised to see me with Lainey. I thought they were talking about me and laughing at me like it made sense to them that the new kid would get stuck with her. Ron came toward us, almost running.

"You two are a threat to the group!" he shouted. "Lainey, you know better. How many times have I told you to keep up. There's no way we are going to be able to do the lake in one day. Impossible. Giorgio, stay with Kenny now. I paired you with him for a reason. Lainey, I think you should do solo tonight," Ron said.

"What's solo?" I asked her after Ron left.

"They put you off by yourself. They think it's a punishment, but I think it's a treat. They isolate you from the group but check on you from time to time to make sure you didn't run away or get eaten. You'll get to do it, but don't let them make you believe that it's bad. It isn't."

Hal helped me string my tarp between two old pines among the scrub as the sun slid behind the red cliffs and their subtle colors blended to gray. Kenny and I cooked some beans, and then I unrolled my sleeping bag under the canvas and the wind stirred up. I could hear it swooshing through the high grass before I noticed how it spun through the dangling bark, climbed the gnarled trunks, and whipped around the thinnest branches, making them move in jerky circles. The sounds of the meadows and the trees braided, and the branches sang. Their voices harmonized. At first, I thought it must be painful how the wind yanked the tree limbs from their resting places, but then I thought it must be good for them. They were stretched by movement, as I was, and maybe they ached as I did. This made me wonder if the hurt I felt wasn't really strength at a different stage, in a different form that I didn't recognize yet, the hint of hidden power.

11

FROM ONE SECOND TO THE NEXT, DR. H WENT FROM BEING a freestanding, fully grown, but miniature female to a heap on the ground sending out a high-pitched radio signal. Some of her massive red hair piled on the left side of her face as her body curled into a fetal position on the sidewalk. Pavement dust and grit ornamented her pantsuit. Benjamin couldn't have taken his eyes off her for more than a few seconds before she had collapsed on the ground.

"Are you all right?" he asked, kneeling and leaning over her. "What happened? Suddenly you were gone."

"My heel broke. Can you see where it went?" She tucked her chin into her chest to retreat further into her body. Benjamin clocked the area around them and, through the wilderness of passing shoes and pant legs, saw the missing red spike almost five feet away from where she had landed. He threaded through the traffic to retrieve it and, proudly, held the errant heel up to her before tucking it in the handkerchief pocket of his jacket as if it were a ballpoint pen.

"Can you walk? Are you hurt?" he asked. She didn't answer. He thought maybe she hadn't heard him, so he leaned closer to her ear and whispered the questions again. She moved her head slightly in a way that he was unable to decipher. He decided that what he needed to do was to lift her up and put her in a taxi. In the crowd he couldn't see whether there were any near them, and rather than leave her alone on the side-walk even for a second, he thought he should scoop her up first and then locate a vehicle. She couldn't weigh that much, he reasoned. He shoved one hand under the back of her black jacket encrusted with pavement grit and the other under the knees of her matching slacks and bent his knees so he would gain enough momentum for the lift. Instead of re-sisting him, her mass seemed to leap into his arms. She weighed so little he almost toppled over backwards. Benjamin thought he had carried heavier shopping bags home from the supermarket . With one of her arms stretched around his neck, he stuck his arm in the air, not caring what type of taxi or car stopped for them.

"Are you hurt?" he asked again while they waited. She moaned into the shoulder of his jacket, and he could feel the moist heat waves of her voice against his skin. Gingerly, he climbed into the milk van-style taxi that had stopped for them.

"Where to?" the driver asked in a heavy Baltic accent.

"One second," Benjamin told him. "Should I take you to the emer-gency room for an X-ray, or would you feel better at home?"

"Home," she said, mumbling her address.

The doorman gave Benjamin a quizzical look as he carried her through the lobby and up to her floor. She whispered the combination to the keypad adjacent to her front door, and it buzzed open. As soon as he saw the eggplant-colored velour couch, he made a beeline for it and lowered her onto it. For the first time since the incident, he noticed that there was a bemused look on her face.

"What's so funny? I thought you were hurt?"

"I am, but I was just thinking that if my secret desire was to get you to carry me across the threshold of my own apartment, which it wasn't, I couldn't have planned it better if I'd spent days and nights obsessing over it. The place is a mess. Sorry. But that's proof."

"Proof of what?"

"That my fall wasn't staged. No woman would pull a stunt like that unless she had tidied up first."

"Well, how hurt are you?"

"Maybe I twisted my ankle. Is it swollen?"

He knelt next to her and cautiously pulled up her right pant leg. She was wearing black sheer socks that made her pale skin appear murky. Until he saw how puffy her ankle was, he was transfixed by the pallor. Clusters of freckles clumped on her calf. Before passing the heel back to her, he palpated the steel slenderness of it in his pocket. It was like a dagger, he thought, or a miniature stilt, as his fingers felt how it tapered from its broader top to the tiny pad on the bottom that had been scratched by her footsteps.

"Your ankle is the size of a softball," he said. "I'll get some ice."

"Vodka would be nice with that, too. It's in the same compartment. Glasses are above the sink."

Benjamin retrieved the cubes from the freezer and placed a bag of it wrapped in a kitchen towel on her ankle and then went back for the bottle. He found shot glasses with pictures of the Eiffel Tower on the side.

"The Eiffel Tower never made me think of vodka until now."

"Well, now it always will. Eternal light. Pour us each a finger, Benjamin."

"Not sure I'm up to it, and I have to keep my wits about me," he said, pouring out two shots. "Our son just returned home. He's been gone for almost three years. We knew where he was but it felt like we had lost him. He was moved from the place we sent him to a place we'd never heard of. We talked to him on the phone a few times, and were allowed to visit once. It's a new situation to have him back."

"You didn't know where your son was? You weren't allowed to visit? How is that possible? How could a child be misplaced? Is that what parents are like these days? I wouldn't know."

"It's a long story. How does your ankle feel?"

"It feels like it was twisted, but I don't even think it's a sprain. Would you get me three Advil from the bathroom cabinet, please?"

Benjamin groped along the slick wall tiles of the bathroom for the light switch. When he found it, it illuminated a cavernous space that was packed with gadgets and products. It was like a junk shop of beauty and pills, full of hair dryers and curlers and bottle after bottle of fluids, liquids, and lotions. Dita's arsenal of cosmetic products and hair equipment was modest by comparison. When he opened the mirrored cabinet door, he saw sepia-colored prescription pill bottles lined up two deep on the glass shelves. He couldn't prevent himself from looking through them and reading the labels: contents, dates, quantities, and the ominous warnings. "Do not operate heavy machinery," several commanded. Dr. H had enough painkillers, antidepressants, and opioids to numb herself for the rest of her days. Pills as simple as Advil, belonging to a lesser class of pain, were harder to locate.

"When were you in Paris?" he asked.

"Many times," she said. "I'm fluent in French you know. *Toi?*"

"No French, but my Italian is getting a lot better since my wife was reborn as *una Italiana*," he said, adding air quote marks with his hands. "She shouts at the television in Italian. She changed our kids' names to Italian ones. She cooks only Italian dishes. She mouths Italian curses at the table and ogles pictures of Italian Romeos lounging on their Vespas. What would make a woman suddenly wake up Italian one day?"

"So you misplaced your son and your wife has been reborn as an Italian? I guess that's what passes for a stable home life. Could be worse. I read about a woman named Omm Sety who fell down the stairs, lost consciousness, and awoke as an Egyptian pharaoh. That must make you the healthy one. The one she clings to. The port in the storm. Is that how you were with Spence? Was he your training ground for chaos? When is it Benjamin's turn to be a rebel?"

Dr. H's grasp of the situation left Benjamin awed and annoyed. He had never felt it as she described it, although he suspected that Spence was training him for something, even if he was uncertain what that was. When they were growing up, Spence's volatility had enveloped them. Benjamin had been proud to be its counterpoint, a constant object. This, he suspected, may have been a proof of some lack on his part: lack of imagination or initiative or fortitude. He had hoped that his experience promised a tranquil future without confronting the fact that he needed the confusion as much as it needed him. Yet he pondered what she said. Maybe it was his turn.

"Spence was uncontrollable. And then there were times when he was shockingly thoughtful. He'd blindside us, but we knew better than to count on him. Good times came and went on a whim."

"What happened to his wife? What was her name?"

"Anna. We've never been sure," Benjamin answered, barely able to remember how Anna looked or sounded. "It's been ten years since we've seen or heard of her. She got sick of him. Or maybe she ran off with somebody else. We heard a rumor that that's what happened. Who knows? Or he threw her out. All we know is that she disappeared. There was never an explanation. As you probably know, Spence doesn't explain things. He just does them. We know better than to ask." Benjamin could feel the vodka's serpent-like head snaking through his innards. The coldness, in addition to Dr. H's rapt attention, prodded him to keep talking.

"Did you like her?"

"Yes, but she was flighty. You never knew what to expect with her or whether you'd get anything at all. We'd invite them over for dinner. They'd accept politely, then send bouquets of flowers, bottles of champagne, when they didn't show. They were a little more reliable with our kids, but not much."

"Hold it. Spence had an interest in your kids? I have never in all of the time I've known him seen him or heard him even refer to a child. Never."

"Alessandra didn't interest him much, but Giorgio was a different story. He'd play catch with him or teach him how to tie a bow tie or take him to a concert. If it had been anyone else, it might have been heart-warming. With Spence, we'd hold our breath."

"I know what you mean. For all you know, he could have been teaching him how to chop up lines of coke."

"Please, God, I hope it wasn't that. I thought Spence stopped using the idiot's powder years ago."

"Seriously? What makes you think Spence could ever give up anything that excites him? "

Benjamin almost forgot that, as they were talking, he was still holding a sack of ice cubes on the ankle of a woman he barely knew, until his hand became numb. He turned away from her to knead his frozen fingers, and while he was distracted he felt a spidery touch on his jacket. No, her hand was actually inside his jacket and climbing the back of his shirt. No, it was under his shirt and traveling laterally. He froze. The chill, inten-sified by alcohol and the ice, spread through his body. He remembered how she had caressed his hair at his first appointment and flattered him and Dutch's warning. Did Dutch mean only to be guarded about what he said to her, or did he mean something more sinister than that? Maybe this answered that question, he thought. Maybe she had left her place messy on purpose so she could use that line, or intentionally worn the stilettos with the loose heel. He felt his trust in her slipping away.

"Got to go. Will you be all right?"

"Benjamin, don't be afraid. I'm not going to hurt you. Tell me why you're here. I'll believe whatever you say."

"You fell. I brought you home. That's all."

"Are you sure? Are you sure that there wasn't any more to it than that? You could have left me in the lobby."

"I thought you were hurt and couldn't walk," he said, and stood up abruptly, as if he were trying to break out of an invisible cage. "I don't want to play games with you. Working with Spence is complicated enough."

"I could tell you liked me the first time we met. Be quiet now and listen to me carefully. Come back. Are these protests what you really feel?" she asked as he knelt beside her. She raised herself up on her elbow and whispered into his ear in her hushed but clear audiologist's tone, the aphrodisiacal pitch of the human voice. She knew all of its modulations. "We're adults. We can keep a secret if we need to, can't we?"

"Keep a secret until when? What secret?" he asked. "Until it's revealed, you mean? Or do you mean keep a secret that no one ever knows? No one. That type of secret?" His voice trailed off, but he spoke with a directness he barely recognized in himself. "I don't want to, but I want to," he murmured to himself, and slumped against her side.

"Yes, the crypt-like kind," she said, and slipping her left hand into his she felt how cold it was.

"Spence will worm it out of one of us, and that's just another hold that he'll have on me. I already owe him money I can't pay back."

"You borrowed money from him? Are you insane, or didn't you have a choice?"

"The latter," he said and he could feel his spine buckle, one vertebra caving into another and his certainty collapsing. "I have an idea. Let's wait."

"Wait for what?"

"Let's wait for tomorrow or the day after. That will give us the guidance we need, and today has no answers. *Allora!*" he said exuberantly, as if he had survived his skirmish with temptation and could walk away intact. "It is decided! Apologies for the Italian. I try not to use the few words I know, but they slip out when I'm stressed. Are you all right if I leave you now?"

"My ankle will be fine. I'm more worried about my pride, " Dr. H said, then sat up suddenly and yanked the upper half of his body over on her chest with a force he never imagined she possessed. She lifted his head and turned it to the side as if it were a puppet's. She plunged her tongue deep in his ear. Its lushness, hardness, and softness made him feel like he had lost his grip on geography and balance. He felt ravaged and plumbed.

"What? What are you doing?" he nearly shouted in a scared voice, breaking away from her.

"You already know I'm attracted to you and I dig ears. Come on, Benjamin. It's not just the mechanics I like. I like the curves and canals and those little electric pulses and how they dance all over the place. They are so small and finely sculpted and the skin on them is like pure silk," she said in a state of rapture.

Benjamin stood up indignantly. He surveyed the room to make sure that he hadn't forgotten anything, but all he noticed was her shape, the small, feminine body sculpted on the sofa, her face framed by her auburn hair, her hands now rigid at her sides. He wanted to leave her, yet he couldn't move. The tension between the twin impulses upset him so much that he walked out abruptly, and the door shutting behind him made the sound of a trap closing. His footsteps on the marble lobby tiles hammered doubt out of his body. The fresh air that greeted him at the open front doors restored him, but he retained the image of her form on the sofa, studying him, listening to his questions, reading his mood. Devouring him.

As he walked home, he realized how the routines of the streets pacified him. The exercise of walking was calmative; people rushed past him with such indifference that he began to think that the incident had never occurred. Even without hearing aids, his ears picked up intrusive noises along the sidewalks: trucks beeping as they reversed, garbage cans crashing into one another when their lids were slammed down, buses exhaling at their stops. He could even detect a flick of wind whipping along the street and tilted his head back to see that the sky was yellow in patches, a late-summer shade that could mean infernal heat or a cold front approaching from the west. He thought of himself in the streets as a warrior, a grizzled soldier, striding through the skirmishes of the city, nicked by glancing blows, coughing at the smell of gunpowder as he did at the fumes of garbage trucks. Despite the urban dangers, he kept marching.

Benjamin opened his front door to the usual greeting of a news program playing on the kitchen television. The aroma of a spice he couldn't name, not the usual sage, filled his nostrils. Dita's chair was vacant, so he searched for her. She was seated at the dressing table in their bedroom, one made of rare, interwoven woods with a multitude of drawers and adjustable mirrors. He could see her face reflected back to him as he stood in the doorway.

"Hello," she said, as if they hadn't seen each other in days. She wasn't used to him being out of the house for so long. "How's your brother?" she asked idly. *"Dove sei stato?"* she asked, wanting to know where he had been. Benjamin put his arms around her neck and clung to her, thinking that if he could hold her devotedly, his reward would be the erasure of Dr. H and her anesthesia—her prescription bottles, vodka, shot glasses, clinging arms, and her tongue probing his ear.

"He's a jerk, but that isn't news, is it?" he asked, gesturing toward the cable channel's cacophony. Rare laughter from the talking heads on television caromed down the hall toward them. He could recognize the tone of derision that accompanied it. True humor wasn't a standard part of their trade.

"He sent some tickets to Giorgio today. They're on the table. He's invited him to a concert. I could see through the envelope. Rolling Stones. Giorgio isn't home yet. Maybe it will be a nice surprise."

"Maybe. He shouted at me in our meeting today, and then he took a phone call without missing a beat. I left with the others and we had a beer at the bar next door. They tried to cheer me up. They know how cruel he can be as well as we do. They're as cursed as we are." Benjamin spoke in low, solemn tones.

"Come here, *amore*," she said, and patted the seat next to her. He sat down on the bed instead.

"Where is Giorgio?" Benjamin asked.

"He said that he was going to see a friend and wouldn't be back until dinner."

"So we're alone again?" he asked, and snaked his hand around her waist up to her wide breast.

"Don't be foolish," she said. "He could walk in at any second and he'd catch us. Sit next to me at least," she said. He moved from the bed to the bench. The room was quiet, and there was an ochre streak of light across the ceiling. Suddenly, the room became dim. The feeling of the two of them being alone returned with stealth and pleasurable familiarity. The simple solitude of their recent lives was briefly restored.

During a lull in their conversation, the front door creaked open and Giorgio walked in and shut it behind him. They heard him pick up Spence's envelope from the front table, and then there was no sound at all, as if Giorgio were paralyzed where he stood. They looked at each other, waiting for the next clue to his presence. They heard what sounded like his shoes being kicked against the wall. His jacket sliding to the floor made a slithery, slumping noise, and then the corridor was quiet again. The next thing they heard was the sound of the envelope being slapped down and Giorgio scream, "Fuck him!" That was followed by the sound of paper skidding across the floor.

"Giorgio," Dita called. "You're home. Come talk to us."

"I don't want you to call me that anymore. I'm sick of it. Giorgio isn't my name. I want my name back. I didn't want to be Italian three years ago. I'm Mark!" he shouted from the door, his face dark and distressed.

"Don't be upset, *caro*. I meant it to be affectionate, just a nickname, and Giorgio is so much prettier than Mark, isn't it?"

"I don't care if it's prettier. I don't care about any of that. It's fake. My name is Mark, the name I was born with. Mark."

"Benjamin," Dita said to her husband. "You better listen to this too. We can't call him Giorgio anymore. Now he is just plain Mark, and never forget it," she added.

"He's right, Dita. He can be called by whatever name he wants," Benjamin said.

"Of course, darling. I love the name Mark too. It carries me to the day you were born. I held you in my arms in the hospital, you were so small and velvet, and we asked ourselves how many ways are there to mark this extraordinary day, and that's how the name came to me. It felt *divino*," she added.

"Well, don't forget to use it!" Mark said emphatically. He turned away from his parents and tramped down the hall, his stocking feet making dull reverberations along the wood floorboards. He had waited three years to say that to his mother, and finally mustered the courage, carrying out the oath he had made to himself during the haunted, freezing nights he had slept outside. How many times had he screamed out loud, "My name isn't fucking Giorgio!" where no one could hear him, and finally he'd been able to say it to the one person it was intended for.

Dita retreated to the bedroom floor, curled up on the thin blue rug, and began sobbing. "Giorgio, Giorgio," she muttered. "Maybe we shouldn't have sent him away, maybe they should have let us see him, speak to him more..." She stretched her legs out and rocked forward and back on her side, heaving as she cried. Benjamin wanted to comfort her, but even with all the power of his will, he couldn't make the words come out of him. The memory of that day and her role in it stopped him. The dark images of Vesuvius behind glass on the wall next to her dressing table, one of a calm Neapolitan town in the lee of the mountains and the next with dark puffs of smoke sailing above the peak, glinted in the strange light.

"You shouldn't have provoked him. I should have stopped you," he said. She gave him a fierce look and hugged herself more tightly.

"Was it all my fault? He attacked me, and that ruined our lives. He had to go, but now I want him to come back for good. Tell him to come to me the way he used to be, Benjamin. Make him come back," she said when she caught her breath between sobs and gulps.

"I can't do that. You know I can't," he said slowly and deliberately, and they sat silently in the shambles of the afternoon. A few minutes later they heard the front door close.

12

THAT NIGHT I WOKE UP SCREAMING. A CRAZED ANIMAL had snuck into my sleeping bag and was running wild. I couldn't tell what it was. It was prickly or furry or both. It stuck a paw or a tail or I was scared to think what else between my legs and around my arms. It brushed its foul coat against the bare skin of my back. I tried to catch it with my hands or trap it between my knees, but it rushed out leaving the sack twisted around my hips. Whatever it was, it stank, and was a lot quicker than I was. I tried to reach my arms out of the bag to unzip it, but somehow the bag was twisted around the top and I couldn't maneuver my hands out. I was frantic. I screamed as long a scream as I could, pushing the air out of the deepest part of my chest. Kenny didn't stir. It was as if he had been run over by a garbage truck. The animal that stopped a few feet from me, I could see its neon eyes. My mind contorted trying to think what I should do.

A few seconds later I saw a flashlight beam jumping through the leaves on the trees. It swerved from side to side as it came closer toward me. I could hear someone's feet pounding on the ground. The stride was rapid and steady and didn't stop until whoever it was reached me.

"Get me outta here!" I yelled, begging, when he came into focus. It was Hal. Thank God. I had never felt more grateful in my life.

"What is it?" Hal asked, and knelt down to me.

"Get me out of this bag. There was something in here. Fast!" I shouted, still not sure whether it had been real or not. Hal released the drawstring and unzipped the bag. I jumped up and started slapping my hands against my legs and running my fingers over my skin to check for blood and bites. I couldn't see or feel anything wrong. That was weird.

Hal lifted the unzipped bag up into the air and beat the insides with the flat of his hand. There was nothing there, just a few crumbs from the cracker that I was munching on before I fell asleep. He waved my sleeping bag in the air and shook it in the wind like it was a pair of damp pants. He set it down and then shined the flashlight beam on the dirt around where I had been sleeping.

"If there are some paw prints, maybe I can figure out what it was, but I don't see any," he said, pointing the light around my feet.

"You don't?" I asked him. "That's impossible. I'm sure it was there. I could feel it." I almost shouted to prove that I was right. Hal pointed the beam at my hands and feet. There were no marks. That was when I started to worry that he must have thought that I was crazy. Or delusional. Or both.

"It could have been a dream, Giorgio. It wouldn't be the first time that a new kid had one like that on his first night or two out here. You're not used to sleeping outside. And this life isn't used to you," he said in as kind a way as possible. He handed me his water bottle and urged me to have a sip. "Go back to sleep now. Nothing happened. This is between us. I won't tell anyone, even Ron. He's as hard a sleeper as Kenny is." Hal placed my open bag on the ground and shined the light so I could see that there was nothing in it. He zipped me up, and I felt like I was being tucked in in a way that I hadn't been since my mother folded me under the covers when I was a little boy. "You'll sleep well now," he said. My eyes followed his light as he walked away from me across the plateau.

The moon glared at me through the bare branches of the cottonwood trees with a flickering, skeptical eye and twigs for eyebrows. It was so bright that I blinked and closed my eyes. My breath lengthened and my chest became quiet. If the animal wasn't real, then what was it? I asked myself calmly. Maybe it was my distance from home that my brain manufactured into a villain. I shivered again, remembering my terror, how I had been attacked by the invisible. Then I fell asleep gently and soundly, as if none of it had happened.

The next thing I knew Hal was standing over me again nudging my feet through the sleeping bag with the hard toe of his hiking boot. Even this he did with care. It wasn't just Lainey that he treated with patience and respect in spite of her obvious hiking flaws. He treated everyone that way. I didn't really know what to think of someone who was so consistently kind. It felt unusual and valuable. Yet almost fake.

As I approached the ragged but noisy group around the breakfast campfire, I didn't want to see anyone or anyone to see me. I thought they could somehow tell how scared I had been. Except for Lainey, the rest of them were talkative, even boisterous. She stood in the back, her eyes with their long lashes nearly closed. Her fine nose was pointed downward, and the sun cast the shadow of it on her pale, freckled cheek. I wasn't sure whether she was tired from the effort of the previous day or hadn't slept during her solo or both. As Ron reviewed the daily schedules, I slinked over to where she was standing. She looked up and smiled so tightly that it was almost a grimace.

In his speech, Ron kept referring to the blue water jugs that were placed along the trail that would lead us to our destination for the day. He told us that we should ration our water to get to the next "bluey," as he called it, without dying of thirst. The morning's coolness fooled me again into thinking that I wouldn't overheat. My hood was pulled over my head, and I wore my bandana tied at the base of my throat. As soon as we started marching, Lainey slowed down and ended up in the rear of the column. I drifted back to be with her.

"Let's talk about food," she said, and gave me her pixie, sideways smile. "What would you like for breakfast today if you could have anything?"

"It's my least favorite meal. I usually skip it."

"Skip it? You can't skip a meal now. I used to skip them all the time. If I survive, I will never do that again for the rest of my life," she said emphatically, stopping to stare at me to make sure I knew how seriously she meant it. The others slipped further and further away from us.

It must have been the thought of food that helped Lainey propel herself forward again. She walked with a sudden energy I hadn't seen in her before. She leaned forward into the incline and swung her arms with conviction. For a few steps, I struggled to keep up with her until I realized how badly I wanted to be next to her and pushed myself to catch up.

The heat intensified as the sun rose higher. Lainey kept walking but peeled off her Pomona sweatshirt and tied it around her waist. When I told her that she should stuff it in her backpack, she shook her head and said that she didn't want to stop walking. "If I stop," she said, "I may never rev up again." She sighed. I nodded. I knew exactly what she meant. I felt the same way.

"Me too. Let's talk some more about breakfast. Let's talk about donuts. I'd like a twisted chocolate cruller with coconut shavings on it," I suggested as if I had been obsessing about them the whole time.

"That sounds scrumptious. Would you share it with me?" she asked.

"I promise that I would share anything with you, Lainey." In case it wasn't obvious, I could already feel that she had taken up space inside me, and I trusted her there. She was in my head and my stomach too. She was everywhere that I was.

"I think I'm getting fixated on donuts because it's almost my birthday and no way I'll be getting a cake out here. Donuts are at least a possibility. But remote."

"How old will you be?" I asked.

"Eighteen," she reminded me but it was hard to tell how old people were without knowing what grade they were in. I had no idea she was only four years older than me. It felt like more.

In the distance, I could see that Hal was loping down the trail toward us. His approach made Lainey drag her feet and start shaking again. The shivers were most noticeable in her torso and shoulders, but her back spasmed too, and when she lifted her foot for her next step, it wobbled from side to side. There was definitely a connection between Hal's approach and her symptoms. She sat down on a rock by the side of the trail and patted the space next to her. Each of us took a deep swig from our water bottles; already some grit had found its way into the thermos. Hal had told her, she reported to me, that the red dust only made the water taste better, and at that moment I would believe anything that either of them said.

"You guys are doing well. Don't sit for too long. You'll overheat. The sun will make you sick," he said, gazing out over the valley below us. "You don't have that far to go. Do you think you can make it?" We nodded at the same time. Neither of us was sure of anything.

Ron appeared out of nowhere, trailed by a swirl of dust, his face distorted and indignant. "Hal, you've got to stop babying these two. We can't make the whole group sit down in the sun to wait for them. What don't they get? Don't they realize that they're holding everyone up?"

"Take it easy, Ron. Lainey was just sick. They're doing a lot better than they were, so let's give them a break."

"I'd like to but I can't. The ridge is where the trackers dropped our supplies. If we don't make it at least that far tonight, nobody eats dinner. And we won't have enough water for tomorrow. Is that clear enough for the two of you?" Ron asked, turning to us. "So if you want to be thirsty and hungry tonight, that's up to you, but you can't prevent the others from eating and drinking too. Come on. Pick it up."

As Ron spoke, Lainey's face lost the splash of color and joy that it had been wearing. She turned blank in front of me. I wanted to pull her up, lead her magically to the ridge where her imaginary meal would be arrayed on a white porcelain platter. I looked into her eyes and gave her what I hoped was a sign that I was with her whether we made it to the ridge or not. I thought that we both could reach it if she wanted to. She stood up and threw her damp sweatshirt at me. I stuffed it into my pack.

"He's right. Let's go," Lainey said. Ron started back up the trail at a jogging pace, leaving us behind.

From that moment on we kept our heads down and our legs moving. We barely spoke for the next two hours. Every so often Lainey would stop by the side of the trail for a sip of water and bend over the trail bank lined with dry bushes and thorny branches as if something invisible to me had sparked her interest. She stopped and pointed to a broad plain in the distance tucked into the mountain. It was a bluish shade a color that I hadn't seen yet in that landscape.

"What's that?" I asked.

"Sage. A whole field of it. I can almost smell it from here," she said.

"It can't be sage," I said. "Sage is silver green, not blue. My mom always had it in our kitchen."

"That's what you may think. The leaves are green but its flowers are blue and the light does funny things at this altitude. The last time we went by here I asked Hal what it was and he said sage, and I said that was impossible, exactly as you did. He explained to me how the sun distorts colors up here and everything else, and besides there is such a thing as blue sage he told me." I looked at the distant field again. It was as blue and as broad as the ocean. It was one of the most beautiful things I had ever seen, but it was even more beautiful on that day that until then had only been filled with humiliation.

When Lainey caught her breath and stood up straight, she put her hands on her hips, threw her shoulders back, inhaled in a loud, exaggerated way, and squared off against the ridgeline. I could feel her determination and her sadness. They made her beautiful to me and moving, as moving as an unexpected field of blue sage that I knew I'd never get close enough to wade in or pick.

"Hallelujah!" I heard her scream suddenly. "Look!" she shouted. I could see a tiny blue dot in the distance. I was overwhelmed with relief. We knew we were going to make it to Ron's finish line. We weren't going to be mocked as we had been the day before for falling short. I wasn't going to be jeered at for being the new boy, the only one crazy or stupid enough to keep Lainey company.

"Aren't all dreams sort of true?" I asked her. The question came from my encounter with the nocturnal, nonexistent creature. "Last night I was sure there was an animal in my sleeping bag and started screaming. Hal ran over and showed me that it wasn't true. I had dreamt it. I think it was my biggest fear."

"I heard you, but I knew you weren't in danger. Yes, I believe they are, dear Giorgio. I think they're more true than anything else once you learn the language. They are how the brain works at night when we're not directing ourselves to think what we've been told to think. It's like a thought that doesn't know what it's supposed to think or how and it gets curvy. I talk to my brother almost every night in my dreams, and when I wake up I can't believe that those conversations weren't real. The words he uses, his tone of voice, the dawn coming through the curtains in our living room where we used to stay up all night together, are perfect recreations of real scenes and conversations that we had. But then there are strange details in them that force you to think differently. In last night's dream I could see a spider climbing the curtain behind his head. I wasn't sure whether I should say anything to him about it, but it distracted me. In the dream, I froze. I was paralyzed. I tried to lift my arm to protect him, but it wouldn't move. I couldn't open my fist or make a sign to warn him. So why was that? You tell me. I want to know what your interpretation is."

"So what did you do?"

"There was nothing I could do to save him, but when I woke up I thought it might be a message from him telling me that what happened to him wasn't my fault. There was nothing I could have done that could have helped him. He knew there was danger, but there was no way he could prevent it. I thought that maybe he had already accepted what he was going to do to himself. That it wasn't a whim. It was a plan." We walked silently as we absorbed the gravity of it. I didn't want her to blame herself for what she hadn't done in a dream, but I had a feeling that I couldn't spare her from her dreams any more than she could spare me from mine.

When we reached the bluey, it was like we had reached the end of an uphill desert marathon. Both of us were elated even though we were hot and sweaty. From where we stood, we could see the area where the groups had already started their fires. We strolled in the direction of the smoke as though we were experienced trackers and a banquet awaited us. Kenny saw us and waved me over to him. Lainey wandered away, and I sat down and slithered out of the straps of my pack. My shirt stuck to my back.

"I'm glad you guys made it. We weren't sure that you would. Now you know what she's like, right?" Kenny asked.

"I was waiting for her and she was waiting for me a little too."

"We've all done that with her and got sick of it. She definitely wins the slowest camper award."

Instead of taking off my socks and staring at the blisters on my feet, I took out of my pack the diary that Dave had given me when I'd arrived. He'd called it a "pass tracker," whatever that meant, and said it was a journal that we were allowed to keep that was completely private. And just in case I didn't get it because I was new, he added that neither the shrinks nor the guides were allowed to read it. When I opened the flimsy tan cardboard cover, the fragrance of fresh paper brought back memories of school and classes and classrooms. Blethen already seemed so far away. Another continent. Another era. Almost not real, a hallucination.

I was writing about the sleeping bag incident and Lainey and the field of blue sage when Ron came over and asked if he could have a word with me privately. He took my arm and walked me away from Kenny and the others.

"I know you just got here, Giorgio, and are doing the best you can, but I think it would help you concentrate better if you were off on your own tonight. It's not a judgment. You did well today, but I think you'll like being alone a little," Ron said in a way that made me think he was trying extra hard to be caring and it didn't come naturally to him. "Hal will set you up. You're not going to be far from the fires or the rest of us, so don't worry. You'll be fine," he said with finality, patting my shoulder. "Oh, and don't forget to count off if you leave your sleeping bag. Loud. That way we know you went out and came back."

Hal led me to a grassy area a little back from the cliffs but I could still see out over the red rock ledges into the abyss below us. It was hollow and quiet. The light was dim, but I could still write a few more sentences in my notebook when I wasn't watching Hal work. Every step he took in evaluating the strength of the trees and stringing up the tarp was slow and thought through. If I had met him in the city, I might have thought he was a little slow, but in the wilderness his experience had taught him lessons I hadn't begun to consider, let alone learn. Already, I had seen enough of him to know that he was intelligent and maybe wise too.

"Don't worry about last night, Giorgio. It won't happen again. The wind is picking up and some clouds rolled in. We may get a few flurries tonight," he said, and started walking away. Then he turned back as if he had remembered something important. "Use your eyes and your ears and nose. There is a lot to learn out here," he added before he left.

Hal was right. As soon as most of the light was gone everything turned into its own map: the stars, the scents, how the trees swayed in the breeze depending on how strong it was and the direction it came from.

Every movement and sound and smell had its part in the whole order if you paid enough attention to figure out what it was. I drifted off to sleep and then woke up again. The stars were covered in clouds, and I could smell a trace of dampness in the air. I fell back to sleep.

"Giorgio, Giorgio." Someone was whispering my name. It wasn't a dream this time. I lifted my head and looked around. There was no one, but I could see that a few snowflakes had stuck on the rocks next to me. Then I saw a figure with dangling hair sneaking next to me in a crouch, as if ducking from gunfire. I knew it was Lainey. She bent her head to get under the tarp and kneeled next to my head.

"Can I get in with you? It's cold out here. Are you awake?"

"I keep waking up. My heartbeat is so loud, I can't stay asleep."

"It's the altitude," she said. "That happens to everybody when they get here." She unzipped the bag and stuck her feet inside and then stretched her body next to mine. There was barely room for both of us.

"How did you know where I was?" I asked.

"I've been here long enough to know where they put us if we're not in the camp. Is it okay that I'm here?" she asked. I wasn't sure what to say.

"What if someone finds us?"

"They won't if we don't make a lot of noise. It's only if you scream like last night that they'll come."

"I was in a complete panic."

"Yes, I could tell. I saw Hal running toward you. Or his flashlight. You poor boy," she said, and kissed my cheek. I liked how soft her lips felt.

"Am I your first girlfriend?" she asked, and pressed the palm of her hand against my chest as if she could soften my heart or help it find its natural rhythm.

"Yes."

"I really like you, Giorgio. You are my only friend. The rest of them hate me."

"They don't hate you. They just think you hike slow. I don't care if you do."

"Kiss me back, Giorgo." I turned my head toward her and pulled closer. It felt dangerous. In her hair I could smell the smoke of the fires she had sat next to and the dirt from the trail that had blown into her face. I wanted to kiss her. I meant to kiss her. She turned on her side toward me and she put her free hand around my waist to bring me nearer to her. I put my fingers on her forearm. Immediately, I could tell there was something wrong with her skin. It was dry and raw. She had a rash there. It felt scratchy and rough. And then Uncle Spence's face popped into my mind with his bright-red cheeks and his too bright teeth that looked phony and evil. He had broken skin like that on the back of his hands, his wrists, and the backs of his legs. Then I could picture Uncle Spence's hands encircling my body like hers were doing. I could feel them fishing around in my pockets where they didn't belong, where nobody's hands but mine should have been. My whole body went stiff.

"I feel sick, Lainey."

"What's wrong? What did I do, Giorgio?" she asked.

"You didn't do anything," I said. "It's something else. My brain feels stuck." The crazy animal was loose again in my sleeping bag, rubbing against my legs, and I could sense the looks on the faces of Walt and his friends when they opened the stall door and stared at me. Rage surged through me. I did everything I could to restrain myself, to not be angry at her. It was an accident. A coincidence. I balled my hands into fists and jammed them into my pocket so they wouldn't fly out. So they wouldn't attack her.

"What's wrong?" she asked. "Tell me."

"I can't. Not now," I said, using all my strength to control myself.

"Someone made a demon out of you, didn't they?" she asked. She put her hand in my hair and pulled my head to her chest bone. It rested there until she lifted it off and drew her legs out of the bag. It was too dark to see her face clearly, but I was sure I saw humiliation and shame on it. I watched her scurry away as if she didn't have any weight, a ghost flying between the snowflakes.

13

BENJAMIN LIKED SITTING UP ALONE IN THE QUIET OF THE living room with the television set off, the absence of chattering experts a blessed relief, an open space. In late September the air conditioner still hummed in the corner, the forced air a stale patch more than a few feet beyond the vents. Light from the surrounding buildings cast geometric shapes and figures on the walls—rhomboids, abstract heads, and tangent curving lines. The lamp glowed next to him, and he attempted to focus on the words of the book he was holding on his lap, but his mind kept drifting. It sailed through a montage of images: Mark opening the door that first night as they were eating dinner and dumping his backpack on the floor, the thumping he'd felt in his chest at his son's return, an end to his paternal fears, Mark's new assurance. Carrying Dr. H into her apartment and her kiss inside his ear which jolted and thrilled him. Spence's tirade of insults burst in and left jagged tracks on his other imaginings. The scenes scrambled together were no match for even the most muscular prose.

Less than an hour later the front door groaned open. Mark kicked off his shoes, which slammed into the baseboard and dumped his jacket onto the floor. The front hall table scraped on the wood planks. An expletive hung briefly and sharply in the air, and then the light switched on in the kitchen. The refrigerator door sucked open and Benjamin heard the clank of bottles before it closed with a sealing sound. A bottle cap rattled on the counter.

"Mark, I'm in here," he said. "I didn't want to spook you. Come sit with me for a few minutes."

"Okay." Mark answered from the kitchen, his voice sounding despondent. "I'm coming." A few minutes later Mark shuffled in his socks across the living room and sat down on the light-blue sofa in the corner not too far from his father. The reading lamp left half of his face in shadow.

"You know what I was thinking about?" Benjamin asked.

"No, no idea." Mark exhaled impatiently. Across the space that separated them Benjamin could smell beer on his son's breath.

"Do you remember when you were a little boy and you'd look up at the sky when you heard a plane flying over us and you'd point to it and you'd ask us where it was going? You were sure we knew. You were sure we knew everything. The first few times you asked us, we tried to read the writing on the side of the plane so we could give you the correct answer, but then you did it so often, we started to make up goofy stuff just to amuse ourselves. Terrible parents. Mea culpa. We'd say Mozambique or Vladivostok, waving at the clouds, when probably the plane wasn't going any farther than Cleveland or Boston. We thought it was kind of funny and you couldn't tell the difference, so what was the harm? Do you remember that at all?"

"Not the exact places, but I do remember believing whatever you said about the planes and asking you to show me those places on the globe."

"Kids wonder about unknowable things when they're two or three. They're trying to organize the world. Put objects in their places, in an order they can understand. Adults don't think they have to do that once they reach a certain age. That doesn't mean they're right or know the correct answer. It just means they've given up and have gotten comfortable not knowing, so the question becomes not where is that plane going but who cares where it's going, I'm not on it and neither is anybody I know. What about you? Have you reached the crossover age yet?"

"No, not really, Dad. I wish I had. That would be progress. But now that you remind me of them, I still wonder where those planes are flying and then I start to imagine what those places are like," Mark said.

"You do? Really? I'm impressed, I guess. Oh, before I forget, Spence sent an envelope for you on the table. Did you see it?"

"Yeah I saw it. I wasn't expecting that. He didn't say he was sending anything."

"Oh, when did you speak to him?"

"A few days ago. He called me."

"Mom said she thought it was concert tickets. Sometimes he's not as bad as I think he is. I started doing some work with him, in case you didn't hear."

"Claire told me. I don't understand why you would do that."

"What do you want to do now?"

"I think I'd like to be a pilot, learn how to fly one of those planes. Maybe learn how to be a navigator."

"Is that true, or are you making fun of me?"

"Both." Mark's voice wavered between surliness and candor without stopping on the notes in between. Benjamin didn't know which mood to expect from one word to the next.

"What kind of plane would you like to fly?"

"I'd like one of those planes that could store megaton bombs in its bays. A bombardier like the ones in World War 2 that set Dresden on fire or the B-29 Superfortress or one of the Vietnam ones. I think it's the Stratofortress that carried so much ordnance that they had to dump it in Laos or they wouldn't have enough fuel to get back to the aircraft carriers. I wouldn't want to be the one to drop them, but I'd just like to have them in the hold so that if I ever needed one, I had it and knew what to do with it."

"Would that make you feel safe, Mark?"

"I'd have my weapons and I would always be protected," Mark said. "Believe it or not, I'm not the violent type. I'm a pacifist."

"What do you mean, protected? We protected you," Benjamin said.

"You protected me? Right." Mark scoffed. "From who? You couldn't even save me from my mother, let alone Spence."

"What do you mean with Spence?" Benjamin asked.

"I didn't tell you about him, did I?"

"Tell me what?"

"Your brother put his hands where they shouldn't go," Mark said with an edge that broke through his sarcastic tone. "I figured it out in the Fremont. That's what I mean!"

"What?" Benjamin asked, not because he couldn't hear what Mark had said but because he was sure he didn't want to. It was incredulity, not deafness, a sudden violent ringing in his ears like a broken smoke alarm. Benjamin opened his mouth to ask the next question, but Mark anticipated it and cut him off.

"Yes, I'm sure. It took me a while to piece together. Yes, I wouldn't have told you if I wasn't," Mark said with confidence and finality.

"Oh, Mark!" Benjamin groaned. "When? How?"

"I was around ten when it happened. You were in the other room with Mom and some of our guests. The rash on his skin was the first clue I had. It took me so long to remember all the details. You of all people should have known how crazy your brother was, Dad."

"Of course I knew, but how could I have known this part of it?" Benjamin said, his tone pleading.

"You should have known," he repeated, and began to hyperventilate. The panic spread across his face. His breathing was short, filled with high-pitched, terrified exhalations.

"Oh, Mark," Benjamin said in a wailing voice, leaning forward toward his son. "How could he do that? How could he?"

"He... has eczema.... all over his hands and legs... It is one of his distinguishing... features. Didn't you ever notice it?" Mark stammered. He was almost shouting, indignant at his father's incomprehension.

"Is it possible that you just noticed that from his playing on the floor with you and it stuck in your head because it's ugly? Of course I knew he had rashes. He always had them. Nothing helped get rid of them, or he wouldn't use what the doctor gave him."

"I saw it on his hands, Dad. I saw it on his hands for as long as I can remember him, and then his hands touched me. He put his hands in my pocket. I thought I'd catch his disease or whatever it was. I was too disgusted to move."

"You should have told me."

"I was a kid. That was years ago. How could I tell you? I thought it might have been my fault in some way. I was scared you'd defend him, that you might say I made it up, so I tried to forget about it to make it go away, but I kept feeling that people were sneaking up on me from behind. I'd never attacked anybody before. Ask Mom if you don't remember. Up to the time Walt and his friends walked in on me, I had never reacted like that and never thought about my hands, where they were or what they were doing. But after that I didn't see why I had to control them. I lost my grip with Walt. My hands hurt all the time, like I had arthritis. And then I wasn't sure whether I could ever control them again. Or could any idiot provoke me whenever he felt like it. Those kids laughed and pointed at my body like they knew something was wrong with it, that it was weird or damaged or stank." Benjamin listened with his head in his hands trying to piece together what Mark was saying. The words left him speechless and then murderous and frozen.

"Please tell me this isn't true, Mark, or you're not certain. I'm glad you trusted me. Have you told anyone else?" Benjamin asked. He looked over at his son who seemed to be having a panic attack. His body was shaking. His eyes, stuck open, not blinking, jumped around the room unable to settle.

"I don't trust you," Mark said. Benjamin kept his mouth shut. "I told a girl in the Fremont. She's the only one."

"Who was that?" his father asked. Mark didn't reply.

Benjamin felt something dead in his stomach, as though he was carrying a stillborn baby that was pressing down on his intestines. The malignant weight sank and spread out through his belly. He wondered who had died, what had disappeared. His son? His brother? Or was it the web of the family, its pride and past, its slight profile in the world? All of that yet nothing quite like it.

Benjamin didn't speak. He noticed that the moon, a magnesium white strip, split the floor between them. As he stared at it, Benjamin thought of it as a line of corrosive lime that had been laid down between them, the injured son separated from the father who hadn't shielded him. Mark saw the moon as an agent of his realization, one that had revealed its knowledge to him in the Fremont, night after night in that strong, pure air, one that had left him sick when he realized his vulnerability and nakedness, struggling to discover how he could become human again.

"Where's the envelope?"

Benjamin handed it to him. Mark tore it open, read the note inside scrawled in Spence's bold lopsided hand, glanced at the ticket and dropped the package to the floor, where it tipped into the moon's path. As Benjamin reached down to pick it up, Mark kicked it across the floor and the contents flew to separate parts of the room.

"I can imagine how angry you must be."

"You can? How could you? Your brother stuck his hands in my pants with his flaky fucking fingers. How could you know how that felt? How could you know that I thought it was my fault? How could you know how disgusting it was? If I was going to hurt anyone, it should have been him!" Mark yelled.

"I'm sorry," Benjamin said. "I'm sorry. I thought he was teaching you stuff I couldn't."

"He was, you moron!" Mark said with a cackle. "He was. Now do you get it?" Mark exhaled loudly and the muscles in his upper body relaxed.

The agony of that question hung in the air above Benjamin's head. The longer it was suspended there, the sharper it became. He knew that the ramifications of what Mark said ran everywhere. It sucked everything into its distorted field. In addition to the damage it caused his son, it was a billboard that shouted out Benjamin's inattention, his aloofness: the father who had been too distracted to notice his son's vulnerability. Whether he had ever suspected it or observed some part of it or missed clues was irrelevant. He knew that he should have known. He had been there. It was his son. His brother.

Benjamin gave himself no excuses. There was no one else to blame. Not Dita. She hadn't played any role in this. If anything, she would have preferred never having to invite Spence to their apartment. She knew who Spence was, or enough of it. Benjamin's instinct told him that she mustn't learn about this yet, and he sensed that Mark didn't want her to know either, or he would have told them at the same time. The magnitude and misery of it needed to sit between them for a little, or at least until the most lethal layer of it had boiled off and he could see clearly what he needed to do next.

Many times Mark had envisioned sitting with his father late at night, just the two of them, and telling him what he had figured out or at least part of it. But he hadn't been able to imagine the equanimity he would need for that conversation. Now he knew why. The pain went beyond equanimity.

Nor was he ready for his mother to know. The risk of her tipping him into even greater chaos was too real to discount. And if he lost his footing with her, he would revert to being the out-of-control child in a tantrum, who said so many vicious things that it was impossible to tell if any of them was true. And that would jeopardize the whole of it, and its burden would remain stuck in him. That was too frightening to consider in his new but shaky stability.

"What's wrong?" Dita asked from the doorway. A light sleeper, she had been awake since Mark opened the front door.

"Spence got him a ticket to the Stones, and he's not sure he wants to see Spence right now," Benjamin said quickly. Mark stared out the window at the moon, not turning toward her as she entered the room.

"I always hated the Stones too, Mark," his father interposed in a light if barely believable voice. "No, that's not quite right. I hated the people who liked them. I can make up some excuse for you if you don't want to go," Benjamin added more earnestly. "If you think it would be hard for you to tell him yourself, I can tell him when I see him tomorrow. Why is it called the 50 and Counting tour? It's amazing that those old men can still stand, let alone dance, if that's what you would call it. How many more times can they tour the world, rush through the same riffs, and charge thousands of dollars for tickets? They're not so old that they've forgotten how to make their fans pay, I guess," Benjamin added nervously to avoid an uncomfortable silence.

"It's nice of your uncle to invite you," Dita said. "That's all I can say for him. You have to call and thank him."

"How gracious, Mother. Of course. I will do that first thing tomorrow," Mark said in his most mocking tone of voice.

"We don't have any illusions where Spence is concerned, Mark, so we should accept his generous impulses whenever they occur," Dita said.

In her presence, Benjamin and Mark conspired to keep his story safe from her, at least for the moment. Mark had rehearsed telling her too, but later. He had wanted to start with his father. Practice would steady his nerves and prepare him for her. He anticipated her operatic response—the Italian, the curses, her falling on the floor grabbing his legs and begging forgiveness for her flaws. He wasn't ready for that yet, or the compassion that would come after it, so he said good night to her and gave her a hug before he went back to his boyhood bedroom.

As he walked down the hallway, Mark felt a discomfort he couldn't ascribe to his father, who had responded as Mark thought he would. Hearing the details out loud made it different from how he heard it in his head. Gritty details, subterfuge, and advantages taken were more clinical, more accusing than in their previous incarnation. Reaching a truce with them in the outside world, even if that world was only the apartment he had grown up in, was going to be as treacherous as it had been to grapple with them in the first place. Entering his room, he was consoled by the thought of sleeping in his old single bed, among his boyish knickknacks and trophies, even if the pride of winning them had long drained out of them. His ancient things, his younger self invigorated him. He took off his clothes and put on the T-shirt that he liked to sleep in.

Mark had designated a special cubby in his closet for his pass tracker and Lainey's sweatshirt, and they served as his talismans. They hadn't eliminated danger, but they spotlit it, and that drained away some of its shock and malice. He had come to recognize how malevolence presented itself in the world, how it appeared first with the pretense of solicitude and kindness that wasn't explainable on its face. Evil flattered him, using its clever, sweet voice, and as soon as he recognized those notes he knew he must be sober and vigilant to prepare for what could follow. The hard-won knowledge armed him with instincts he hadn't been born with nor been taught.

14

MANY WEEKS WENT BY. LAINEY AND I STILL HIKED TOGETHER and chatted, but our conversation didn't have the same closeness it had had before the night she visited me in my sleeping bag. The mood had shifted. I could tell she felt awkward about it, or rejected. Or maybe she felt punished for being so forward. I had punished myself, too. I had pushed away someone who had seen things in me that didn't scare her. I didn't mean to do that, but my intention didn't matter. The hurt was in her, and I had caused it. If it were ever to heal, it would take a long time. Avoiding her would be a double wrong, so I stayed near her. Both of us pretended that nothing serious had happened.

In the meantime, Kenny showed me how to stick food in the fire so it was edible even if entirely tasteless. Beans and beans punctuated by a night of noodles or a nugget of bacon. When you got that bacon flavor in your mouth, you almost went crazy. You wanted more. You wanted as much as you could possibly get. I had a theory that the smell of it, not to mention the taste, could seep into a person's dreams, wake them up and lead them to the kitchen no matter their state of alertness. It had that much power, especially when you were in a wilderness camp separated from your home and your family.

After one of our longer hikes, Kenny and I were sitting around trying to get up the energy to start cooking. I couldn't concentrate on anything, and I watched the horizon line like it was the best show I had ever seen on television. Broken pieces of shale were scattered across the red, pebbly ground between giant boulders that had rumbled down from the high rock ridge behind us. Rows of chunky, cubist faces, enormous and mute, stared down from the rims that towered above us. Facing forward, I looked over the edge into the canyon below. The enormous valley filled me with awe. Behind me I heard a whiny, whirring noise. Kenny was trying to start a fire.

"Watch what I'm doing. Hal said that I had to teach you this so you'd know in case of an emergency. Tomorrow night it's your turn." He was sawing a wooden bow back and forth with the attached string wrapped around a spindle jammed into the notch of another piece of wood. A thin curl of smoke wafted up from the friction into the twilight sky, and in the notch I could see the tiniest orange shimmer of lit coal. He stuck the tip of his knife into it and dug out the little spark that he deposited into a nest of juniper bark that he had rubbed furiously between his hands to dry. Within seconds, it had caught fire and he tucked it inside the teepee of twigs he'd built. The flame that leapt out of the top felt like a miracle.

"Not sure I could do that," I said, shaking my head.

"Are you thinking about Lainey? Do I have to quote more Keats at you?" he asked and glanced at me with the trace of a smile.

"I don't know. Do you?"

"He wasn't much older than we were when he wrote this. I think it was in a letter he sent to his brother, my dad said. 'What if a man could exist in uncertainties, mysteries, doubts, without an irritable reaching for fact and reason.' Or something like that. The 'irritable' part is important. Without it we're calm. Without anxiety. We can dwell peacefully in doubt. My dad said it was called negative capability, but that doesn't make any sense. Your doubts reminded me of it."

"You mean about the fire or how neurotic Lainey is?"

"Well, yes, either one. Like wouldn't it be better if we weren't as neurotic and twitchy as she is. Or maybe we are. We have to blame ourselves for some of that rather than just our cell phones. Although they're not innocent. Every time my dad quoted that to me it pissed me off, but when I think about it now, out here, it doesn't feel so annoying. It feels like a real thing, a pure state."

Kenny and I gazed silently into our dented pot. Watching the water boil that would cook our noodles was the most exciting thing I could think of. At first the bubbles were reluctant and small around the edges, but when the water heated up they expanded and moved to the center. The wind blew in little bits of debris, but Kenny didn't move to spoon them out, and I didn't either. Seasoning, Kenny also quoted Ron, referring to the specks that had fallen into the pot. Kenny dumped the hard clump of noodles in, and in my hunger I boiled my fingers checking to see if they were soft enough to eat.

Kenny twirled the ramen around his spork, transfixed by the fire. We didn't have much more to say to each other, and watching the flames was hypnotic. I was exhausted from the hike and too little sleep. Almost as soon as I put down my plate, I crawled into my sleeping bag and fell into a motionless state. I don't know how long I'd been out when I heard the shouting. I burrowed deeper inside my sleeping bag even though the shouting got louder and more and more desperate. When I realized that I couldn't block it, I stuck my head out to see what was going on.

The stars were bursting above my head, and there was no trace of smoke from our campfire. Judging by the moon's position near the horizon, it must have been between five and six in the morning, or ten hours after we had eaten. Kenny's sleeping bag was empty, and he was hard to wake up, so I knew it must be important. Trackers and kids were running back and forth to the main tent in a frenzy, flashlights leaping around the scrub and the goblin-like undersides of the trees. The activity was concentrated on an area a hundred yards from our campfire. I walked toward it with a sense of foreboding. Had someone been attacked by an animal? Was there a runner?

The air was freezing. There was frost on the desert grass that made a crunchy sound like Rice Krispies when I walked on it. What was left of the tree leaves were wrinkled and dangled lifelessly on their branches. I could see my breath. When I got closer, I saw Hal kneeling next to a figure stretched out on the ground and not moving, surrounded by onlookers. With a partial view I could make out the pleats of Lainey's gray skirt. Why was she lying there?

I pushed my way to the center of the circle. Lainey was dressed as I had last seen her—her black hiking pants beneath her skirt, the light-gray fleece she'd worn under the Pomona sweatshirt that was balled up in my backpack, and her boots splayed out. She was radiant but rigid, like a queen carved out of streaked, white marble. Her half-open eyes were ice white, and her skin had an eerie tint to it, as though she had used a make-up brush to apply a thin layer of blue powder. Ice crystals had formed in a glimmering trail that traveled from her hairline across her left cheek, swirled around her lips, and ended in a glistening pool on her chin. Above the serene face, her hair was bunched up like a matted woolen cap. The ice that poked through the heavy weave of her hair sparkled like the tips of diamonds. Her fingers, hands, legs, and left arm were straight; her right arm was bent at the elbow, fingers spread unevenly, palm out, as if to stop the cold from taking possession of her. That gesture was the same one she had used with me often. Or maybe her forearm frozen in that position was saying to her life, Halt, I've battled you for long enough and I lay down here to surrender to a loss I can't accept, to acknowledge a force greater than myself. And this is the only possible expression of my will.

Hal put his cheek to her chest to listen for a heartbeat and held his thumb on her thin marked wrist. It was unclear whether he could hear anything or feel a pulse. He lowered and raised his ear several times and looked around without catching anyone's eyes. He pressed his hands against her left breast in a rhythmic way to stimulate her heart. He gave her mouth-to-mouth.

"Get blankets!" he shouted at Ron. "We need to move her to the tent right away. She may still be alive."

When someone came back with a blanket, they lifted her onto it with caution, as if they were moving the glass statue of a saint. She looked so fragile that it seemed she might shatter into pieces if handled carelessly. When they raised her body, there was no sag to it. Her right forearm stayed lifted in the air. They carried her away as though she was already dead. I didn't know whether she was alive or unconscious, but it felt like she had moved to another dimension, outside time. She was tranquil, free of any reaching, irritable or otherwise, released from her haunted dreams. Maybe at peace. I was devastated. My brain foamed. I could still feel her next to me in my sleeping bag, my forehead against her body, her hand on my heart.

When she was gone and the kerosene lamps had been carried away, the rest of us stood around the ground she had left in the same oval formation of mourning. We were a group without a center. The sky was showing a faint blue light she could not see. At that moment I couldn't imagine how I would get through the rest of the Fremont without her. Or even the day ahead of me.

In the mist before dawn that swirled around us it was hard to see each other completely, but we knew we weren't alone. No one said a word. Even Kenny, who could nervously break a lull in any conversation, was silent. Little by little, we drifted away from the spot where Lainey had been and went back to our sleeping bags. I shuffled my feet and huffed into my hands. The skin on my face tightened in the cold like a mask that was incapable of expression. When I stretched back into my sleeping bag and my shivering had calmed down, I reached into my backpack, which was just behind my head and pulled out Lainey's sweatshirt and put it over my jacket. It was the closest I could get to her.

We tried to get some more sleep but couldn't. We gravitated back to the spot where Lainey had lain down as though we were being sucked into a vortex of ice and memory. Frost glistened in the blades of Indian ricegrass bushes around the silhouette of her absent body. The clearing in the pine trees felt holy. I was left with so many unanswerable questions about what had brought Lainey there, silent and alone, while I slept. We had been together the day before, and I had been with her more than anyone in spite of our mutual discomfort. What had changed in her, and when? Where had she been taken? Was she still alive, or was she gone? The morning bell didn't end my thoughts of her.

There was the usual all-group morning meeting. I thought that one of our leaders might fill us in about Lainey, but explanations of any type were not in Hal's range. For him to provide updates to the group that might contain intimate information was also beyond his sense of discretion, one of the critical features of his character. Ron was even more tight-lipped but for different reasons. The less said, the better was his position on every subject. The minimum was always preferable: less food, less water, less to carry, less baggage. He didn't have Hal's compassion, despite the austerities they shared. I thought Ron's instincts were especially misguided in the Lainey situation, and not only for me. He should have told everyone what he knew, even if it was incomplete. Since nothing was said at the meeting beyond the day's goals, our minds formulated new scenarios. Lainey had revived and fled. Lainey was dead. Lainey was in a coma in a hospital and had been flown to another part of the state.

When I returned to pack the rest of my things, my stomach launched on its umpteenth turn. I realized that I had to speak to Hal. If there was no one to hear us, I could ask him quietly about Lainey and he wouldn't stonewall me. I looked over at Kenny. He was already dressed and stuffing his sleeping bag into his backpack with so much energy that I knew he was as disturbed as I was, as we all were.

The last thing I wanted to do was to walk another step. Walk where? For what reason? It wasn't like we had a destination, and hiking with

Kenny was such a different sport than hiking with Lainey. He didn't like to hang back and talk. He was a dynamic walker with long, purposeful strides that quickened the farther he went, and the weeks he had spent in the Fremont ahead of me had only made him stronger. He bent forward at the waist as we ascended the trail, his feet skimming the ground. He barely lifted them. The only time he stopped was to yank his bandana off his head to wipe his face. The first time he did that he yelled at me to wait for him. It crossed my mind that for Kenny walking was the whole point and it didn't matter where you were going or why.

"Look what I found," he said, turning his back to the sun and opening his backpack as if it contained contraband candy and chewing gum. "I don't want to pull it out because I stole it. Poke your head inside. See it?" In the dim, reeking interior of his pack, I could see a creased map with topographic lines on it.

"Where did you get that?"

"Last night in all the confusion I grabbed it out of Hal's tent. So this is my idea. Everyone is going to be exhausted tonight no matter what, so let's make a run for it. We can get to Bicknell before anyone knows we're gone."

"That's a long way, isn't it? Then what? What's the point of that?"

"To get out of here, and I thought you might like to come so we can get to Lainey at the clinic. That's probably where they took her. Maybe you can sneak in to see her."

"They won't let us in even if we don't get caught before we get there. Dave or one of the ghosts will snatch us before that. And then who knows what will happen to us."

"God, you're a slug. Don't you think we should even try? How could you not care enough to do that? Where's your nerve? We all thought you two were in love. Aren't you? Weren't you?"

"They'll catch us and they'll tell our parents and that means we'll have to live in tents a lot longer or some other worse punishment. Is it really worth it?" I asked. The last thing I wanted to talk to Kenny about was my feelings for Lainey or love in general. Especially not then.

"Yes, it's really worth it. Freedom is worth it."

"We don't have money or phones or anything."

"I do," Kenny said. "I kept some bills in my socks that they never found. We can get pretty far on them, and I can get more once we're moving. We can look at the map later and find out how to go."

The whole group hiked all day. Once it warmed up, the trail was as hot and dusty as it had been on the previous days. As we moved, I imagined Lainey frozen in the same holy position in which I had seen her only a few hours before. I wanted her to wink at me, to peer into my head as she had done that first morning as she sketched me, to wake up, to lean toward me and speak to me again. I needed her to help me and wait for me. Now she was too far ahead of me. Was that what love was? I wondered. Was it that someone you barely knew could see deep into your brain and cherish what they found there even if it was hideous? And did it mean that then that person would be mindful of your injuries and scars and help you trace them back to the beginning in a way that you couldn't do by yourself? Those questions went haywire in my head. I tried to connect them somehow, but they were too disjointed and out of control, so I kept my feet going in front of me rather than stalling to ponder what would have been obvious to anyone but me. After only six weeks I had fallen in love with Lainey. Everyone, even Kenny and all of the other filthy campers, had seen it.

It took almost six straight hours of slogging along the trail, but we made it to the summit of Thousand Lake Mountain. Over the long day, the group's energy had surged from its mournful, distracted start. We had all begun slowly as we struggled collectively with Lainey's fate. We pushed ourselves past our stray thoughts, hoping the exercise might relieve us. We pushed ourselves to reach the lake that she thought she would never reach. The notion that we were supposed to see it for her sounded like bullshit to me. Ron had uttered the slogan that morning as if the day was some kind of dedication. I knew that was camp counselor/psychologist nonsense. There was nothing we could do for her now.

There were a few lakes a hundred yards or so below the summit, but as Hal told us later, that wasn't the point of the ascent. He said it was better known for the sheer beauty of its reddish crags. In fact, he said, the people who had named it Thousand Lake Mountain had made a mistake. It was really supposed to be Boulder Mountain, but the cartographer screwed up and the wrong name stuck. I didn't give a fuck. I wanted to jump into that lake so badly, wash everything off me—the dirt, the night, Spence's lingering, leering face, the loss. I imagined all of it rinsing off me and puddling in the glacial pool before it was swept over the edge. Fat chance of that, was my immediate reaction.

The water was clean, crystal clear, and cold. It made me want to splash and take a sip although Hal had warned us not to drink the water. He said that animals pissed in the rivers upstream that drained into the ponds and that could make us sick. I didn't give a shit. My pants and shirts ballooned up to the surface. I lay on my back and looked at the sky, and Kenny's speech my first night echoed in my mind. How the sky didn't see me and couldn't care less about me and what I'd done or what had been done to me. The sky simply didn't care. The sandstone walls and slabs didn't care. The dumb boulders and burnt red cliff tops with their snakelike, colored bands and markings didn't care either. They had stood as witnesses to the lives of people far wiser and far stupider than I was and would outlive me by a trillion years. I knew too that it was hardly original to think this, as if I was the first person on earth who'd ever pondered eternity, but it helped me see that if I didn't care about what I had done, no one else would except for my parents or Lainey, not to mention Kenny.

Hal waved to me from the bank that it was time to get out. I doggy paddled up to the bank. I stood up in the breeze that hadn't yet begun to turn cold and felt as alert as I had in days, even though I had barely slept the night before. I wasn't dried out or aching. My wet clothes hung from my body and sprayed water on the ground around me.

"Can you tell me where they took her, Hal? Please. Is she still alive?"

Hal stroked his chin, pressed his fingertips into his jaw, and looked at me sympathetically. His thin hair was lifted by the breeze and settled back down. "You know I can't tell you that, Giorgio. Lainey had acute hypothermia by the time the EMTs got here. The medics didn't tell me anything, so I'd just be guessing and then you'd be passing on all sorts of misinformation. So nothing to say, Giorgio, except how sorry I feel for you. And her. This never happened to us before."

"Come on, Hal, you know how close we were. You saw us together. You waited with us. You knew what we talked about. You were the only one who did. She could see into me. I think she cared for me. You have to tell me where she is. If she's alive, I have to..." I paused. At that moment I realized how young I was or how young I sounded to him. I knew he couldn't tell me anything or I might interpret it as permission to go to her. I was afraid that I was going to burst into tears in front of him. I wanted so badly not to do that, but I could feel my throat getting tight and a pressure inside my eyes that I couldn't manage. Tears spilled over my cheeks and ran into my mouth.

"Her heartbeat was slow, very slow, but it wasn't gone," Hal said out of nowhere to no one. "I was pretty sure I heard it, but it was hard to pick up out there. There was a lot of other noise around. Yelling, kids stomping in the grass. I thought I could feel her pulse, and then it went away and then I picked it up again. I wasn't sure."

"When will you find out? Will they tell you later or tomorrow? Where did they take her?"

"You can't go, Giorgio. I don't know where they took her. They wouldn't let you in. Her parents have been notified, and you're not her family. That's all I can say, and it's already too much."

"Is there even a hospital in Bicknell, Hal?"

"No. There isn't a hospital, just a clinic, but I don't know if she's still there if she even survived the ride down. They might have transferred her to a hospital in Salt Lake."

"What would they do if she was still alive?"

"I just don't know, Giorgio," he said, pronouncing my name slowly. "Maybe warm IV fluids."

I fixated on Hal as he spoke. My breath caught in my lungs. My chest and back were suddenly cold. The wet clothes that had been blissfully cool a few minutes before hadn't dried completely, and they chilled my skin. The sun lost its warmth behind the clouds. I shivered. "What do you think her chances are?"

"I just don't know, and I shouldn't put numbers to it. It would be a meaningless guess," Hal said quietly. He stared at his hiking boots and clutched the creased, red skin on the back of his neck. His instinct was to move away from me, but I could tell that he couldn't. He was stuck too. She wasn't just another kid under his supervision. She intrigued him in a way that he couldn't let go of, either. It hadn't really occurred to my young brain before that moment that he shared some of my feelings for her. Her antlike pace and her sweetness had caught him, too.

"Would you send her a message for me?" I asked, and looked up at him. He regarded me with a mature person's pity, I thought.

"I doubt I'll see her again even if she's alive. I'm sorry, Giorgio. I really am. I wish I could take you wherever she is. If we hear something, I'll let you know or we'll make an announcement to the group. We never had this conversation, right? I'm sorry, Giorgio. I really am. Time to make dinner, isn't it?"

Hal walked away. I watched his long, loping gait. The breeze was slow, nearly still. I bent over to pick up my socks and banged my boots together to shake the dust loose from the treads. I would have to get used to her absence somehow. Maybe I would be able to, but that seemed too hard to contemplate. My next thought was that it might take me forever. I wished someone who was wiser would tell me how to get used to what I felt. How and where should I keep these feelings?

Kenny was pulling the bow and spindle from his pack when I got back to the camp. He shoved them toward me to say that it was my turn "to bust a coal". My arms were slack and tired.

"Come on!" he shouted at me in frustration. "Put some muscle into it. You're not dead yet, are you?" I looked at him but my eyes smarted. To hide my hollowness, I started sawing the bow frame back and forth more and more wildly, like the mad violinists I'd watched in the string section when my parents had taken me to the symphony at Lincoln Center, but there was still no trace of smoke.

"Am I doing something wrong?"

"No, keep going. That's all you have to do. Don't stop, keep going. It will come. I think I know what you're thinking about. Don't. It will only get in the way. 'Fled is that music,' as my father would say. That means she's gone. Let her go."

"Is that what's his name?"

"Yep."

At some point that night Kenny jostled me awake. He was already dressed and his pack was full.

"Put her sweatshirt on. Maybe that will help us find her. A homing device," he said. He stopped for a second and pulled the map from his pack. "Do you want me to show you where we're going?"

"No, I trust you."

"It's pretty far. Farther than I thought, but I think we can make it before dawn. Stay close to me. If we get separated, we could be in real trouble. And don't turn off your head lamp. Parts of the descent are steep."

We went over the first rise and followed the trail down that we had walked up that afternoon. Beyond its bank, I saw the pond where I had cried in front of Hal. There were still tears stuck inside me. In the moonlight, the water looked serene and solid, a landscape of sand and metal. Hiking at night had a mystical quality to it. The bushes and rocks that took on bizarre human characteristics during the day became dark monitors of our progress. In the night, they judged us and lost all of the sympathetic human features we'd endowed them with.

After an hour on the trail it forked. Kenny took the left leg, which wound around the hillside. We could see a small bunch of lights in the distant valley. To me they looked like torches of hope. I fixed my eyes on them to encourage myself on the narrow path down. I didn't know whether they were in Bicknell or not, but I felt myself being guided by them as if they lit up a landing strip of an airport that was near my home.

After a couple of hours we stopped and drank some of the water that Kenny had put in our plastic bottles before we left. Even in the cold, the liquid felt good on my throat. It had barely been a day since Lainey was gone. I ached so much for her, I didn't feel tired. I had no idea how the next morning would be and the one after that. My thoughts had turned into broken pieces that rattled in my brain when I tried to think, so I stopped trying. I forced myself to focus on the trail, the rocks and bushes.

Kenny took out the topo map and traced his finger along the dotted line to show me where the trail had split and where he thought we were. I was indifferent to our route and to him. As badly as I wanted to see her again, how we found our way was beyond my patience. Kenny understood that without saying it and didn't consult with me about the map or the contours of the ridges and dips that lay ahead of us. That made me like him in a way I hadn't before. His intensity didn't annoy me as soon as I realized how much it left me alone.

We kept walking and passed through endless cottonwood groves and culverts. The trail that was supposed to be descending took us up and down. It felt like we were going in loops and would never reach the valley.

It took another two hours until we found the path that led to the road. It was almost five o'clock in the morning, Kenny said. We walked in the direction of the lights I had seen a few hours before. There were no cars, but we hugged the shoulder of the two-lane road. A sign told us we were in Bicknell Bottoms and we had another mile to walk.

As soon as we started in the direction of the streetlights, random thoughts about Spence pushed my need for Lainey aside. Or maybe she had inspired them. I wanted to speak to him, not to accuse him or yell at him but to identify him, hear his voice and the pauses in his breathing. Their spacing would confirm what I already knew. Would I recognize him when he was listening and quiet? I was sure I'd be able to tell immediately as soon as he said hello and asked who was calling. His breathing rhythm would be the final clue. Before looking for Lainey, I had to find a pay phone.

"What's the first thing you want to eat when the diners open?" Kenny asked me.

"Is food all you can think about?"

"Yes, sorry. Everything else will have to wait. No meeting without eating. I think I want pancakes and bacon. What about you?"

"Pancakes and bacon," I repeated mindlessly. Kenny's head was on another planet. I didn't care what I ate.

As we got closer to the town the lights became bigger and brighter. Fog hid the tops of the telephone poles. Little birds crowded together on the sagging electrical wires. I felt like I had spent years in the desert rather than months and it had almost become my home. Neon signs farther down the road, the mile markers, the lines dividing the highway—all were alien to me. The only measurements of distance that we had in the Fremont were the blue water jugs spaced along the trail to goose us from one camp to the next. But here on the edge of this small town in Utah, every feature suggested some measurement, and that substituted for the kind of looking that I hadn't known I'd developed. It was more a searching than idle looking, a probing of my surroundings without calibrated information to assist me. I had begun to learn the striations of color in the cliffs. I wondered what caused them and thought about the history of water levels in the valleys we had crossed. Hal had told us how high the flow used to be and how it came and went, and I knew that must have affected the shading of the stone. In the Fremont the rock was full of information and I could tell by the indigo between the rim of the sky and the stars that it was about an hour before the sun rose.

In the distance I saw a phone booth with its silver sides and dark metal interior. I knew that I had to stop and call Spence before I went another step. I nudged Kenny and pointed at it. He gave me a look that said "so what." I picked up the receiver and dialed the operator. I gave her Spence's number, which I knew by heart, and she asked me how I'd like to pay. I said collect. What is your name, she asked me. I stammered for a few long seconds. I couldn't give my real name. My name is John Keats, I heard myself say. The line rang once or twice before I heard Spence's sleep-heavy voice. Who's this? he asked. Will you accept the charges? the operator asked. Umm, okay, he muttered. Who's this? he asked again. I listened to the cadence of his breath and the few words he had spoken. They were wheezy, and that carried me back to my room when he rested his chin on my shoulder and snaked his hands into my trousers. I didn't say anything, I just listened to him as hard as I could. His breath became deeper and slower. He asked again, Who's this? Who's John Keats? I could feel him exhale on my neck and the scratching of his beard. Is this a game? he asked. What do you want? I held my breath so he wouldn't know it was me.

I placed the receiver back in its cradle. There was no possible confusion. It had definitely been him who had acted that way and done those things. I knew it as surely as I knew my real name. As I walked along the road the rest of the way into Bicknell, a teenage runaway from a treatment program, I could feel him swarming over me with a hunger that

I couldn't escape from or understand. I could feel it again. It sat on me and I was paralyzed. I could sense him around me, so close. I wanted to throw him off me, slip away in the cool dawn air, but it hung on me like my own skin.

Kenny walked down the road, and I followed him, barely able to make out his form in the distance. My eyes couldn't focus. As we got nearer to town, a few cars whizzed past me. Their speed took me by surprise. I hadn't seen anything move that fast in the mountains. Vehicles came from behind us, out of nowhere, and vanished in front of us just as quickly. Getting used to the world again was going to take time.

Kenny led us to the first diner that was open. The neon sign beamed its name: Stag and Heather Restaurant. We plunked ourselves down in a booth. I used the toilet, and when I got back a stack of pancakes, syrup, and a heap of bacon were piled on a plain white plate in front of where I had been sitting. The sweet aroma was cloying and seductive. We never had pancakes at home. Mom was against them. So American, so bad for you, she claimed when I begged her to make them. She said she didn't even want to hear the word in her kitchen, although we were urged to eat the crepes that she made in a heavy cast iron pan and sprinkled with powdered sugar.

Kenny pushed forkful after forkful into his mouth, hardly stopping to chew. He acted as if he had never tasted real food before and couldn't get enough of it. When he saw how little progress I was making, he reached his fork over and speared some of it. I tried to appreciate my freedom and the breakfast in front of me, but after the phone call and the chilling recognition, nothing interested me. Even the idea of seeing Lainey again seemed strange. The only thing I could really feel was Spence overwhelming the space I took up in the world. Kenny devoured what I left on my plate.

"Hey, boys," somebody said in our direction. We looked up. It was Dave, the ghost in charge of supplies who had let the bear romp and snack in his unlocked truck. "How was your breakfast? I thought I might as well let you finish eating before I came over. It's cold out there! Jesus! Do you have money to pay for this, or do I have to do that too?" he asked.

PART THREE

15

WHEN BENJAMIN AWOKE THE NEXT MORNING FROM A fitful sleep, the ambient light had already soaked into the curtains and through the sheers next to him. The sun hadn't risen yet; it came up later and later each morning. Through the swishing tides in his ears, he listened for the noise of the streets to orient himself in time: the muffled tweets of birds, ambulance sirens and police cars, the late-night or early-morning motorcycles. Traffic density helped him set his clock. He'd stopped wearing a watch years ago, so listening to the sounds of the night or morning situated him. Urban echolocation, he called it.

The subject of the Belphonics meeting that morning was Dutch's report. One of Dutch's roles at the company was new product licensing, and he'd had a preliminary discussion with the CBGB representative, a downtown overgrown ex-biker type, he reported, with a grouchy voice, gray-white stubble, and a skinny ponytail. On any other day, Benjamin would have been interested in Dutch's remarks while bracing himself for Spence's outbursts. But that day he was dreading it. Mark's revelation from the night before intruded on him long before his eyes were fully open. Although Benjamin was a stoic, Spence's behavior was too much to tolerate. It stabbed him over and over again. His ears were bleeding into his heart. No matter how he tried to blunt the blows or defend himself, the knowledge attacked him again from another angle. Benjamin was still hoping or praying that Mark had made some mistake of identification, but he had a hunch that once he was seated at the table opposite his brother, the sickness and starkness of it, its visceral truth, would be indisputable.

Benjamin shut himself off from his wife and son as he dressed and left their apartment to walk to the Midtown office. He felt jumpy and vulnerable to every sudden squawk on the sidewalk and the street. He knew that even he could not pretend that nothing had changed. This was simply too much to absorb. He had accommodated Spence's devious, reckless behavior for too long, although he refused to believe that not confronting it had made it worse. He felt a nagging loyalty to his brother that he couldn't explain. His role as Spence's older sibling and guardian was more enduring and stubborn than he had realized. Benjamin derived his sense of maturity from it, the notion that he was worthy of the trust that had been placed in him by their parents—a trust that had survived for over fifty years and their passing. Or maybe the excuses on Spence's behalf were due in part to how grateful he was that his brother had bailed him out of a crisis. A flimsy irony, Benjamin thought, that Spence had paid to heal the wounds that he had been most responsible for inflicting.

The mood in the conference room was cheerful and light. Spence beamed at Dr. H, who shone in a turquoise linen sack dress studded with square pearl buttons with rounded edges. She had matched it with beaded earrings embedded in suede that went with the nacreous studding on her aquamarine stilettos. The effect of her red hair against the blue was enthralling and distracting. Benjamin couldn't stop himself from staring at the long thin heels that she stretched out in front of him and found himself mentally testing the physics of their design. Her smile weighed on him, feeling sad and alluring. Spence's teeth glimmered as he waved his brother over to an empty chair next to him. Dutch was tight and testy, as if the news he had to deliver might be less than the boss had hoped for.

"So, how did we make out with the heathen downtown?" Spence asked, referring to the CBGB representative. He exhaled toward the table in an exhausted way as if he didn't really care about Dutch's response.

"They want to make a deal," Dutch answered. "They think it's worth a shot and would like to know our time frame. I don't think we'll need to pay much for the rights. Maybe we can get away without paying any advance at all if we sweeten the royalty."

"And they'll arrange for us to launch there in December?" Spence asked.

"If we can finish by then, Spence," Dutch said.

"So I was thinking," Spence said, ignoring Dutch, "I was thinking that the Stones are playing soon, CBGBs is a great name, a great license, don't get me wrong, but nothing says deafening rock and roll, nothing says loss of hearing, like the Rolling Stones."

"What about Bon Jovi?" Benjamin asked.

"Who?" Spence asked with incredulity that morphed into outrage.

"Bon Jovi," Benjamin repeated, deadpan.

"Are you fucking with me, Benjy? They are beneath us. A bunch of pretenders, and they hardly suggest a quality product. The Rocker must be quality, or how do we charge for it?" Spence asked, thrusting his stout midsection forward for emphasis, his face flushed a carnation pink. Dr. H simpered at the mention of quality. Technological refinement was her department, and one Spence had relatively little interest in or respect for. The science of sound was beyond his patience.

"Bon Jovi! My own brother. Fratricide. Are you trying to offend me on purpose? How could you say something so inane, so treacherous, so stupid, Benjy?"

"Well, they are loud," Benjamin stated, and then felt an odd turn in his stomach: it was a dizzy, churning defiance he hadn't allowed himself to acknowledge before, a swan dive off a cliff into the unknown. He knew that there was a pool of water down there, but he had no idea how deep it was. His long experience with Spence had taught him that hope of any kind was an illusion,

"The Rolling Stones would laugh at you," Benjamin said, sneering. "They wouldn't even let you in the room, and if they did, it would only be to crap on you, Spence. What would they want you for? Steal your idea maybe? That would be a shame, since this may be the only original idea you've ever had." For once, he felt fearless. Mark had filled him with courage to the point of carelessness.

Benjamin felt the colors in the room draining out. The light turned hazy and glossy as though they were experiencing the flash from an atomic explosion, and in its aftermath their eardrums had been ruined by the sonic disturbance. If there had been a real detonation, papers would have been flung around the room by the whirlwind mixed with dirt and grit. There would have been panic and mayhem. Instead, the calm was paralytic. The table and the objects on its surface were untouched.

"Meeting adjourned," Spence declared after a few awkward moments of silence. He leaned over to Benjamin and motioned him back to his office. As soon as the door was closed behind them, he said, "Who put you up to this, Benjy? This isn't like you. Was it Dr. H? I've been having my doubts about her. And she is way behind on her deliverables. Has she put the moves on you yet? Maybe she's trying to undermine me. I probably should have warned you about her."

"I want to know one thing, Spence. And I want you to tell me the truth or else. Could you promise me that?"

"Or else what?" Spence nodded.

"What did you do to Mark, and how many times did you do it?"

"What are you talking about? I love that kid as if he were my son, and if I had a son, I'd like him to be just like Mark. What did he tell you?"

"He said you'd interfered with him. Stuck your hands in his pockets and touched his privates. Did you do that, Spence? Did you?"

Spence walked over to the couch, sat down, and propped his feet up on the glass coffee table with nonchalance, as if they were having one of their long- ago chats and no more serious topic was on the agenda than what sandwich to order for lunch. Benjamin squared off against him and glared.

Spence's face ran through its cycle of tics. "How could he make up something like that? I just don't get it. What an imagination that boy has. Nothing could be further from the truth. I adore him. I haven't seen him in so long. I miss him so much. Is this why you sent him away, so he could come back with garbage like that? Was the point of all that therapy and exploration and self-understanding to invent this type of bullshit? Like he needed a straw villain to take the blame for the stuff he did and I'm it? I'm not even angry, Benjy. I'm dumbfounded. I'm in shock. When did he tell you this?"

"Last night. I didn't want to believe it. I said he needed to think about it some more before he made accusations that he couldn't prove."

"You shouldn't believe it. It's not true. It never happened. He made it up."

"Why would he do that, Spence? What would that achieve? I'm having a hard time with it too. You're a weirdo and paranoid and you turn nasty about stuff no one else notices, but it never crossed my mind that you were more depraved than that. That you were evil. Are you evil, Spence?"

"Don't be ridiculous. You've known me my whole life. Some kids do this, you know. You may have read that they invent stuff to protect themselves from what they are afraid of. There was a case I read about a few years ago. Invented memory it was called, I think. Maybe he needs to blame me for what he did to Dita and that kid. Maybe that's just easier than taking responsibility. All that time he spent in the desert and that other school you sent him to that I paid for, you'd think he might have learned that. Wouldn't you? What does Dita think? Does she blame me, too?"

"I haven't talked to her about it yet. I wanted to speak to you first."

"Here," he said, handing Benjamin a thick magazine. "Cover your head. You're going to need protection. And you might want to think twice before you pass this nonsense on to her. You know she will somehow turn it around to be your fault, don't you? Or mine. But that's your problem. So what do you think? Should we try for the Stones?" Benjamin realized that Spence was doing what he had always done when he was confronted with uncomfortable information. He changed the subject and distracted his victim in as many ways as possible, like the gifted apprentice to a master magician.

"Waste of time." Benjamin said.

"Yes but—" Spence started. "Do you know why Dr. H is acting so strangely? She hasn't given me any specs. It's like she's trying to sabotage me. How are we supposed to have a launch in December?"

"Wing it?"

"Yes, wing it. Good idea. Great idea. How could I have managed without you?"

Benjamin let Spence's sardonic question hang in the air. He wanted to leave, but he was pinned to the chair by an unsettling but familiar force of gravity. He'd lost his bearings and didn't know who to believe. Was Spence capable of lying about something this substantial? Probably. Spence was capable of making almost anything appear plausible. Was it possible that Mark had been led to a false conclusion by someone else or misled himself? Benjamin didn't think so. While Mark could be violent, he was also disarmingly, almost naïvely honest. And how many times in their brotherly lives had Benjamin had to defend Spence when he suspected that Spence was guilty despite his urgent protests of innocence?

To Benjamin this was a level of violation way beyond Spence's usual deceit and cruelty. And this was not to a stranger. This was to Mark. No son could make a false confession to his father about something so humiliating. That was as strong a reason as he would ever have to make

Spence admit his wrongdoing and offer whatever contrition he could. This was his chance to exert maximum moral pressure on his brother. To force him to do what he had never done before. But the Belphonics office wasn't the time or place for it, and Mark needed to be there to hear it.

"Yes, wing it," Benjamin repeated, as though nothing had happened, and stood up to leave.

"Don't go, Benjy. I think Dr. H has got the hots for you. She didn't tell me so, but I've got good instincts about these things."

"You didn't put her up to it by any chance?" Benjamin asked.

Spence made a leering satyr's face, part grin, part lizard, and flicked his tongue out.

"Of course not. Why would I do something like that?"

"Maybe because you can't help yourself?"

"And maybe you can't help loving and defending me, Benjy. Such a shame, such a waste. You really do have a thing for hopeless causes, don't you?" Spence asked in a taunting voice.

When Benjamin got home, Dita wasn't there. He called her and asked her to come back as soon as she could. In his text he said it was urgent. Mark was gone, too. The empty apartment spooked him. As much as he usually enjoyed the quiet of the rooms, now the solitude unnerved him. The door creaked open.

"Anybody home? Ma? Pop?" Claire's voice inquired before she appeared in his small study. She was wearing a palette of iridescent shades of orange, like the sun in its full range of sunset colors. She sat down next to her father.

"God, you look bright today," Benjamin said with an artificial enthusiasm he couldn't sustain. "Is today the day?"

"Which day?"

"The day when the spaceships come to whisk you away."

"I doubt it. I don't think they've spotted me yet," she said.

"Have you talked to your brother much since he's been back? He's scaring me."

"What did he say?"

"I'm not sure I should tell you."

"Well, you can tell me, I'm his mother." Dita's voice boomed from the kitchen.

"Yes, that's why I came home early. To speak to you."

"What is it?" Dita asked with a troubled look, her handsome features crumbling, then fixing into an expression of suspense mixed with dread.

"I guess Mark wouldn't mind if..." Benjamin paused.

"I'm his mother. He better not mind," Dita said righteously.

"He said that Spence bothered him, messed with him is how he put it. I asked him when and how many times it happened. He said more than once. I asked him when the first time was and he said he was ten. He said that was what made him so angry he couldn't control his actions but he couldn't take it out on Spence so ... he took it out on others. Walt. You. That's the secret that he said he discovered in the mountains."

Benjamin didn't look at his wife and his daughter as he spoke. He didn't want to see the surprise and pain register on their faces. That would be too much for him on top of what he had already tried to accommodate. Finally, he turned to look at them. Both of them seemed to be holding their breath. Their facial muscles were strained in unusual positions, their eyes stuck open.

"I can't believe it, but I can believe it," Claire said.

"I always thought he was evil, your brother. The devil. How could he do that to our son, his only nephew? Did he think that we would never find out? I always wondered if he was gay after Annie left him and we never met another woman. Of course, he wouldn't confess that to you. That would be way too self-aware of him. And too shameful and too brave. What a coward! What a pig! He will never set foot in this apartment again! We have to report him to the police. He's a pedophile. We have to tell someone. We can't sweep it under the carpet for the sake of the family. That would kill me," Dita asserted dramatically.

"You're right, Dita. You're right. He is the one who should have been sent to Utah, not Mark. Do you think there is the slightest chance that Mark could have imagined it or made some mistake?" Benjamin asked, still in a state of shock about the extent of his brother's depravity.

"I don't know, Pop. I doubt it. I truly doubt it. He's not crazy like that," Claire answered, not looking at her father, staring out the living room window into the gap above the buildings.

"My poor Giorgio!" Dita shrieked, and bowed forward sobbing, his relinquished name barely a solace. Her deep, heaving moans made her rock back and forth. "We blamed him the whole time. We didn't think what made him do the things he did. We were so stupid. Such a bad family. Such a bad mother. We don't deserve him."

They sat together silently as though it was a wake. Details of remorse washed over them. Feelings swerved wildly from believing Mark to not believing him enough, not paying sufficient attention, withholding affection, being too self-involved. And all the distractions. Benjamin conjured up the picture of the goons as they had entered the apartment that night almost three years before to take Giorgio away and the look that he gave them of profound distress and confusion. Or was it one of betrayal? Benjamin wondered. He and Dita, who devised and set the plan in motion, had watched them lead their son away as if he was guilty of a heinous crime, not bad behavior.

Benjamin spotted the concert ticket that Mark had kicked into the corner of the living room. He leaned over to pick it up with the note that Spence had written to accompany it. What he could make out from Spence's scrawl was banal, something to the effect of "I can't wait to see you. Let's grab dinner before." Benjamin stuffed the items into his pocket. It was the smallest piece of order that he could bring to the chaos of the situation. In the background, he heard Dita moaning like a wounded animal, her self-recrimination drowning out her pleas for revenge. Claire rocked back and forth, her coiled black hair yoyoing in front of her dark eyes, then parting to reveal the tears that wet her eyes and cheeks and chin. Her shoulders curved over her chest. He had to go; he couldn't absorb their grief, too.

Benjamin left Dita and Claire in the living room as he slipped out the front door. They couldn't find anything else to say to one another; words were simply inadequate. Dita's nerves were not calmed by her daughter's presence. Usually, when Claire came home to visit, it was a celebratory occasion, but there was no trace of delight in what they had just heard. As Claire slumped on the couch, Dita stalked in and out of the room without putting on her favorite cable station, which usually acted as a calmative. Without reflection, she picked up her purse and left too.

It was rare for Claire to be alone in the apartment that she had grown up in. Like Mark's, her bedroom was mostly the same as it had been when she had moved out five years earlier, a memorial to her former, unformed self. She had outgrown the photographs and mementos that had been stationed there for so long that they had lost meaning or the power to remind her of a cherished moment. Her little bed, flocked with dolls, was pushed against the wall, and she flopped down on it as soon as she walked in.

Almost immediately she heard the front door open but didn't jump up to see who it was, as she used to do. Collapsed on the worn quilt bedspread, she stared at the ceiling, as she had done so often. She pulled her old blanket up to her shoulders, a crocheted one in faded yellow and pink fractals that she had knitted at one of the girls' camps her mother had selected for her. She closed her eyes as if the hideousness of what had been done to Mark would put her in a dreamless sleep rather than stir her to outrage.

When she opened her eyes again, her brother was standing in the doorway, and he was so broad and tall it was as if he could support the frame he was leaning against by himself. A brief smile crossed his lips before he sat down on the stool facing her makeup table. Because Claire was still not used to having him back, still thought he was an apparition, she stared at him for a few seconds before either of them said anything.

"Tell me what happened, Mark," she said. "I won't repeat it to them or anybody if you don't want me to. I have to hear it directly from you. What did Spence do? How did you figure it out?"

Mark didn't say anything. It wasn't that he didn't trust her. He trusted her more than anyone. It was that he didn't want to go completely back to that time and place in Utah, let alone the day itself and how it lingered in his head. He didn't want to revisit the first revelations, the unfolding of painful details and the rage that came with it and hadn't left.

"I knew the whole time," he said, stretching his fingers and interweaving them as he spoke. "Even if I was just a little kid when it happened. I always knew what he did. I shelved it. Put it as far in the back in the dark as I could until I was ready for it. But I wasn't ready when it came."

"What do you mean?"

"I don't know about memories or how they come to you when you hide them from yourself, but it was a little thing that set me off. A girl in the Fremont had a rash on the arm that she was holding onto me with. It was the same skin rash Spence had. I freaked out. The girl ran away. I'm not sure that she ever forgave me. We didn't have a chance to talk about it. She disappeared soon after that. I don't know what happened to her. And then it all kind of straggled back to me piece by piece. I felt Spence's face pressed against my cheek, his beard scratch my skin, his heavy breath. And his neon teeth. He said he had a present for me."

"A present? He never got me anything!"

"You were lucky. It was a bow tie. I don't think you would have wanted a present like the one I got. He said he was going to show me how to tie it, like that explained why he was standing so close to me. He was going to show me the steps so I would learn how to tie it myself. And I remember how badly I wanted to learn, how badly I wanted to impress him. So I could get it just right and prove to him that I was good at it. Dumb little kid. I watched everything he did and made him do it over and over again. And then he let the bow tie drop on the floor and he didn't pick it up."

"Why didn't he pick it up?"

"Because that wasn't really why he was there."

The pause between them was uncomfortable and long. It made them feel that no matter how much they trusted each other, they were suddenly on uneven ground together.

"Then Mom came in while he was hovering over me. She didn't see what he had been doing. He'd yanked his hands back by then, but she knew something bad had happened. And in case she wasn't sure, Spence left the room abruptly."

"She didn't say anything? She just appeared?"

"Yes. I hadn't shouted out or called her, I was all quiet, but she must have known Spence was with me. I guess some instinct made her come in to check on me. I think she spared me. It's hard to know if he would have done anything else, but if he was going to, she spooked him and he stopped. I feel I should be more grateful to her than I am."

"Did you tell her?"

"Not yet."

"I think I want to kill him. If Mom doesn't first that is. Do you think there is any way you can forgive him?" she asked.

"Forgive him? Should I?" Mark asked, and smiled. "Maybe I already have a little. No, not really. But then there are times I know I can't. He always made me feel like he liked me. That I was a little special. He knew stuff that Dad didn't know. Real stuff, not book stuff. I liked that, too. There were so many things I thought I could learn from him."

"I never felt that. I guess because he wasn't interested in girls. Are you going to see him?"

"He invited me to a concert. I don't know if I'm ready, but maybe I'm as ready as I'll ever be."

16

"**W**HAT TOOK YOU GUYS SO LONG?" DAVE ASKED AS HE drove us back up the mountain in his chewed-up truck. He was cheerful in spite of the early hour and showed no sign of anger toward Kenny and me. He almost seemed happy to have an off-site job on such a fine morning and to be behind the steering wheel, maneuvering the vehicle between ruts in the dirt road, rocks and puddles of unknown depth. Like Hal, he belonged here. He knew the land, and it felt welcoming to him. Whatever dangers might have been lurking ahead of him, he had wrestled with them before. Thousand Lake Mountain wasn't the kind of place where he would be undone.

"Usually runners are at the diner by six," Dave added. "I suppose you went looking for your girlfriend and couldn't find her. She's long gone," he said, without elaborating. I wanted to ask him where, but I stopped myself. I wasn't ready to know any more of the truth that morning.

I never saw Lainey again. Or I never thought I did. Or I wasn't sure. After I left the Fremont, if I noticed a girl wearing shimmery black warm-up pants under a pleated skirt over dusty boots, my eyes traveled up her legs to check whether she wore Lainey's purple fingerless gloves or had her blank white skin or her cascading tangle of black hair. Or her green eyes that saw everything. I tried not to stare at those girls, but it was hard not to search them for clues. I wanted to find Lainey so badly, and at the same time I was afraid that I might discover that she was gone for good and the conversations we'd had were the only ones we'd ever have.

Over the next few weeks I cornered Hal whenever I had the chance. After the first couple of times I stopped him to ask if he had any more information about Lainey, he started to avoid me. Soon I had the feeling that he was starting to feel sorry for me. He would turn sideways and ask me if I didn't have something else I should be doing. I did what I was supposed to do, not caring whether it was well done or done at all. I wondered if he was keeping Lainey's information or memory close because he didn't want to share what he felt with me or because the news was bad and he was trying to protect me. Either way I didn't have the guts to press him beyond those first insistent questions.

After Dave had paid for our pancakes and bacon and drove us back to our tents, no disciplinary measures were taken against us. That made me nervous. It was almost as if our escape had been overlooked for some reason. Ron didn't make a point of admonishing Kenny or me alone or in front of the group, which was out of character for him. As far as we knew officially, we were both going to "graduate" at the upcoming ceremony and be reunited with our families, who had been invited to join us for it. By that time, I would have spent over eight weeks in the Fremont and adjusted to more variations of weather, feats of physical endurance, and emotional events than I had had any idea of less than two months ago. I could barely imagine myself as I had been before I had arrived.

Kenny didn't blame me for getting caught. He wasn't more or less friendly than he had been before. He remained the same skittish, neutral character that he had always been. He was still twitchy, bug-eyed, and shifty. It was as though the whole episode hadn't made a noticeable dent in him either. He handled his fire-making and cooking tasks with the intensity and agility that he always brought to them without referring once to the botched escape or much else, although he was quieter than he had ever been. At the end of each hike, he took off his red cowboy bandana, dunked it in a pot of water, then wrung it out and put it back on damp, as if nothing was different, even though it was. He didn't quote any more Keats to me that I can remember, but since I had used the name on my phone call to Spence I wondered whether I had violated some sacred Keats rule of impersonation and was banned from receiving further knowledge.

Inevitably, thinking of Keats brought back Spence's breathing into the receiver. The cadence of his breath, his mumbling and confusion, would always be fused in my mind with the search for Lainey and the question of whether she was still alive, still breathing. That she had been the first one to help me see Spence's interference in my younger life meant that the two were intertwined. I would have liked to split her off from him, but that wasn't possible even though she represented the better side of the equation—realization and understanding. My love for her rested on her powers of insight. Subliminally, she was still messaging me that any truth was bearable if it was examined clearly and deeply no matter how bad or embarrassing it was. The truths that weren't bearable, she had suggested, were the murky ones, the ones that could bite you like a snake if you weren't careful and didn't watch where you put your feet or your hands. The few venomous snakes we saw sunning themselves on the red rocks by the side of the trail were in plain view and took no notice of you unless you waved your hands at them or did something extra stupid like trying to kiss them. In those idiotic cases, according to camp lore, you got what you deserved.

Lainey and I never had the chance to discuss how I might handle my grievance toward Spence, but I could feel her support for any nonviolent confrontation that I was capable of. I felt in my bones that she would endorse a quiet but pointed discussion, and I kept that belief alive in the front lobe of my brain. One day in the future, facing Spence might be a fine way for me to scrub away the past, cleanse the record, but I had more immediate issues given that my parents were coming to the graduation that would be taking place very soon. My awareness of Spence's act was still too raw to mention to them. I couldn't hear the words that I would need to describe the scene, to set it in its right time and place so that it would be believable. I wasn't prepared for their doubts about the incident or their agony for their son, their upset at failing to protect me or just the dismal whole of it.

After Kenny and I were apprehended and returned to camp, I had my first letter from Claire. Her handwriting sprawled across the front of the envelope, and she was still using the canary-yellow stationery that had rays of sunlight bursting from the multicolored hand-drawn stars and a floating pink unicorn in the top left corner. She must have kept that stationery in her desk drawer since she was a little girl and had nothing else to write on. I pictured her huddled over the bright sheets, writing by hand as if she were engraving it. "Where are you?" she opened with, as if I knew where I was and we were speaking in real time. "What are you wearing? Is it cold there?" The first paragraph was only questions until she left a space and started again. "Mom and Dad are in shock. They mumble to me and to each other. They are sleepwalking. I think they can't believe you are not home, although they were the ones who sent you away. They don't really grasp what they have done, but they keep muttering to each other that they had to do it. There was no other choice, I hear them say. And I can assure you that now they are far from sure. They are wrestling with the idea but not blaming each other yet. They don't have much interest in me or anything else in their lives. They never go out, let alone have a laugh. They are restless and inactive. The television is always on so they don't have to talk to each other. It's one congressional hearing after another. The same tedious inquiry over and over again. They barely have the energy to buy food for dinner, so you know that there's something seriously messed up with them. I am really not sure how they make it through the day. They are so depressed. Whenever I am there, they pretend to dote on me or at least when I walk in the door. They ask me a ton of questions, but they don't wait for an answer, and then they ask the same ones all over again. They want to talk to you and hug you. Mom shrieks, "If only I could..." You can fill in the blank yourself. They are sorry for you. And sorry for themselves. It is so weird to be there. I stay away as much as I can unless they force me to come over by using one of their tricks. I really don't want to be there. No. I don't want to be with them."

I shoved her letter to the bottom of my pack but couldn't help picturing the scenes that Claire described. The kitchen, the dining room, the den. The rooms were small and everything felt toylike inside them; the miniature chairs were rickety, nearly weightless; the small dining room table was an assembly of plain oak planks shoved and glued together; and the living room sofa and my bed didn't have much padding. Just some coils that had lost their spring.

After the upcoming graduation, I wasn't sure that I wanted to return to those airless indoor spaces with those dark rooms, the tiny furniture bunched together, the conversations that those walls had overheard and absorbed, the sunlight turned by the towering buildings into uneven rows of shadow. I missed those rooms in some ways, but I didn't miss what happened inside them. In the Fremont, space wasn't at a premium, it was endless. Ron and the rules aside, nothing said you couldn't go somewhere except for your stamina or your instinct for caution. You could see everything as far as you could see. You could climb a hill or sit down when you were tired, make your own fire, and with some experience, catch your own food. You were free there. The idea of graduating from that to go back to my room was miserable.

The day before the parents' arrival Ron was in a frenzy of cleaning activity. Everything had to be dirt free. Our hands and faces had to be dusted and scrubbed, not to mention that our hiking pants, boots, socks, and packs had to be spotless. It was already hard for me to recall what people looked or smelled like who took a shower every day and wore clean clothes. That reminded me how disheveled my group was the night I had arrived. I remembered wondering whether this was how I would look soon and how long that would take.

The morning of the ceremony was windy and bright, so we strolled slowly down the trail trying to kick up as little dust as possible. The location was less than half a mile from our campsite, barely enough mileage to register on our legs, which had become used to much greater distances, distances that we had become proud of. What was left of the leaves on the cottonwood trees toward the end of autumn swung in the breeze in a giddy way as we passed under them. The air was clear and thin, and luckily, it wasn't too cold. We were still at almost seven thousand feet. We had stopped noticing the effects of the high altitude weeks earlier. I was as adjusted as I'd ever be.

During our walk, I noticed an unusual jauntiness among us. "Esprit de corps" I heard that it was called in the army. We thought of ourselves as a troop of survivors who had been challenged by the elements and made our peace with them. We had faced the enemy even if that enemy was mostly ourselves. Ron really wasn't that bad. Somebody had to organize the mechanics of the place, and he was good at it. Or good enough. Fortunately for him he had Hal to be his human side. I couldn't imagine how hairy the experience would have been without him.

My first thought when I saw Mom and Dad at the ceremony was that they were city people. Their clothes were useless in the Fremont. My father's lightweight blazer with its fake gold buttons and his gray gabardine slacks would be shredded in a day. And his shoes horrified me. They didn't have laces. His arches would collapse and his feet would be aching in minutes. The low-level polish that he liked to maintain would be soiled instantly. Tall and thin with dangling arms, he wouldn't have enough strength to do the hikes we had done even if he had been training before he got here. And the sun on his mostly bald head and pale face would scorch him. My mother's darker skin might protect her a little, but her attitude would be busted in days. She wouldn't take well to a defeat like that, and I didn't want to imagine the fallout. As Kenny put it, she would still be shouting at the hailstones months after she got there. The contrasting colors of her clothes and her fabrics were equally useless. I imagined my parents in tatters, stupefied and lost, wandering in the canyons.

Appearances aside, my emotions jammed up inside my brain. Revenge, betrayal, and even the pleasure of anticipation fought over me. I wanted to run to them, kick clouds of dirt on them and mock their preposterous clothes and ridiculous assumptions about me and the Fremont. A dumb quick fix. Is that what they had thought? I didn't know, and it was too late to care. At the same time, I wanted them to take me in their arms and hold me there for as long as any of us could stand. Please don't let me go, I heard my inner voice plead. My mother enveloped me and held me close to her solid silk-blouse body. My chin rested on her shoulder, and my father caught my eye. He looked at me and then he looked away. He was embarrassed, I thought. Embarrassed by his part in such a radical decision.

We barely knew what to say. We fumbled, used verbs without objects, subjects without verbs. We were always on the verge of a finished sentence without reaching it. Although I had written a few letters to them describing our daily activities, they did not seem prepared for seeing me in the flesh. I could tell from their faces that they hadn't expected to see a change in me so soon, but even after eight weeks they could sense a difference that was far from subtle. I liked the idea that it was impossible to ignore. Side by side with my previous self, anyone would have noticed it. They could call it whatever they wanted to.

"You look like you've been in a basic marine training boot camp, *caro*? Don't they give you food or sunscreen here? You look like burnt earth, like the desert, but a little cleaner than I expected," my mother said in her sharp voice. "Did they get you ready to be inspected by your mothers? How many times do you wash in a week?"

"Not once, Mom, unless we find a pond. There were supposed to be portable showers, but they broke on the first day I was here. I got used to a layer of dirt after a week. The dirt protects you, keeps the flies away."

"Even the girls?"

"Even the girls, Mom."

"Giorgio," my father said. "There's something we need to tell you."

"Yes," I said hesitantly.

"Ron doesn't think you are ready to come home yet. He said to us that you would really benefit from spending another month or two here until the next semester starts at a special school in Omaha. He told us how much progress you have made and what happened to your friend. Is that why you tried to run away? To visit her. Is that right? He said that more than half of the kids stay beyond their first commitment. Is that true?"

Almost before he could finish the sentence, Mom added, "We came here to bring you home, *carissimo*. They warned us you weren't ready to leave, but we came anyway. We don't care what they said. We wanted to ask you ourselves. Do you think you are ready to be home again?"

My thinking stopped when I heard the word *home*. It was untranslatable. Or meant something different in every language to every person there was. Either I was in a state of shock or I already knew that I wasn't ready to leave and probably didn't want to, so the news didn't startle me as much as they thought it would. The mere idea of going back to Blethen and New York City and that whole life made me sick. I nodded my head a little as my dad spoke to let him know that I heard him. My parents were definitely more surprised and upset than I was by the news.

Ron interrupted our reunion to announce that the ceremony was about to begin. We sat together on makeshift board benches propped on logs. Once it started, he stood in front of us and strung together upbeat bullshit slogans that mingled with and drifted in and out of the idea that I was staying on. He ticked off details of our discipline and effort, endurance and learning that we had begun to exhibit. All of these qualities, he said, like taking care of our stuff, cooking our meals, looking after one another, et cetera, were becoming second nature to us. He didn't say so exactly, but it was as if he was laying out a lot of what we already assumed: that we had come to Camp Fremont as incomplete humans, with huge missing pieces and obvious flaws, parental or otherwise, and our experience there was making us whole. While he listed our achievements, I could feel Lainey's ghost pass over me as if she were an angel of wisdom and protection watching over me. She wasn't just in the sky. I could feel her in my chest and in my forehead between my eyes, the spot where she had peered into me. The sensation of her being close helped me breathe evenly and think cleanly. In the weeks since I had known her, even after she was gone, I didn't feel any pressure inside my head. All the traces of my brain irritation were gone. I was convinced that she was the one who had cured me of it or, perhaps, replaced it.

"It was supposed to take us a day to reach the top of Thousand Lake Mountain. We had been training for it for weeks," Ron continued in his clipped, matter-of-fact way. "Instead it took us three days. Some of us are stronger than others, so the fitter people had to wait for the slower ones. That's hard to do. Patience is hard to learn, hard to practice. But we have begun to accomplish that." He was so full of shit, I thought. All I could remember was how often he had yelled at Lainey and me to hurry up and shamed us for endangering the group. I wondered if that had been one of the last straws for her.

"Yes, it did take us three days," he intoned, like he had been suddenly turned into an evangelical preacher offering uplift, "but when I think about what we gained in that extra time, the delay was worth it. We saw more. We spoke to each other more." The parents sprinkled among us nodded meaningfully. I wondered what they made of Ron. Did they think he was showing them up, underscoring the fact that he might have been a better parent than they had been? At the end of the row, I spotted Kenny sitting between his mom and dad. His father was as swarthy and twitchy as he was. I wondered how he would react to the news of my failure to progress. Maybe a Keats quote that Kenny would repeat to me down the road. His mother was a small, carefully composed woman with a swirl of black hair and dark, sharp eyes. She listened as thoughtfully and as skeptically as anyone to Ron's list of our accomplishments.

Toward the end of the talk, Ron praised us in a way that felt even more phony, if not totally false. We were, he said, model citizens who, having been put through these tests of character, were better prepared than any to be future community leaders, to further, to deepen the meaning of being a citizen. Toward the end of that thought, he referred to those of us who weren't "far enough along" by saying that while we needed more seasoning we had made "important forward progress." It crossed my mind that he might be right, but if he was, why did he never say any of this to us before our parents came? Why had he needed them to show us a sign of encouragement? This struck me as a manifestation of his cheapness as much as his hypocrisy.

At the end of his speech, Ron handed out awards. Each of us got one, rendering the distinctions between us meaningless. Mine was for personal growth, whatever that was. It seemed superficial, maybe arbitrary. I wondered who had made the little suede squares embroidered with white, red, and aquamarine beads. Was there another camp nearby that specialized in Native American crafts? Comparing them later, we noticed that the designs were identical regardless of achievement. An attempted escape hadn't prevented us from getting the same badge as those who had slept more or less peacefully through the night in their sleeping bags.

My parents sat on either side of me during the picnic lunch that followed. The news that I wasn't going home had progressed from feeling right to feeling demoralizing. Maybe apologies were needed, but whose? Mine or theirs? I didn't know, or I thought that there was maybe enough apologetic material available for everyone. We were all sorry for everything, and there was nothing to say about any of it, so we just sat together and I realized that that was better than talking. At least then. There would be enough time in the future for mountains of words and apologies and confessions, but it was too soon for those.

Our good-byes were physical, too. I clung to them and nuzzled my forehead against the soft shoulder of my mother's jacket, but I couldn't look her in the eye. When would I see them again, and where? I had no idea. But I decided that I didn't want to be with them until I had figured out the rest of what had happened to me and could say it without violence or blame. I had the beginnings of that composure, but I knew that I had a long way to go

They described the school that I would be sent to when the time came to leave the Fremont. It had more freedom, they promised. It was more like normal life. I'd live in a dorm as one of a group of kids overseen by a married couple who were both teachers. I could finish high school there. It did have a disciplinary element they said, but I didn't listen to that part of it. It didn't really matter at that moment where I was going next or who would be there or where it was.

I watched them walk away with remorse. The urge to be more open with them was overwhelmed by my reluctance to do that before I was ready. The farther away they were, the harder it was to repress the desire to run after them, as if my pursuit would fix what was wrong and the reset would be permanent and strong. I stood next to Kenny not waving but wanting to believe in that with all of my best will.

17

WHEN BENJAMIN EXITED HIS APARTMENT HE HAD NO destination in mind, but he found himself walking west and toward Midtown. He stayed out of the late-afternoon sun that was still warm given that it was already December. He kept close to the buildings, as if the chill of their stone siding might keep him shadowed and inconspicuous. Within minutes he realized that he was retracing his steps to Dr. H's apartment, reversing the path he had taken home after he carried her up. He knew that he didn't want to go there, but at the same time he felt himself drawn to her. He made arguments to himself using convincing, logical reasons why he should not return, but they didn't slow his stride or change his course. He kept moving toward her as if she were summoning him, saying tell me what happened so I can explain, so I can console, saying Spence would never do something that hideous. That was what he wanted to hear her say, he realized. He wanted Spence to be exculpated without him having to divulge the details of Mark's confession. What could a seventeen-year-old remember of a traumatic event that had happened seven years before?

When Dr. H opened the door, she had an orange lipstick smile on her lips that made him think that she was expecting him. She reached up on her tiptoes to put her arms around his shoulders and pulled him in. His eyes adjusted slowly to the near dark. Beneath her makeup and the meticulous chaos of her hair, he observed that she had the face of a warrior.

"It's usually a good idea, Benjamin, to give a woman some warning before you turn up. We're not so good at the impromptu. You're old enough to know that, aren't you? Anyway, you're here. Vodka? Too early? Do you want to tell me what's wrong? I knew there was something off with you when you started yelling about Bon Jovi in the meeting this morning. Bon Jovi? Really? Nobody in their right mind would question Spence's hierarchy of rock and roll. You must know that by now. You might as well have proposed the Monkees. Or Satan. No, wait, Spence might have gone for that."

Dr. H didn't wait for any comment. She walked to the open kitchen area across from the front door. Her heels made hypnotic clicking noises on the tile. As she bent over the freezer drawer, she retrieved the same frosted bottle of vodka and the Parisian glasses that they had drunk from on his previous visit. Her calves bulged above the heel strap as if they had been carved from a lump of clay. Benjamin tried not to stare at her stockings but couldn't look away. Blue was one of her most flattering colors, he thought to himself.

"To what do I owe the pleasure of this visit?" she asked, extending the Eiffel shot glass toward him.

"I want to talk about Spence."

"Oh no, please not that. I'm sick of talking about him, analyzing him, making excuses for him. What has he done now?"

"Are you sure you want to know?"

"Are you sure you want to tell me?"

"No, I'm not sure."

"So don't. Let's talk about happier things. Spence is work. You didn't come for work, did you, Benjamin?" She reached her hand up toward him and cupped the back of his head. She twisted a curl of his gray-black hair around her index finger as if it were a piece of yarn that had come loose from a sweater.

He didn't answer and looked down into his lap. In case he had any doubt before, he knew then with her finger spinning his hair into twine that it was wrong for him to have come. It was as wrong the second time as it had been the first, but that hadn't stopped him. He wanted someone besides Dita who knew how evil Spence could be to reassure him that blaming and hating Spence for what he had done to Mark wasn't a part of his brotherly obligation. It was separate and grievous. That awareness made him shaky and alone no matter how long her hand resting on his shoulder might be her form of approval.

"Come here," she said, and pulled him gently but forcefully toward her on the velour sofa where they sat. He bent forward on his knees in front of her as if he were praying to her for something he thought he still needed. His knees hurt; his trousers yanked at the hairs on his shins. "I know how to help you," she offered.

That was enough of an assumption to push Benjamin out the door. Any invitations beyond the ones she had already offered could be too tempting and too frightening. He made worthless excuses for his intrusion and thanked her, although she didn't know what she had done for him. Walking home, he realized that he wanted to be free of all commiseration, even hers. He wanted to be released from his lifelong commitment to a brother who rolled over everyone, him most of all. In his imagination, he was walking heroically free through a new city. The colors and sounds around him were amplified, and the ruins of his former city, his previous self, trailed in the distance. Then he noticed his drab local deli and the soot on the sign of his dry cleaners and realized that he was almost home.

When he slipped through the front door of his apartment, he tried to be as unobtrusive as possible, holding his breath and turning his head sideways. Before he was confronted, he wanted to assess the situation. The hall was quiet and still, but as he walked toward the kitchen he could feel an early winter breeze flowing through an open window. Mark stood against the sink cradling a glass of water, dressed in his old blue jacket that barely fit over his shoulders that made Benjamin think his son was going out.

"Where are you headed tonight?" Benjamin managed.

"Brooklyn, Barclays Center," Mark answered.

"I thought you were going to skip it?" Benjamin asked.

"So did I," Mark answered. "But I can't."

"What if I forbid you?" Benjamin asked.

"You can't do that."

"Too much could go wrong," his father stated.

"You mean more than went wrong already?" Mark queried.

Benjamin examined his son and envied his courage. He hoped that Mark with patience and reason could persuade Spence to look at and examine the damage he had done. As unlikely as he thought that would be, he admired Mark for having the temerity to attempt it.

"I've had three years of thinking about this," he said, a little more nervous than his strident words, nibbling the inside of his lower lip.

"I think it's a bad idea. Would you at least let me protect you now? Spence is unpredictable. Stay in tonight. Give it some more time."

"I made up my mind. I'm going. Watch me."

They stood facing each other. Slightly taller, Mark regarded his father fondly. When Mark learned that Benjamin was working for Spence, he had realized that a larger capitulation had taken place, even if he didn't know the details. He hoped for his father's emancipation from Spence as much as he hoped for his own.

"Earplugs?" Benjamin asked and smiled. "You'll still hear the songs. Don't worry. You couldn't miss those chords if your ears were filled with cement."

"Give the Stones a chance, Dad. They couldn't be as terrible live as you say they are. They are the biggest band in the world, and besides, they're probably on their last lap and I've never seen them before. Did you ever hear them live?"

"Never. I've never wanted to. The thought of being with twenty thousand of their loudest fans ..." He didn't finish the sentence. The rest of his opinion was obvious.

"Maybe you should go instead of me," Mark suggested.

"They're not for me but I heard someone say once that seeing the Rolling Stones play in an arena is like seeing a Sophocles play performed at Epidaurus. It is an event of equal historical importance. Once in a millennium. A cultural touchstone. But, more important, what do you plan to say to Spence?"

"Can we not talk about that? Please trust me." Mark said and stared at the floor. His shadow leaned away from him and spilled across the tiles.

"All right. I trust you. How is your mother?"

"She's upset. No, she's very, very upset. She stormed out Claire said. I don't know where she went. I think she wants to murder him."

"Nothing new about that. Let's hope she waits until tomorrow. I have something to say to you that may be hard to understand."

"What is it?"

"I completely accept what you told me as the truth. I know that you didn't make any of this up. But be warned. That's what Spence will say, so I hope you're prepared for it. Spence is a wanton, destructive human being, but he is my brother. I wish I could separate those two things, but I'm struggling. I blame him for everything he has done, and I've always hoped that he could be better. He can't. Can you understand that?"

"Yeah, I think I can. Or I would like to. But if you believe me as you say you do, you have to confront him, too. You can't pretend it didn't happen either," Mark answered. After a moment, Mark left the room and Benjamin heard the front door closing, which abandoned him to the whooshing in his ears, the empty apartment, and the cacophony of his thoughts.

Although Mark had tried to avoid the claustrophobia of the subway in the weeks since he had returned to the city, he headed eagerly down the nearest steps of the Eighty-Sixth Street station to go downtown and under the East River. Spence had chosen a steakhouse restaurant near the venue, so it was a straight ride, no change of trains or waiting through the deafening clatter of other cars passing through. The number 5 train came almost instantly, and, since he'd been away, he didn't remember the New York subway working so effortlessly. When he walked into the restaurant's dark front room, where sides of beef hung from hooks on either side, his uncle's flushed face beaming above a red checked tablecloth at one of the front tables summoned him.

Even though he had prepared himself, seeing Spence in the flesh after three years was a shock. He looked even beefier than he remembered him. His teeth were not only white, they were shining and reflected on his squirrelly cheeks, which were still tan and plump from summer. Encased by a too narrowly cut gray suit, Spence looked like a sausage squeezed into a tight casing. When he hugged him, Mark realized that he was at least six inches taller than his uncle, but his height only made him feel that he was at a disadvantage: gangly and awkward. He sat down and glanced at the menu with no more than a nod.

"How do you like your steak? Bloody?" Spence asked. He was glaring, his cheeks a shade of medium rare.

"That's fine," Mark answered. Spence ordered him a Bloody Mary in spite of his age and prime-cut sirloins and home fries and broccoli, and the waiter nodded as if the two of them had agreed to it in advance. Mark wondered whether Spence had said something to the waiter so that he didn't ask for Mark's ID. Group after group of diners arrived in their vintage Stones paraphernalia. Each pin stuck into their lapels or caps or blouses showed off the scarlet lips curved into a sneer and the lascivious tongue. As if they were participating in a conspiracy, their excitement for the event built upon itself and burst into hilarity as they jostled one another between the table and chairs.

Mark felt as though he was in a congregation of the wrong faith or age, or maybe he was in a cult. The band didn't mean enough for him to share his father's animosity toward them, but their fans clamoring around him increased his suspicions about the concert. They were so adoring of one another and their heroes that the quality of the concert seemed like a foregone conclusion. They had already decided that the evening would be an event of epic dimensions.

"Tell me a little bit, Mark. I've heard bits and pieces of your travels from your parents, but I'd like to hear it from the horse's mouth. I could never spend a night in the wilderness, let alone as long as you did. How did you survive?"

"I liked it once I got used to it. I liked it a lot. Much more than here."

"What does that mean, 'once I got used to it'?"

"Once I got used to the dirt and bugs and the cold and how much the packs weighed."

"I see. How should I ask this? Did it fix what you got sent for?" Spence asked.

"No. Yes. It did and didn't," Mark said, and clammed up. He wasn't sure if this was the moment to bring up what was pressing on him or whether he should wait until after they ate. He regretted that he hadn't asked for his father's advice.

"What did you eat out there?" Spence asked, sensing Mark's hostility and trying to direct the conversation to neutral ground.

"Bugs, Spence. We ate bugs and beans and rice, "he said flippantly.

"No wonder you're such a beanpole," Spence answered, and grinned. "Well, we'll do much better than that tonight. You mean you never caught a trout and fried it? I did that once, and I still remember how delicious it tasted."

"No fishing rods. We had enough to carry. After a while we got used to the packs, but I wouldn't have wanted to add another ounce. I called you once, but you probably don't remember. I used a different name. Woke you up."

"You did? How long ago was that?"

"A few years ago. Right after I got to the Fremont. You picked up."

"What did I say?"

"You didn't say anything. You didn't know it was me. I pretended to be someone else."

"Why would you do that? What name did you use? I have no memory of it at all."

"Keats. John Keats. Ever heard of him?"

"Of course I have. Do you think I'm ignorant? Why would you use a fake name? Why did you call and not tell me who you were? You could have said hello at least. I would have liked to hear from you. I have missed you a lot."

Before Mark could answer, the waiter set a sizzling plate on the table. It contained the rare sirloin slices Spence had ordered. After rubbing each one on its side against the rim and soaking it in juice, the waiter arrayed them on the edges of their plates. The aroma of meat and blood and juice wafted up into Mark's nostrils. It was a meat lover's ambrosia. For a moment, the other questions and answers and animosities were suspended in its flavor. Mark loved the reddish raw color and the charred taste of it in his mouth and put his knife and fork down after finishing the first slice.

"The reason that I had to call was to ask you a question, but I didn't ask it. I didn't have to," Mark said.

"Mark, if you have something to say, say it. Don't make me guess. I hate that. It makes me feel like I'm a fifth grader again. You know that time in class when the teacher calls on you and everybody knows the answer to the question except you? I'm sure it's happened to you, too. It happens to everyone sooner or later. Please don't put me through that. What did you want to ask me?"

"Remember when you taught me how to tie a bow tie? You brought me one as a present. I was ten or eleven maybe. We stood in front of the mirror in my bedroom. All of this came back to me when I was in the Fremont. You were behind me and took me through the steps, except that in the middle of your demonstration you stopped. That's when you put your hands in my pockets. Remember that?"

"Hmm. Not off the top of my head. I need to give it a little think. Rummage around a little, you know. Stuck my hands in your pockets? That's a long time ago, isn't it?" he asked.

"You must be thinking of someone else," Spence said. "It couldn't have been me. I didn't wear bow ties back then, so I know for sure that something is wrong. Let's do the math together. You were ten or eleven when you say this happened and you're seventeen now, so according to my calculations that means it would have been 2005 or 2006. I didn't start wearing bow ties until 2008. Before that, I wouldn't have known how to tie one if my life depended on it. And here's how I know for sure. I started wearing them after Anna left, and that was 2007. How can I be so certain? you may ask, so I'll tell you. I wanted to break the jinx. Anna jinxed me, and she loved how ties looked on me. Those were the only presents she ever gave me, so I realized I never wanted to wear a tie again. That's what made me switch to bow ties. It took me forever to learn to tie them, too. I'm sorry," Spence said. "You have got the wrong man. Must have been someone else, and you were so young then it would have been hard for you to remember so much. So many details for a little kid. Let's finish up so we can get to our seats."

Mark hadn't expected Spence to break down and confess. He knew his uncle well enough for that, but he hadn't anticipated such a spontaneous and agile rearrangement of the facts. The dates, Spence's mangled personal history with Anna, the prevarication, confirmed more than any other facts that his conclusion was solid. He wasn't sure how to refute his uncle's version of the facts.

"What about the eczema, Spence?" Mark asked.

"Under control. I've always had that. Even before the bow ties. Why do you ask?"

"Because I saw the dry flaky skin on your fingers and wrists when you reached around my neck to teach me how to tie it. Before you did what you did."

"Hold on. You're accusing me of molesting you, my own nephew, based on some oddball memories you had three years ago? Am I understanding that right? Do you know how many people have eczema? It's one of the most common skin diseases in the world. Did your father know you were going to come up with this shit? This is crazy, Marco! Please stop, please, I beg you just cut it out, everything you think you remember, all of this anger and your hypotheticals. It doesn't add up to a truth. So let's just go to the concert like we planned and listen to the best band that there has ever been, okay? I promise that I will discuss it with you again, whenever you want. But no more tonight. Okay, Marco?"

Mark hadn't been called by Spence's pet name for him, his uncle's version of his real one, since he had gone away. It had been a joke between them. If she can change your name to Giorgio, then I can change your name to Marco, Spence explained with a mischievous smile similar to the one on the Stones merchandise. At least that has some relevance to your actual name, he'd added, rather than being a complete fabrication.

Mark decided to let his uncle's question linger in the space between them. Since his days in the high desert, Mark, like Hal, had become comfortable with the absence of speech. It reinforced some of the instincts he had learned there, and he treasured it. Silence meant that he could hear the sonic environment and, through the encrypted sounds, he could realize danger and safety. He could tell that there was a river in the canyon too far below to be a threat to him. He knew with certainty that the animal that was scratching a hole in the dirt made a light, high-pitched pawing noise, perhaps a rabbit or a vole, so nothing large enough for him to feel threatened by. When he had learned to listen hard and understand what he heard, he felt invulnerable and strong. Nothing would surprise him.

After Mark didn't answer his question, Spence started to fidget in his chair. He lengthened his spine and slumped again. He raised his right hand so the white cuff of his shirt showed. He twitched his head in the direction of the waiters' station to scan the group of black jackets for the one that had been attending to them. He looked up suddenly when some boisterous concertgoers, the lips and tongue on the logo inexplicably pale blue as if they were the deep-ice version of fire red, bumped his chair. He harrumphed, turned condescending, as though he knew that they were already stoned or inebriated before the first note had been played. He looked pleadingly at Mark as if to say, Can you believe how rude those people are?

Mark felt no tension as they walked the few blocks to the arena. He was proud of himself. He hadn't backed down, and he had laid out his case as sensibly as he had intended, without aggression. Nor had he overreacted to the pseudo-logical alibis that Spence had offered him. He was calm. The night was cool but not cold. Above the buildings, the stars were bright in spite of the masses of electric lights that clustered beneath them on the corners of each block. Night darkness in the city wasn't close to the purity of the nights he had come to know in the Fremont. Light pollution, he muttered to himself.

They claimed their seats in the sharply banked stands. From halfway to the rafters, Mark stared down into a mouth full of people. How many were there, he wondered. Ten thousand? Twenty thousand? More? He had no sense of the size of crowds. Excitement among the enormous throng around him burbled through the blur of voices. Anticipation engulfed them as they expected to witness that night some extraordinary feat of music and communion, a ceremony that could fuse them together despite their unlikely, unmatched ingredients. It would unify them, transform them into one being.

The house lights dimmed, and a soft pinkish wash bathed the mammoth stage. A spotlight appeared on a lowered screen, and a sequence of talking heads offered filmed testimonials about the band. Mark thought he recognized some of the faces and voices, but he wasn't sure. He didn't try to listen to specific comments until a shot of lightning crackled through the public address system snapping him to attention, an electric spark that vanished as quickly as it had flashed. Then more bolts of lightning, then darkness, and the crowd around him rising and shouting like they were at the Roman Colosseum when the lions entered the ring to sniff and sample the Christians. After a few seconds, Spence tugged on his arm and pulled him to his feet.

Seven or eight shadowy figures appeared on the stage far below them. A few random chords ricocheted across the arena. Some drum strokes pounded into the cavernous air. A voice mumbled something into a microphone. Silence. Spence gripped Mark's arm as if to steady himself. The band started in all at once. Mick Jagger, the singer, a thin man, twitched around the stage, his longish hair the only undisciplined part of his body. His voice hurled through space. Klieg lights swept the crowd and the white padded ceiling like spotlights raking the sky at an outdoor summer carnival. Mark thought he recognized the song and turned to watch Spence mouth the lyrics. It traveled through verses and choruses and ended abruptly in a crash of notes. The next one started up raggedly, and the next. With each song, Spence reached a higher level of rapture. He closed his eyes, mouthed the lyrics, moved heavily from one foot to the other.

Almost an hour into the show Mark wished it was over. He imagined himself home, stretched out on his bed. The crowd, the noise level, and the disorientation frayed his nerves. His ears hurt, and that made him remember his father urging him to use earplugs. In his mind, he imagined his eardrums throbbing like the skin of a struck tambourine and prayed that they could withstand the repetitive impact. To breathe different air and give himself a rest, he headed out down the narrow row, afraid he might topple into the seats below him. In the concrete hallway he bought a soda and sipped it as slowly as he could. His shoes stuck to the spilled beer on the concrete floor, which reeked. He wasn't sure how much more patience he had left in him. It may have been one of the great cultural experiences of his life, but its importance was overshadowed by his unique discomfort. Spence acting like a participant in the revels didn't make it easier. He forced himself back into the hall. The ballads were easier to sit through. The audience calmed down. Some even sat. Mark could make out the words above the plaintive steel guitar and hum with the melody until it was over. Then the next pounding of rhythm, bass, guitar, and drums started up and the same intense dread returned.

Between a few songs the stick figure at the microphone who, Mark thought, resembled a cricket posing with his neck and head craned forward, muttered a few words of introduction that Mark couldn't decipher, and next a new performer magically emerged from the back of the stage. The music cranked up again, and then that new person traded phrases and verses with the singer and the chorus, acting as if the spontaneous guest appearance hadn't been rehearsed repeatedly, and walked off the stage. After the special visit ended, the crowd exhaled and sank back exhausted into their seats. The first few bars of the following song quieted most of them except for Spence, who stayed on his feet without ever sitting down. The beatific look that had blossomed on his face at the beginning of the concert never left.

Until "Sympathy for the Devil," most of the Stones' songs were an indistinguishable mush to Mark, but this one he had heard his father play on the record player at home. He had liked it even though he had never paid much attention to what the lyric said, but with those chords and the general frenzy of the music, the singer's posing and posturing felt even more vapid than it had before. If Jagger had ever been regarded as a satanic figure, it was obviously due to mass delusion. To Mark, he appeared more idiotic than demonic, a flimsy speck, barely human. He knew his father was right. The Stones were hateful, but their fans were worse. From the opening lines of the first verse, Spence and the crowd went into spontaneous, uniform, howling ecstasy like they were summoning an ancient oath out of themselves that they had been repeating secretly during the intervening decades. They knew all of the words. Everyone did except him. "Please allow me to introduce myself, I'm a man of wealth and taste/Pleased to meet you, hope you guess my name." Mark started to cringe, feeling a seizure that flexed the muscles and tendons in his body and made them ache. He tried to shake the spasms off, lift up on his toes, let his arms dangle down, but the intensity escalated like peristaltic waves of nausea. They crashed over him, seethed against his blue jacket, straining his entire body.. The physical power of the sound mixed with the emotion of the moment overwhelmed and engulfed him, and he became wild. As if he were being controlled by someone or something else, he turned toward Spence, bent over him, locked his powerful right arm around Spence's neck, and started to squeeze with incremental force as Spence flailed. Jagger sang all of the verses about the famous people who the devil had assassinated and reached the chorus that said "but after all it was you and me." Mark knew it was Spence. Spence was his devil. And it was Spence who had helped bring Mark's devil to life. Lamely and weakly, Spence slapped his hands against the grip of Mark's biceps and forearms, which he had built up into levers of force. Holding up lighters, closing their eyes in an oblivious, reflexive euphoria and swaying on their feet or grooving in their seats, the audience was transfixed by the chorus. No one beside them noticed Spence whipping his hands through the attenuated air.

"I want you to confess, Spence. Tell me that you know what the truth is and then I'll let you go. Did you or didn't you do that to me?" Mark shouted into his ear through the noise and loosened his grip on Spence's throat to let enough breath heave out of his chest so that he could be heard. Spence cleared his throat and sputtered but didn't say anything. The malevolent song played on, and the crowd, still enthralled, sang along.

"What is the truth, Mark? You tell me," Spence rasped as his chest heaved.

"No, you tell me," Mark answered, and tightened his lock again.

"Maybe it happened. I don't remember. Let go for Christ's sake. If you let go, I can talk." Spence huffed at him. Mark released him again partially as the song was winding down. Spence gurgled something inaudible.

"What?" Mark demanded. "Say it again."

"Maybe I did something like that. I don't remember. If I did, shame on me. I'm sorry if ..." Spence coughed out. The song ended in a crescendo of cheers and whoops and a cymbal crash. Mark kept his uncle in his grip. He wasn't ready to release him yet, and he didn't know how far he would go. "I'm sorry if I hurt you," Spence said.

"Is that what your lawyer told you to say? Did he tell you to say 'if I hurt you' like there was the tiniest chance that you didn't?" Mark shouted straight into his ear. "Yes, you hurt me because I was a kid and admired you. Is that why you took advantage?" Mark seethed, holding Spence's head and neck snug against his blue jacket, one of his arms clutched over the other to make the lock tighter when he wanted to.

"No. What lawyer?" Spence asked.

The rest of what Spence had to say was drowned out by the sudden rise of soprano voices singing a cappella. The ethereal chanting didn't come from the band or their backup singers on the stage. Mark couldn't make out the words or where they were coming from. Who was singing? Where were they standing? They were the most beautiful voices he had ever heard. The figures on the stage were not moving or standing near the microphones. The voices were clear and pure as if they belonged to a school or church choir of children in perfect harmony. Then Mark noticed a parade of children dressed in white floor-length robes moving slowly along the lower walkway. The ethereal sound was coming from their opening mouths. Who were they? Were they real? Their voices were otherworldly. The voices of seraphim and cherubim. The melody was familiar, and he began to distinguish the words. "You can't always get what you want/ You can't always get what you want," they repeated. Transfixed, he dropped his arms from Spence's neck and let them hang at his sides like dead weights. A French horn played a fanfare that sounded as if it was in a different key before Jagger started singing the first verse against the background of the choir. His voice was gruff and a little off-key, matter-of-fact, affectless compared with the children's heavenly tones.

Mark was motionless. The melody built surely and slowly. Mark paid no attention to the meaning of the lyrics as he mouthed the words. His body was enervated, as if it had been through an ordeal of endurance. In his mind, he imagined making Spence say more, admit to more, but he didn't think he had enough energy left for that or that there was anything more that Spence could say that Mark would believe. Spence's face was a lifeless, wrinkled gray. He listened to the music in his seat with his eyes closed, head bowed, and hands flat on his cheeks, as if in a state of awe or repentance. Uncle and nephew sat stupefied, side by side. The notes rose up as if they were wishes for a better world that were flung in the air and caromed through the upper spaces of the arena that had been transformed into an extraordinary cathedral. The crowd was now silent and awestruck. The spotlights were stationary. The band played their instruments with-out flourishes. It was a moment of grace.

When the song stopped in a slow, halting way, Mark knew that it was time for him to go. Spence stared but didn't say anything to his nephew to stop him as he put on his jacket. Spence looked dumbstruck, his face a composition of embarrassment, anger, and perhaps love. Love for what,

Mark wasn't sure. His own wounds. The music maybe. Whatever it was, he had had enough of Spence to last him for a long time. Mark didn't look at him as he pushed past him or glimpse back as he inched down the row. The crowd whooped and shouted at the band to keep them onstage, to hear encores, to sustain the spell. As Mark climbed the aisle steps and walked to the exit he could hear the rhythm engine of the band rev up again, but nothing had the power to pull him back inside the arena. He never wanted to hear the Rolling Stones again. He wasn't sure he wanted to ever see his uncle again, either. There was nothing more to say or do.

18

A FTER THE CEREMONY IN THE FREMONT AT WHICH I HAD
failed to graduate, I spent two more months camping and
slogging with Kenny and Hal and Ron. By the time I left there,
I would say that we had reached a stalemate. I had learned most of the
outdoor skills I was supposed to. The rest, Hal said, might come with
time, by which he meant a gradual progress toward maturity. More important, I was also able to pass my know-how on to the new kids who
arrived at the Fremont as dumb and disoriented as I had been when I
first landed. That made me happier than even the counselors' choicest
words of praise. The arrivals appeared every few days or so like stunned
calves, eyes crazed and wandering, feet not necessarily pointing forward
or in the same direction. Little by little, Hal entrusted some of them to
me. His confidence in me helped me remain afloat, but I knew that when
Lainey exited for wherever she had gone, what was left of the kid in me,
or most of it, had fled. Fled is that music, as Keats had written.

I was transferred to the school in Omaha after I finally graduated. I
spent the next two and a half years there living in a so-called family that
wasn't my own. There was a mom and dad who didn't resemble mine in
any way. They were kind, plain people. There were no shows of aggression,
nor were there magnificent displays of affection to compensate for the
previous attacks. Facts were facts. The rules were clear, and if you stuck
to them, you'd stay out of trouble, more or less. If you didn't, the mas-

ters of discipline descended on you without mercy. Scores were kept and marks were made in a book hidden away in an unseen ledger. All of these activities took place in cement-block buildings squatting on the edges of a city I only entered once or twice. Omaha may as well have not existed. Compared with being in the mountains and using my body every day, it felt like being in a juvie pen.

As much as I tried to live by the school's and my "parents'" code, my time there was marred by an escalating series of skirmishes. When I had my final growth spurt and wasn't in firm control of my reflexes or my limbs, other boys started to refer to me as "the giraffe." Over time that got shortened to the nickname Raff. "Hey, Raff," they whispered or shouted at me when they wanted my attention in class or passed me in the halls. Most of the time I was good-natured about the name. It was kind of true. I was definitely awkward, and it showed as I walked, my feet flopping and my arms waving aimlessly in the air. After a while I stopped noticing the nickname altogether.

Of course, that ended badly. One overcast fall day, I was already feeling bugged and this kid who I'd never liked had it in for me, not just calling me Raff but sticking his elbow in my ribs more than once. Finally, I couldn't take any more of it and I followed him when he headed back to his dorm via the side door. When he was behind one of the big ash trees scattered around the campus, I ran up and sucker-punched him as hard as I could. He collapsed on the ground, and before I ran for my room not looking back, appalled by what I had done, I watched a thin line of blood trickle from his left ear. Kenny had told me with his usual air of authority, not quoting Keats, that if you ever had to sock somebody, do it in the ear because there was less of a chance that you'd break any bones in your hand and your victim would get instantly dizzy so he couldn't hit you back. I always believed Kenny when he fed me information like that.

The penalty in Omaha for a physical assault of the kind I had perpetrated was expulsion or detention at least, so that's why I decided to take off in a hurry. I grabbed my long winter coat, pulled my sweater on, gathered the few things I cared about and the only money I had from the back of my desk drawer, and flew out the door. Everyone at Omaha knew that the place to hang while you were waiting for your Greyhound was the Heartland of America Park next to the Missouri River. You could sleep under the bridge without getting hassled, and your fellow vagabonds weren't aggressive. They were stoners and dabbers, not thieves. Luckily for me, I only had to spend one night there sleeping in my clothes, my head on my sack, and lucky for me too, it was a mild night with a crowd of stars to keep me company. Even the constellations made me feel good that I was leaving. Reaching home in just a few days meant that I might beat the formal letter that my parents were sure to receive. If it had arrived already, they must have been too distracted by the sweetness of my return to mention it.

In the weeks since I had been home, it was obvious that the Fremont and Omaha hadn't cured me of all my "impulse control" issues, as my problem was called. I didn't believe that they were worse than before, but they certainly weren't gone. I still hadn't got the hang of the "delay" mechanism that Mom tried to fix in me. Like if you want to punch someone, count to three and in those three seconds try and decide whether that is as good an idea as it first appeared. What trips me up about this trick is that there is no textbook situation. Each provocation is ever so slightly different, so I have a recognition problem. If I were presented with the one in the textbook, I wouldn't have any difficulty ticking the time off, pinning my hands to my sides, et cetera.

Of course, I knew that choking Spence was wrong, a wrong that lingered in my body like a useless bone or organ that had no other purpose but to haunt me or get inflamed. I tried to convince myself that this time it wasn't the same. The anger had pooled up during the three years since I had first realized Spence's obnoxious behavior, and there was no other way to siphon it off. So, therefore, the incident was excusable. Once it had come and gone I thought I was cured in a way that I couldn't have been without this form of closure, my own special brand. And, not to overlook it, I could tell that I had scared Spence enough to make him tell the truth. His eyes had bugged out in a Bugs Bunny way, and I could feel a little whimper of breath on my right forearm that I had choked out of him. I hated to admit it, but that made me feel cocky in a shaky, yet superior, yet ephemeral way.

When I got home that night, the apartment and my parents were asleep. I padded down the hall in my socks and closed my bedroom door softly behind me. I went straight into the closet and rooted around for Lainey's Pomona sweatshirt. Finally, I found it at the bottom of a bag of clothes that my mother had filled during one of her periodic purges. Neither Claire nor I had ever been able to see those coming. From one minute to the next, she would transform into a tornado. Her bagging cyclones usually touched down in fall and spring and with no obvious warning signs. She would just start tossing our stuff into random sacks. Yes, our closets looked tidier as a result, but everything that wasn't hidden would be moved to a new place and we wouldn't be able to find what we were looking for. Claire said she was as upset by it as I was, maybe more so, since she was a female. I thought she might be wondering if it was a uniquely maternal trait, one that she was destined to inherit one day. I think it was. What Dita was doing, I realized, was bagging up my childhood. She decided what would survive, so she became the shaper of my memories. Those plastic contractors' bags were filled with the good and bad of it, and when the items were removed from sight, recollection was banished with them. It was fortunate that I got to them before they got tossed down the chute. Or maybe, my more mature brain hypothesized, she was making order and space for the next phase of my life.

Putting on Lainey's sweatshirt brought back to me the night she had vanished. In the years that had passed since then, there had been no word of her. Hal had sent me a few postcards and letters when I was in Omaha asking how I was getting on, but he never mentioned her name. As soon as I thought of her, usually picturing her atop the rock with a sketch pad on her knees, her hands in her purple fingerless gloves clutching her pencil, the pangs started again like an aching song on the radio that keeps looping and lodges inside you and makes you more melancholy and heavier no matter how hard you try to fend it off. I tried to remember instead the pure, innocent voices of the concert choir, and I fell asleep to their echoes, wrapped in Lainey's sweatshirt, dreaming that the burden of Spence's meddling had been lifted from my shoulders.

When I opened my eyes the next morning, I could tell that I wasn't alone in the room. There were little shifty noises coming from the closet as if a team of gerbils were at work in their cage. I didn't stir. I listened and watched the closet door to see who it was. I suspected that it was my mother. Whether she was making order or disorder wasn't clear to me, but her presence was reassuring to me, carrying me back to when I was a little kid and she picked out my school clothes each morning. Her warmth and devotion surged back into me as if in their first bloom.

"Are you awake, Mark? What's this?" she asked, holding up my Fremont notebook.

"Notes I made while I was away. They're private," I said.

"Of course, darling. So I guess you want to keep it." She disappeared for a second in the closet.

"Is the sweatshirt you're wearing the one that belonged to your friend who went missing?" she asked, and gave me a look of maternal sympathy. I had only told the story to Claire, who must have repeated it. "That's so sad, *caro*. Tragic. Were you in love with her?"

I pretended not to hear the question. Wasn't the answer obvious? Three years later I was still sleeping in her sweatshirt. Of course, I'd been in love with her, or as in love as a fourteen-year-old boy can be. Each of us had been for our own reasons : Hal and maybe Kenny too, although we never talked about it. Perhaps even Ron, although he didn't seem like the type. Of course, I was devastated by what she had done to herself.

"Were you, Mark?" she prodded. I nodded. I thought that would be the end of it. But it wasn't.

"Have you tried to find her? She could be alive, you know. Maybe if you put some research into it, you could learn what happened to her. Maybe someone at the program can fill you in. If you'd like, I can call for you. They might be more responsive if a parent calls." I nodded again, not sure if I could bear to find out if she had died that day or after.

"I'm not sure, Mom," I said.

"Uncertainty is a difficult place to be, Mark. You are my courageous son. You survived being sent away, didn't you? You survived the wilderness and that horrible school, and now you're back and you'll survive here, too. How was your uncle? Did he survive the evening? Your father told me you were going out with him. That was brave of you. If it had been me, I would have invited him to dinner and poisoned his minestrone. Don't worry. Of course, I would never do that—for your father's sake. Did you have the nerve to bring it up?"

I stalled. My venom, or some of it, must have come from her. It dripped from one floor to the next, one generation to the next, through an invisible hole, a gap in the boards that only a liquid could find. Her bile soured my stomach, too. I struggled to accommodate it. I had tested it in different positions. I had yielded to it. I had wrestled with it and appeased it, but Spence was proof that it could never be fully eliminated. Only tamed. That's what the counting was for. Hal had also taught me that counting was the key that I was looking for, whether it was how to catch my breath going up a mountain or how to hold on to my temper. Once I started counting, I could stop myself from acting or reacting. If I could use those brakes, I had succeeded in holding myself in check and was the master of the situation instead of its victim. Spence was the obvious exception.

"Yes, I brought it up. Disaster," I answered. "I lost it with him. He was so full of himself, so smug. That fraud!"

"What did you do?" she asked with pitch-perfect nonchalance.

"I choked him a little and then I stopped."

"Mio caro!" she exclaimed. "I'm so proud of you!"

"For choking him or for stopping?" I asked, a little too much of a wise guy for the situation.

"Both."

"I guess you don't want this anymore, do you?" she asked, holding up a sweater that wouldn't have fit me when I was nine. "You looked so cute in it, Giorgio. Sorry, Mark. You're wearing it in all of the photographs." I recognized it, but after a first twinge of nostalgia for that innocent time, I never wanted to see it again. Suddenly, I wanted her to pack everything up and send it careening down the disposal chute. Whoosh! A clean shelf.

"Chuck it," I said.

"And this, *amore*?" she asked, holding up a little black leather belt from even farther back, maybe even pre-Blethen days.

"Chuck it," I repeated. I was getting tired of this triage.

"And this, *carissimo*?" It was the bow tie Spence had given me. Its strands of green, blue, and gold silk threaded over and through one another and wrapped around the ends exactly as I had remembered. It was strange to me that I had ever thought of it as anything more than the impossible knot it was. Or a noose.

"Do you think I should keep it? Like a warning or something. To ward off evil?"

"No, definitely not. Throw it away, and never think about it again. Do you hear me, darling?"

"Yes, I hear you. But I think I need to hold on to it. It will help me remember," I said. Without a pause, she folded it over the hanger with my other ties.

"Don't live like that. That's not a good life, especially for someone your age. How will you fall in love if you are always so suspicious? Falling in love means losing your caution. That's what I had to do with your father. He is a decent man. That is so rare. You probably don't know that yet," she said.

Given how guarded she was, not to mention fierce, I didn't think I was supposed to answer the question about falling in love, and besides, she asked it so often in so many different forms that I was sick of it. I didn't want to discuss Lainey with her. Other than devastated, I didn't understand my feelings about her being gone, and even if I did, my mother was the last person on earth I'd want to analyze them with. The more I thought about her prying into the mess of my feelings, the angrier I became until I realized that this was one of those textbook situations I had been warned about. I shut my eyes, and as soon as I did, the numbers 1, 2, and 3 popped into my head in the shapes of birthday candles on the delicious chocolate cakes she used to bake for me. The white wax numbers, edged in blue and pink, skittered and floated to the top of my skull like balloons rubbing against the ceiling, and I felt an alien calm descend on me.

"I'll take your word for it," I said, returning from my heavenly place. She hadn't even noticed how I had restrained myself. That was behavior that she had not often exercised herself. Shouting at the television was how she regulated. It probably calmed her down as much as it drove the rest of us crazy. It certainly didn't contribute to our domestic tranquility.

"Are you coming to your father's launch party? You must. They have been working on it so hard. And Spence is making him give a speech and your father hates those. It would mean so much more to him if you were there. Of course, your uncle will also be coming, so both of us will have to leave our feelings and our weapons at home."

"I don't want to see Spence again, and he probably doesn't want to see me, either."

"But what about your father? You have to come. It wouldn't be right without you. I know that he would want to see your face in the crowd. He's such a recluse, and this is a big outside event for him. Think about it, will you, darling?"

"I will. I promise I will," I said, but I had no intention of reconsidering, let alone going. Never being with Spence again in private or public was at the top of my list of life priorities. There wasn't another one even close to it. "What's it called again, their thing?" I asked.

"It's called the Rocker or the ... I'm not sure which," she said.

"Rocker makes more sense if it's a hearing aid for boomers."

"Yeah, I guess you're right. It must be the Rocker. Bad name, don't you think?"

"How would I know?"

Mom emerged from my closet and said that if I came out of my room, she would make me pancakes for breakfast. Although she'd always hated them, she knew it was one of my favorite dishes at any time of the day. I thought of the ones Kenny had ordered and I had been unable to eat at the diner after we had run away. As Dave hustled us out the door to his truck, I remembered looking back at them in their lopsided stacks, the round doughy forms limp on the plate. I didn't crave them or the taste in my mouth. I had been way too tired for that, exhausted by walking all night, haunted by Lainey's body frozen solid in the tall grass and my phone call to Spence that confirmed everything I had feared.

19

ALMOST FROM THE BEGINNING, BELPHONICS INC. HAD planned to launch the Rocker at the site of what had once been CBGB OMFUG at 315 Bowery in Lower Manhattan. CBGB's as it was mostly known stood for Country, Bluegrass, Blues; the other letters were for Other Music for Uplifting Gormandizers. There was no other venue that defined the product as the former club did. Although the space had been converted into a men's clothing store in 2008, the year of the club's demise after thirty-five years of dust and debris, the new owners had made a reverent effort to preserve the mystery stains and sweat of its origins. A wall plastered with authentic flyers from its heyday was protected by Lucite. The original, ominous black ducts hanging dangerously from the ceiling were covered in them too. Some of the layer upon layer of graffiti was still visible on the cracked walls, but these features failed to capture fully the earthy, reeking, pounding chaos of the club. The fresher details were worshipful homages to what had once been supremely raw and genuine. In the place of the flimsy chairs and tables, the broad uneven floor planks, the dinky black plywood stage barely a foot high, there were racks and racks of flowered shirts and cashmere-soft suede and military-style leather jackets, items that borrowed their inspiration from the wardrobes of its original musicians and fans. The clothes that were on display were ones that the punks of the seventies might have been able to afford if they had spent the little money they had less haphazardly.

Plexiglass boxes had been designed to hold the Rocker hearing aids that were stuck on the heads of pins. The prototypes had been delivered to the Belphonics conference room the day before, and Spence had asked Dr. H, Dutch, and Benjamin to attend the unveiling. Although each of them had played a part in the launch, seeing the shining models in their finished form took away their collective breath. Cherry, olive, black, and yellow plastic perfectly molded to the ear, festooned with thunderbolts, stars, and wisps of fog, brought them to life. Even Benjamin had to admire their handsomeness. The prose that accompanied them embodied Spence's original inspiration, "The Rocker is the music you loved. Hearing loss suffered in the service of love is not loss. The Rocker is your badge of honor. Your love was never lost."

Spence had not been involved in the minute details of planning the event, but because he could not help himself, he scattered his mercurial whims and commands among his staff. He thought that there had to be music, so he asked Dutch to put out feelers to a few of the former era's surviving musicians. Some responded eventually. Some leapt at the opportunity. Others were discovered in the obituary pages. Too late. Dutch wasn't sure if he was going to be able to assemble a ragtag band to play, not to mention one that would serve Spence's lofty requirements. The musicians who agreed "in principle" had, in many cases, to overcome decades of rancor that had separated them from their former friends and bandmates. A few of them had gone on to long careers. Others still lived in the same tiny Lower East Side apartments with exposed pipes and a bathtub in the kitchen they had lived in back in the day. Dutch and Benjamin used all of their diplomatic skills to convince the erstwhile rockers that they should participate. Three weeks before the event, a bunch of veterans had committed to the gig and had begun to rehearse. The fact that they had been promised a fee in addition to playing in their former clubhouse convinced the most reluctant ones.

Dr. H was in charge of testing the Rocker's controls, design, and market segmentation. She was careful to separate the ladies' models from the men's. She had persuaded the others at the start of the project that women were as critical to the success of the Rocker as men were. She had argued that surely, if the product was based on love, even the love of music and its conspicuous display, ladies were far better disposed and dedicated to that idea than men were. Weren't men the ones who were more likely to conceal their physical and emotional weaknesses? she asked the group rhetorically. Women, at least of a certain age, she argued, weren't so circumspect and understood love more energetically and profoundly. And they were far more capable of coping with vulnerability, she had added, to wind up her argument.

Benjamin felt that he could breathe again as he walked downtown to the final pre-launch meeting. The last heat of the year had expired by late October. Indian summer had passed without a relapse into the infernal conditions of August. Dr. H was in good spirits, buoyant at the idea of the product's introduction and without recriminations toward Benjamin who hadn't returned to see her. Since his last visit, Benjamin had barely spoken to her. She tried to discount their last tryst as one that had no trace of true feeling, hers or his. She was under no illusions about his interest in her. She knew that each visit was related to Spence in one way or another, and as much as she resented being thought of as Spence's explainer, she had to admit that she liked playing that role with Benjamin, who had performed that part for his whole life. Benjamin's serene forehead, the length and pliability of his body, pleased her. That Spence had contrived their meeting to an end only he knew didn't diminish her physical attraction to Benjamin.

When Benjamin had asked his brother what he thought the Rocker's prospects were, Spence shirked the question. Because the Rocker was rooted in their former lives, Benjamin assumed that it had an emotional claim on his brother's heart and, therefore, the product would be handled in a special way in the Belphonics catalog. Spence refused to acknowledge that and declared that it was just another "product" to throw onto the market. To stir them up, he added. We need new stuff to stir them up, he proclaimed, as if "they" were a herd of cattle: dumb, grazing, open mouths stuffed with hay. This left Benjamin wondering if Spence's shift in attitude to the Rocker wasn't the result of the conflict with Mark. It would be exactly like Spence to act in an unrelated and peculiar way to something that was so uncomfortable.

In the conference room, Dutch posed a simple question. What were the songs people would expect to hear given the setting of the former shrine to punk music? "'Venus'," Benjamin said. "'Heart of Glass'," Dr. H offered. "Anyone for 'Satellite of Love'?" Dutch countered. Spence listened but didn't say anything at first. His silence was peculiar, given how pronounced and harsh his opinions usually were. That led Benjamin to believe that something important was distracting him.

"What about 'Psycho Killer'?" Spence spluttered in exasperation, realizing that he shouldn't leave the conversation without putting his stamp on it. Each of them nodded in recognition rather than in deference. "The era really wouldn't be complete without that weirdo's voice singing French, would it?" Spence asked, his face as bright and eager as a kid's.

"Yeah," Dutch growled, and lowered his head, making the yellow tint in his glasses seem opaque. "What about something stronger? Can we really keep the Ramones off the track? Or Patti Smith? Or Suicide? How deep do we want to go?"

"I think we've gone deep enough," Spence answered. "If they have to, they can play the same song twice. Those second-rate has-beens probably can't hold their instruments for longer than ten minutes at a stretch anyway."

"They barely could back then," Dutch added.

"May I ask a question?" Benjamin asked. "Has anyone tried the Rocker on yet? Actually put it in their ears so they can hear what the sound is like?" They turned to look at him angrily, as though he had said something repellent.

"They have been tested over and over again at the lab," Dr. H answered with exasperation. "Would you like to be the first amateur to try them? They won't fit your ear exactly, but you can still get a pretty good idea. How about the cherry ones?" she asked, and smiled slyly, as if she were asking him to wear a skirt and unhooked them from their stand.

Benjamin nodded. The color of the plastic matched Dr. H's nail polish and her crimson patent leather high heels, Benjamin noticed, as she carefully inserted the hearing aids into his ears. She adjusted the volume on her laptop. They fit snugly, and Benjamin's head was immediately flooded with sonic data. In response to her request for ambient noise, Suicide's "Cheree" came rumbling and tinkling through the conference room speakers: drum track like a cat's heartbeat, fugue-state organ, and breathless vocals. Simultaneously, Dutch and Spence began to argue about the order of the songs on the playlist.

In Benjamin's head, the external noise sloshed and slapped against the bow of his brain, which nonetheless navigated through the noise. In his ears there were subtleties and articulations of sound that he had never heard before or hadn't heard in decades. He felt exhilarated and exhausted by their demands and made a panic sign to Dr. H, afraid that he might run out of the room shrieking.

"I lowered the gain. Can you still hear me?" Dr. H asked him in an affected, low, rumbly voice, almost a growl. Benjamin nodded. Then she covered her lips with the palm of her hand. Benjamin studied her buffed, tapered fingernails and the polish that, on closer inspection, seemed to contain flecks of a red mineral. "Can you hear me now?" she asked. He nodded. Dutch and Spence ignored them.

"Were you interested in me even a little?" she mouthed, but almost no sound came from her lips as she leaned toward him and stared into his eyes with her whole torso, sure that no one was watching them.

"I don't know. I don't know now," he answered, knowing exactly what she had said.

"You're not going to visit me again, are you?" she asked. He looked back at her, ashamed, as if she had caught him in a lie. His eyes dropped to the floor. He could hear every word she said and between them her pauses and other, vague brushing noises in the air. It felt to him as if she was breathing inside his ears, inside his brain, as if the hearing aids had given her free passage into his conscience and she could wander as she wanted around his synapses, his tunnels of thought and emotion. He dug them out of his ears and handed them back to her.

"They work perfectly," he proclaimed to the room. No one was listening. Dr. H took them from him and replaced them in their case. Benjamin noticed how carefully she handled them, as if they were precious gems.

Spence rose from his chair and turned off the music. He beamed as he bustled back to his seat at the head of the table. "Does anyone have anything else to say, or are we set for next week? Dutch, is the contract signed with CBGB's?"

"Everything has been agreed to. The lawyers have gone over it, so we're just waiting for final signatures," Dutch said.

"What's taking them so long? How long does this have to go on for? It's not that complicated!" Spence almost shouted and rolled his eyes. "Is there a problem you're not telling me about? Should we find a backup just in case they mess us up?"

"No, no. Don't do that. This is as good as done, Spence," Dutch assured him, although he could tell that Spence wasn't satisfied by his answer. "I'll call the lawyer again this afternoon."

"From your lips to God's ears," Spence said. "Anything else? No. Benjy, come with me for a minute."

Benjamin trundled down the hall to his brother's office. Spence closed the door behind them and sat plumply behind his baroque desk, bouncing in his executive chair in a fidgety way. "There's something wrong here. Something Dutch isn't telling me. What is it? I know you know."

"I don't know anything, Spence. There's nothing wrong. You know how long the lawyers take."

"Yes, I do, and I know it a lot better than you do. But my instinct tells me Dutch is hiding something. See if you can find out what he's lying about."

"He's not lying, Spence. He's said the same thing to Dr. H and me that he said to you. Don't do anything rash."

"Don't tell me how to behave. I have done better than fine without you."

"I wasn't saying that. I was trying to say just be patient a few more..." Benjamin didn't finish the sentence before Spence interrupted him. "Don't lecture me on patience!" Spence shouted, his face turning plum colored and oddly oval. "You can be patient your whole fucking life if you want, but patience only buys you misery. You're proof of that, aren't you? You've been infinitely patient with Marco, haven't you? Where did that get you? He's as deranged now as he was three years ago. Sixty thousand dollars of patience. Do you know what he did to me the other night? He choked me. I almost passed out. And in the Barclays Center, and he was going to leave me there on the cement floor. Unconscious. Is that enough gratitude for you? It is for me."

"And there was no provocation by any chance? Ever? He just choked you on a whim, because the mood took him, as a way of thanking you for dinner and the concert, right?"

"I'll see you at the party, Benjy," Spence said, standing up abruptly. "Could you at least give your family some pointers on how to behave in public, please?" Benjamin didn't respond, and slammed the door on the way out.

Benjamin stalked home vindictively as if it were the streets and weather that had enraged him rather than his brother. He looked at the sky. An innocent blue lurked there, stultifying and banal. Some of the leaves on the little mid-block gingko trees had lost their leaves and were more precarious than usual. He propelled himself home with his long, rapid strides. He nodded to the doorman and to his cousin, who exited the elevator as he entered. He grumbled if only to himself. Suddenly, he felt unseasonably hot inside his shirt, which stuck erratically to his neck and back. He braced himself for the usual house storm. Instead, he found his wife and both children in the kitchen helping their mother prepare dinner as if nothing had happened, as though the family had never been disrupted and was now recomposed in its original state.

It was such a tender scene that he didn't wish to intrude on it. He passed by the kitchen door and went directly to his little room in the back that was already warm from the steam heat of the ancient radiators. He turned on the air conditioner, although his room wasn't as stifling as it often became in winter. The clicking of its gears bewitched him, and he sat down in his white slipcovered armchair and reveled in the artificial breeze he felt on his neck and face. It also blocked out the ambient noise of ambulances and police cars. He realized that the sounds of the air conditioner mimicked and replaced the soft whirring ones he heard inside his ears when the world was still. Sitting, he removed his jacket and unbuttoned his shirt as he pulled the tails out of the waistband of his trousers. There was a soft knock on the door.

"Are you joining us, maestro, or going to sulk in your room all night? Mark and Claire are coming to your event. I convinced them," Dita said triumphantly and grandly.

"Do you really think that is a good idea? After the headlock and all that? Did you hear about it?" Benjamin asked.

"Yes, of course I know. I hear every word that is spoken in this apartment sooner or later. Mark told me himself. Spence is dirt to him, but he would go anywhere for you. That's what counts. Let him, darling."

Benjamin nodded despite his misgivings. The headlock story made him wonder how settled Mark truly was. Had Omaha and the Fremont calmed him down, or had they merely removed the roughest edges? At the same time he was aware again of how admiring if not envious he was of Mark's nerve and power. Mark, he realized, had every right to be vindictive without restraint. His rage was righteous, not impulsive. Suddenly, he felt proud of his son for punishing Spence and no trace of sympathy for his brother's behavior. This was such a change in the way that Benjamin thought of Spence that he could barely contain the repercussions of the realization. His whole life he had been programmed to find Spence eccentric, not guilty, to make excuses for him. It had taken an act this invasive, this perverse, for Benjamin to find his brother unforgivable. He knew beyond any doubt that he could never protect Spence again.

20

O N THE NIGHT OF THE LAUNCH, I WANTED TO GO ON MY OWN to CBGB's as Dad still called it instead of the clothing store it had become. I dropped by his study to say that I was leaving and found my parents sitting side by side on the blue loveseat. His right arm lay limply across her lap. My mother's left hand held my father's wrist, his hand a relaxed paw between hers, while she carefully clipped his fingernails. The contentment on his face combined with her indulgent attention made me want to scream my fucking head off and run out of the room. No, out of the apartment or out of their lives. It had never dawned on me before that I might be jealous of the time she spent calmly with him. Or any period of calm that I wasn't part of.

"Won't you wait for us? We're almost done," she said, but I knew that hanging back with them would be too big a test of my patience. This was going to be my first visit to what had been my father's shrine, and I wanted to see it with my own eyes without anyone else in the picture. When I walked out the front door, a gentle, humid, unseasonable rain for December was falling that was more like condensation. I could feel it around me like soft curtains, as though there were no separate drops. It dampened and tangled my hair. The moisture made me yearn to be back in the high desert where I could see for miles and my lungs were clear instead of in that urban swamp. Since I had been home, Hal had written me to ask if I would come back to the Fremont as a junior counselor.

While I was there and for the years after, the thought of ever returning was inconceivable, but in the thick evening air, among the brutalist
rectangular buildings, nothing else seemed so appealing. The city had
turned me into a permanent outdoorsman.

I exited the train at Bleecker and walked east, trying to imagine what
these streets had been like when my father was my age. In preparation,
I had watched hours of videos of the neighborhood near the club as it
used to be, as well as losing myself in endless crappy footage of bands
playing live on the tiny scuffed-up stage. Barclays Center made CBGB's
look like a janitor's closet. Every so often in the old footage I caught a
spark from the voltage inside the club that must have flared as unexpect-
edly to the audience as it did to the band. And wasn't that what they
were all hoping for—the sign of a singular moment when the music on
that special night, in the close air, rose into another dimension. When
it lifted from its foundation of chorus and verse to become a raw, un-
differentiated sound almost without features, without single notes or
chords, that echoed the sounds they heard inside their heads. Clues that
might foreshadow their exaltation were impossible to read: Was it the
guitars turning so raw and molten that they became a solid roar? Was it
the jumpy spotlights leaping over the heads of the crowd, fusing them
together? Or the singer's strange vocal tones or how he threw himself
down on the stage because the music had shorted him out and no one
knew whether he would be able to get up again? Or was it the sum of
those jagged parts?

As I approached the mayhem of two-way traffic on the Bowery, I
could see that the two-story white stucco building with the CBGB aw-
ning and its mysterious letters OMFUG underneath was gone, as were
the grimy windows and door covered in graffiti. In its place was a sturdy,
freshly pointed and painted brick building with attractive white letter-
ing on black material advertising the clothing store that had replaced it.
Next to it, in the slot once occupied by a fleabag hotel, was a Patagonia

store, everything the local hiker could possibly want for his subway commute to work.

In spite of the change in the neighborhood, I was magnetized toward the club that had once been able to keep my father awake past midnight. These days he was so placid and beyond excitement that I wondered what aspect of it had awakened and transported him downtown, miles from the building where he and I had both grown up. And furthermore, he had made those trips mostly after midnight. Now he could barely stay awake until ten. He'd told me once that only winos lived down there before the club opened. I'd never heard that term before. When he explained what it meant, he relished pronouncing the exotic names of those cheap, addictive wines like Night Train and Thunderbird, as if they conjured up a long-gone era that he had fantasized about, of hobos hopping freight trains from one railyard to another.

For the event, the racks of clothes and mannequins wearing perfectly faded biker jackets with shiny zippers and worn collars had been pushed to the sides against the exposed brick walls. The black plywood stage that I had seen in almost every shot of the interior was not at the end of the room but in the middle, opposite a buffet table laden with hors d'oeuvres—tumblers filled with celery and carrot sticks, and bowls overflowing with a runny dip. Already, groups of people were bunched around the floor talking among themselves, paying no attention to the historic surroundings. On the stage, a few men stood chatting, Fender Stratocasters swinging from their necks, a Ludwig black-pearl drum set up behind them. My father was nowhere to be seen.

In the middle of the room the free-standing pillars with clear boxes on top containing the Rocker hearing aids were positioned in a semicircle like a plexiglass version of Stonehenge. I walked around the display. It was true that the colors were not discreet, but I wasn't sure that this announced love of music and identity that the advertising copy suggested. Or maybe it was hard for me to assess the product, as I was the representative of a different generation.

Absorbed in thinking about the Rocker, I didn't feel Spence's presence lurking behind me. When his scaly hand landed on my shoulder, I recoiled and shook him off with a shiver. I wanted to make a run for it.

"You might want to listen to the announcements tonight. We have something major to say," he said. "You kind of left me for dead the other night. I survived. How are you?"

"I was having a fine day until I saw you," I said, and tried to head to the back to look at the brick wall where some of the original graffiti was preserved, but he held me, his fingers gripped around my upper arm.

"Come on, Marco. You're bigger than that, aren't you? You might want to try and get in the mood at least for your father's sake. I got him out of the house. It's a big night for him. I couldn't have done this without his help, but I'd never tell him that," he said, and released his grip before I could force him to let go.

"That's the only reason I'm here. Don't wreck it," I said, feeling no remorse for my attitude.

Claire and Mom made their way toward me through what was becoming a small crowd. Clusters of men in various shades of gray suits with name tags gathered around the room. Dr. H, who Dad had described to me in general detail, was instantly recognizable, hopping from group to group shaking hands and smiling a giant smile that resembled a rectangle with a scarlet border. In the distance, I could see my father stooped forward in his listening position, towering over a man I didn't recognize.

"Why do I still want to choke him to death?" I asked Claire, without bothering to say hello.

"Because he stole from you," she said, the truth in her voice as direct as her clothes were loud. She was wearing a shimmering, crimson workout suit that matched one of the ladies' pairs of hearing aids.

"What did he take? How do I get it back?"

"He took away your chance to find out for yourself," she said without further explanation.

"To find out for myself." I nodded. Of course, I thought. It was obvious. Spence had interfered and diverted me from my own discoveries, and now I didn't have a clue what those might be or where they had gone. I caught sight of Spence across the room. His short, stocky figure should have made me more angry than I felt, but all I could do was pity him for picking on a kid.

"Mark, hello?" Claire said and looked up at me. "I didn't say that to piss you off or send you on some rumination, so get a grip. You can't know before you know."

"What is that supposed to mean?" I asked, sounding surly even though I didn't feel that way. I felt like she had said this to me before, but I hadn't been old enough to understand it.

"It means that you have to figure it out when it happens. You can't pre-know. You only know when you get there no matter how much you plan and want to know in advance. You will know whatever you want when you're ready to know it."

"I wish I had been ready before. In the Fremont. And it doesn't help that I have to see him all the time and Dad is working with him. And indebted to him because of me."

At that moment I glanced across the room and saw Mom. She had wandered away from us toward our father. I watched as she adored him, placing her hands on his high shoulders, fussing over him, whisking away invisible lint from the ridge of his jacket as she looked up at him admiringly. I thought I could read her lips whispering *carissimo*, which was what she called all of us from time to time, but it resonated more when applied to him. Her superlative. We moved closer to them through the crowd that was big enough to begin to burble with a noise that bordered on excitement.

A man I had never met before went over to Dad and tapped him on the shoulder. Dad leaned his head down, and I edged closer to hear what the man was saying. His somewhat military bearing reminded me of Ron from the Fremont. He wasn't clean-shaven or measured in his grooming in Ron's way, but he had an intense quality that indicated that he was a conflict survivor of some description. I couldn't tell from looking at him what that was. Before I could get close enough to hear, the man stepped away.

"Who was that?" I asked my father.

"That's Dutch. He's a Belphonics veteran."

"He must have scars, too. What did he just tell you?" I asked boldly.

"He said the contract had been signed."

"What does that mean?" I asked.

"It means that we have officially licensed the CBGB name and can use it in all of our promotion and advertising starting tomorrow."

"Is that good?" I asked.

"Let's hope so because—" Dad said before he was interrupted by the band's front man, the lead singer, his hanging, lank hair hiding the sides of his gaunt cheeks as he hunched over the microphone. The band began to play. His guitar swung forward and clanked against the microphone stand as he sang. When he bent backwards between phrases, the instrument's solid black body reflected the stage lights onto the monochrome of the crowd. His voice had a disinterested quality, as though either his heart was untouched by the lyrics or they resonated so fully within him that he was afraid of giving them any inflection that might expose him.

"Things like that drive me out of mind" he deadpanned, alternating it with the three-word chorus, "satellite of love," that he repeated over and over. It was Lou Reed's song, and this was a perfect lip-sync of the original.

The words compounded in my brain, and in their echo, I started to picture love as a spaceship traveling through the bright Fremont sky at night illuminating the hidden ravines below it. I thought of Lainey and the way she had appeared and vanished like an extraterrestrial creature that had swung so close to our planet that I thought she might almost be able to be our friend, that I might be able to love her, before she was whisked away. And when I watched her go, I stood stunned, wondering whether I really saw her at all or made her up. I knew Lainey had been real, but there were moments when I wasn't sure I knew anything— especially when it came to her, especially when it came to love.

When the band finished the song, the noise of the crowd increased again to fill the silence. The band members pulled back from their positions at the front of the small stage and conferred. I studied the singer. His face resembled one of the blank, hawk-nosed faces on the cover of one of Dad's albums. I wasn't sure which one. It was hard to tell them apart because all of them appeared demented: tense and aloof at the same time. I thought it might be Tom Verlaine. I studied the singer again. No, impossible. Why would he agree to play at a hearing aid launch party unless he was desperate, and I couldn't believe that he was.

The singer clunked the microphone with his knuckle to get people's attention. He did it a few more times, but no one paid any attention. In frustration, he thrashed the strings as hard as he could with his fingernails, and a jangly toneless clang snarled through the stacks of amplifiers. The room was immediately hushed.

"Thank you, thank you. I don't have anything to say except those jackets look punk. Kind of. Might steal a few to top up the cash. Just kidding. Not really," he said, flashing a toothy smile with discolored teeth. The audience responded with a collective, guileless smile. "So I'd like to introduce you to Spence Stern, our host and sponsor. He has a few words to say, or would you like us to play one more song first? This is getting good, isn't it? Our first and only gig."

Appearing confused, the audience clapped. I could see Spence seething at the side of the stage. His face was distorted, as if he had a cramp. Dad walked toward him and, in spite of all the anger that must have been stored somewhere inside him, put his arm around his little brother's shoulder, and Spence slumped into his suit jacket in response to the reflexive gesture. He tried to attract the singer's attention but was unable to make him stop before the next song cranked up. The two interlocking guitars sparred as if they were sending each other telepathic hate messages above the heads of the audience. The crowd was engulfed and hypnotized. Dutch grinned on the other side of the room. This was the moment he had been waiting for. I listened, hypnotized, even though the words didn't make any sense to me. It was only when he got to the chorus and announced "Marquee Moon" that I recognized the song and the solos that I had been listening to almost continuously since Dad had introduced me to it.

The riff ended abruptly. The dazed looks on the faces in the crowd indicated that the music was beyond what they expected for a product launch on an early winter evening. It was too jarring for that, too brutal. They struggled to bring themselves back to a calmer center. Spence hopped onto the stage and hip checked the singer to the side.

"Thanks, guys," he said without a trace of feeling. "And welcome, friends. This is an exciting evening for the Belphonics team, our customers and distributors and allies. The Rocker is a product that we have been contemplating for a long, long time. It is close to our hearts. We were fans once too, and this was our home. We were knocked out by this music. Literally. This is our way of sharing the experience with you. Please schedule a meeting with one of our sales team. Before the band plays a few more songs, I'd like to tell you that working on this launch has been especially meaningful to me because my big brother, Benjamin, has been my partner. We haven't always seen eye to eye because he's at least a foot taller than I am"—Spence paused for a beat to let the dumb joke sink in—"but anyway, in a few minutes, Benjy has an exciting announcement to make to you. In the meantime, eat and drink and talk. Talk about me if you want to."

Spence skipped off the stage and down the steps toward Benjamin. He smiled and put his stubby arm around him at the same moment that I joined them.

"Um, Spence, if there is exciting news that I am going to announce, maybe you should tell me what it is because I thought the news I had was already pretty exciting. Dutch just told me that CBGB's had signed the agreement, so we're all set," Benjamin stated.

"Well, that is what I wanted to talk to you about. Let's go somewhere private for a minute. I want to bring you up to speed. Do you want to come with us?" he asked me as they started walking to the back of the store away from the crowd and the street.

I followed along without thinking whether I belonged with them or not. As soon as we were in the spacious men's room that was painted dark gray, Spence turned to lock the door behind us, an action that suggested that Dad and I were both his prisoners or perhaps he was ours. The lacquered walls allowed some of the original crumbling mortar in the gaps of the red bricks to show through.

"Just hear me out before you say anything," Spence said. "I've been in touch with the manager of the Rolling Stones. A nice lady, a real pro. She loved the idea of the Rocker and pitched it to Mick and the band. They're thinking about it and are supposed to get back to me next week. I don't need to explain to you what it would mean if we could have the Rolling Stones instead of CBGB's as our licensors. They are still the biggest band in the world and maybe the best there ever was. Even better than these punks. That's what I want you to hint at when you go on stage. Say something like 'the best band in the world may want to be our partner' without saying their name. Stay tuned' We can always come back to the CBGB's thing if we can't work out a deal."

Dad's face turned a shade of scarlet. He looked like he'd been punched in the stomach and all of the air had been sucked out of him and his blood had rushed up into his head. His eyes were dark and hooded. He resembled a cartoon gangster.

"How could you, Spence? That is a total betrayal," Benjamin spluttered.

"Benjy, contracts are supposed to be broken when there's opportunity. This is one of those times."

"And I will never forgive you for what you did to Mark."

"He made all that shit up. It doesn't even fit. It can't be true. His timeline is off," Spence said.

"I don't believe you."

"What he said I did is impossible. It's a fabrication. Not to mention the fact that I always loved him."

"You've run out of lives, Spence. And lies. I always covered for you whatever you did. But not this time, and never again."

"Did your lunatic wife put you up to this, Benjy? This is just not you. This is not the brother I've always known."

I studied my father's face for a reaction to what Spence said. At first, it was expressionless, as if Dad was paralyzed, too stunned by Spence for the distortion of events to register. I recognized that mask on him. I'd seen it before when I knew he wasn't sure how he felt and was confused about what his reaction should be. I remembered it from three years ago when he walked in on my mother's fight with me. He must have had a thousand emotions racing through him, too many to manage. At the same time, he was stunned, spluttering, frozen.

Suddenly, my father burst into action, overwhelming and tackling Spence in a bizarre wrestling move that threw both of them to the ground. It happened so fast that I couldn't really tell what my dad had done until I saw Spence lying facedown on the gray cement floor and my father stretched out on top of him like an octopus, his long extremities wrapped around his brother's limbs and his elbow pressed into the back of his neck. Spence's face splotched red and he coughed. A line of drool leaked from the left corner of his mouth toward the sunken drain. His tie was askew, his collar twisted, and his pants were pushed below his belly line.

"Get off me," Spence said.

"Not until you admit what you did to Mark. Admit it!" he screamed in a voice that was high-pitched and hoarse at the same time. I'd never heard him sound that crazed before. He had lost all control and didn't care who heard him.

"Get off me and we can talk about it," Spence said.

"No, this is how we're going to talk about it," Benjamin answered.

For once my father completely astonished me. There wasn't even the play of a sly smile at the edges of his lips to signify that his act wasn't as serious as it appeared. Almost sixty years of being Spence's older brother had taken a terrible toll on him. His legendary patience had been worn so thin that it finally split open, and when it did, nothing could stop it. It wasn't just scary. It was righteous, too. How many lies, distortions, and betrayals had he disciplined himself through in his lifetime? Unknowable. Infinite. I reveled in my father's fury as much as if it had been my own all over again. It felt like he was on fire and free. We both were.

From the main room, the band started another song with a sequence of twangy notes that led to a few strummed chords. The pace quickened. The singer's toneless, unmelodious voice gained momentum as if there was something suddenly he needed to say urgently that he had forgotten to say before. "I don't know just where I'm going / but I'm gonna try for the kingdom if I can." Spence squirmed against my father's smothering hold on him.

"Let me up," he said, coughing. "We have to go back out."

"No," my father said.

"Dad, he doesn't look so good," I pointed out. Spence's eyes were a little swimmy and unfocused. His pupils had shrunk.

"Since when are you the angel of restraint?" Dad asked me. Even his aggression toward me was exciting. Finally, he could say what he meant.

Spence turned his face to the floor and then looked at us again. He was begging us. No, he was pleading with his brother to be fair and forgiving as he had always been, but the dam had burst. Dad wasn't in the mood for it anymore. Forgiveness had lost all meaning for my father. What did forgiveness mean if you forgave the same person for the same crime over and over? Did that make forgiveness meaningless? Or crime meaningless? "Cause it makes me feel like I'm a man," the singer taunted from the main room. We could hear every word, as if there were no doors and walls between the bathroom and the outer room. I looked back at Spence to check on him. Tears were blurry in his eyes.

"Please get off me, Benjy," he pleaded again.

"Why should I show you any mercy?" Dad asked. "Give me one good reason. What consideration have you ever given me or Mark for that matter? Zero. I have to force mercy out of you because you don't know how to find it for yourself. You don't even know what it is, do you?"

"Let him go, Dad," I said, not because I thought he was really hurting him but because I thought he had made his point. The tears that spilled out of the corners of Spence's eyes made little marks on the floor.

"I didn't mean to be this way," Spence muttered, and shuddered. "I just do what I do. I don't know why."

"Is that an apology? An explanation? What is that?" Dad asked.

"It's just a fact," Spence said, gasping.

"He means it, Dad. It is a fact. A fact he can't change. He can't be any better than he is. This is it," I said.

"That's not good enough, Mark, even if it's true. Apologize to Mark, and we're done, Spence," Dad stated.

"Sorry," Spence mustered.

"And we're sticking to the CBGB deal, right?" Benjamin asked.

"Come on, Benjy."

"We're sticking to it, right?" Benjamin asked again, pressing his forearm harder against Spence's neck.

The music from the next room became berserk. The reverberations rattled the glass in the framed photographs on the bathroom walls. The singer, despite his previous affectless delivery, added more passion to the next lines: "Away from the big city/Where a man cannot be free," he sang. Even in the bathroom the air seemed to take on a static charge, and then we heard someone pounding on the door.

"Who is it?" I shouted.

"Let me in," came a little girl's voice. It sounded like Claire's, so I went to open the door a crack. She was the only person I would have allowed in.

"What the fuck are you guys doing in here? I have to pee! Get out!" she shouted. When she saw her father's body sprawled over her uncle's, a gasp came out of her. "And take that piece of shit with you!" she added.

The two of them stared at her, but no one moved or said anything, including me. Claire, realizing that none of the three of us could move, walked to the toilet in the corner, lowered her luminous tracksuit pants, and sat down. As soon as Dad realized what she was doing, he leapt up and turned away from her. Spence rushed after him out of the bathroom without straightening his clothes. I stood plastered against the wall. This wasn't the first time Claire had pulled a stunt like this. She simply didn't care who saw her. Very little inhibited her. She liked shocking me. Not just me. She liked shocking anyone.

I trailed my father and uncle to the main room. In the fifteen minutes we had been gone, it had turned into a frenzy. The band had loosened up and played with abandon, pounding the drums and slamming their guitar strings with picks that went flying out of their hands. The singer had taken off his blue Union Army jacket to show off the stringy muscles that ran down the insides of his arms, and his T-shirt rose up to reveal every worked section of his abdomen. It was more a drum than a stomach.

Looking like he was loving the chaos that must have reminded him of the best parts of tour-manager days, Dutch smirked in the corner. He had lost interest in trying to control the band or the mood in the room.

A few people in the front near the stage were dancing so hard, it seemed that they wouldn't be able to stop themselves. The plexiglass boxes of hearing aids had become obstacles in an open field that the rest of the crowd had to steer around not to knock over. Behind the stage, I saw a man I didn't recognize fiddling with the dials on the mixing board. From the noise of it, he was turning them up. The room reverberated with manic energy.

Claire returned from the bathroom and stood next to Mom. She swayed a little to the music. Mom stood stone footed. I didn't think she had ever been much of a punk or Velvets fan. Dad and Spence stood side by side, straightening their clothes but not speaking, staring in an unfocused way and avoiding each other's eyes.

From one second to the next, the song ended with a ripping sound. I watched as Spence nudged my father toward the stairs to the little stage, toward the microphone. Dad usually spent more time clearing his throat than speaking when he had to address a group. But at that moment, even if he wasn't capable of a rallying speech, he felt bigger to me than he ever had. Stronger. Less troubled by something that I was too young to appreciate but old enough to notice. Whatever it was, I could feel the full-scale change in him. I had seen it with my own eyes. My instinct told me that whatever the painful self-discipline and sense of obligation with his brother had once been, it had been vaporized.

Dad adjusted the microphone to his height more than once. He pumped the palm of his hand against it and asked, "Can you hear me?" too many times. "I'm glad you're here, we're here. And they're here. Tonight is for this place because, in spite of everything, it represents who we were when we were good or better or if not good, at least honest. That's what we were hoping for."

Dad had more to say, but I had heard all I needed to know. It was the minimum that was required to release me. I knew then that this was not my place in the world. I had come home and wiped the slate clean. I had shed the scarred, scabbed layer of skin that I had lived in for the last seven years and grown a new layer in its place, one I hoped I'd know how to protect better. I had done more than my part. I was free to go, to leave these places and these people behind. One thing I could say about myself was that I had always known when I was done with somewhere. I knew that in Omaha and the Fremont, too. If I had thought about it more, I would have seen that I was done with New York City the first time I had left, even though I hadn't left of my own free will.

I gave my mother a hug, and she reached her arms around my shoulders, pulling me down to her. I told her that I was tired and going home. I didn't tell Claire either when I leaned down to say good night. While my father was still standing on the podium and speaking, I put my hand to my lips as if to wish him good night with a kiss. He saw my gesture, and interpreted my look as though I was asking for some kind of permission, I could tell that his answer was yes. Yes, Mark, yes.

ACKNOWLEDGMENTS

Special thanks to Michael Zilkha, Nathan Rostron, Chris Heiser, Pamela Malpas, Tim Shortell, Elizabeth Oxley, Titania Minlend and Gale Farnsworth.

To my family for their love and support: Jane, Alexander, Juliet, Delilah and Gabriel.